The Falling Snow

and Other Stories

Other CUA Press Translations
by Robert M. Fedorchek

FROM THE PORTUGUESE:

The Count of Abranhos
José Maria Eça de Queirós

FROM THE SPANISH:

Don Álvaro, or the Force of Fate
Ángel de Saavedra, Duke of Rivas

*

Juanita la Larga
Juan Valera

*

The Illusions of Doctor Faustino
Juan Valera

The Falling Snow

and *Other Stories*

José Maria Eça de Queirós

Translated from the Portuguese by
Robert M. Fedorchek

Introduction by
Maria Filomena Mónica

The Catholic University of America Press
Washington, D.C.

Library of Congress Cataloging-in-Publication Data
Names: Queirós, Eça de, 1845–1900, author. |
Fedorchek, Robert M., 1938–
translator. | Mónica, Maria Filomena, 1943– writer of introduction. |
Queirós, Eça de, 1845–1900. Contos. Selections. English. |
Queirós, Eça de, 1845–1900. Contos II. Selections. English.
Title: The falling snow : and other stories / José Maria Eça de Queirós ;
translated from the Portuguese by Robert M. Fedorchek ; introduction
by Maria Filomena Mónica.
Identifiers: LCCN 2021047078 (print) | LCCN 2021047079 (ebook) |
ISBN 9780813235042 (paperback) |
ISBN 9780813235059 (ebook)
Subjects: LCSH: Queirós, Eça de, 1845–1900—Translation into English. |
LCGFT: Short stories.
Classification: LCC PQ9261.E3 F3513 2022 (print) |
LCC PQ9261.E3 (ebook) | DDC 869.3/3—dc23/eng/20211013
LC record available at https://lccn.loc.gov/2021047078
LC ebook record available at https://lccn.loc.gov/2021047079

For Maria Filomena Mónica:
prolific author, Eça biographer, and friend

CONTENTS

Translator's Preface ix

Introduction by Maria Filomena Mónica xix

STORIES

The Falling Snow (*Entre a Neve*) 3

Master Devil (*O Senhor Diabo*) 13

The Peculiarities of a Blonde Girl
(*Singularidades de uma Rapariga Loira*) 30

Civilization (*Civilização*) 63

[The Wet Nurse] A Topic for Verse
([*A Aia*] *Tema para Versos*) 95

The Treasure (*O Tesouro*) 103

The Dead Man (*O Defunto*) 113

Perfection (*A Perfeição*) 150

José Matias (*José Matias*) 172

The Gentle Miracle (*O Suave Milagre*) 201

The Catastrophe (*A Catástrofe*) 213

The great nineteenth-century Portuguese author José Maria Eça de Queirós (1845–1900), has long been known for his novels, especially *The Crime of Father Amaro* (1880) and *The Maias* (1888). However, he also wrote short stories, and a number of them, having stood the test of time, are now regarded as masterpieces. Although there is no question that Eça owes the lion's share of his reputation to his long fiction, the tales in this collection tell us that we are reading the work of a writer in full control of both genres.

After he obtained a bachelor's degree at the University of Coimbra, Eça journeyed to Lisbon, where he took up journalism. But his was an artistic, intellectual, and literary temperament, and in the November 11, 1866, issue of the *Gazeta de Portugal* there appeared a change of pace by the twenty-one-year-old fledgling author—a short story titled, "The Falling Snow," what João Gaspar Simões has labeled "the first draft of a short story."[1]

If, in this tale about a forlorn woodcutter, Eça was attempting to eschew the *unreal* of Romanticism in literature, he somewhat succeeded; and if he was attempting to introduce the *real* of Realism, he also, somewhat, succeeded. That elements of both the fantastic and the realistic should surface in this first draft as well as in "Master Devil," which appeared the following

---

1. João Gaspar Simões, *Vida e Obra de Eça de Queirós*, 2nd ed. (Lisbon: Livraria Bertrand, 1973), 114 ("o primeiro esboço do conto").

year, is understandable, for he appears to be testing the waters, so to speak. Some of the fantastic calls to mind Edgar Allan Poe, a writer whom Eça read and greatly admired, but his grip on the *real* will take him to different frontiers.

And then, like Guy de Maupassant, who achieved instant success with "Boule de Suif," his first full-fledged story, Eça gained renown with "The Peculiarities of a Blonde Girl" (1874), his first full-fledged story, a tale that already revealed the inspiration and steady hand of a writer of short fiction who seeks to illuminate what we are and how we are in the manner of the Anton Chekhov of "The Lady with the Dog" and "Ward No. 6," as well as in the manner of the Leopoldo Alas of "Doña Berta" and "Change of Light."

*

The eleven stories of this volume range widely in theme and length and, except for "The Catastrophe," are arranged in order of publication.

• The Poe-like exploration of what constitutes the netherworld, between what actually surrounds us and what we believe surrounds us—our minds playing tricks on us?—is at the center of the despair of the woebegone woodcutter whom we see in "The Falling Snow" (1866). Can we say for certain that an "ominous bird of yore," like the *ebony bird* of "The Raven," is present in this tale? With Eça having read and admired Poe, it seems likely. And although no Lenore appears, there is very possibly another echo, for like the lover-narrator of Poe's poem, the woodcutter looks out over a nighttime of snow and sees naught but "Darkness there and nothing more." In this first piece of short fiction Eça already displays his ability to evoke atmosphere through the chilling presence of a murder of crows.

• To depict a Lucifer who is the "pontiff of the black Mass," humor, irony, and satire are the means that tell of the fantastic, religious, and miraculous happenings in "Master Devil" (1867). The tale moves quickly as Eça enumerates, in short, punctuated paragraphs, the evil that the Devil has perpetrated since his expulsion from Heaven. He has had his wicked way with both man and woman, he has poisoned and tyrannized, and he has tortured saints, but when—in deceitful disguise—he seeks to wreak havoc in the pure love of two youths, his efforts will be foiled by a power that is much greater than his, for it is a Force he cannot command. And he will then make a most astonishing admission and decision, because "Master Devil" is also—when all is said and done—a story of the hope of love, of the promise of love, rendered in a tenderness that reaches beyond words.

• The power of love becomes the obsession of love in "The Peculiarities of a Blonde Girl" (1874), the story that would secure Eça's standing in short fiction. Although the title tells us that the peculiarities are the girl's, the obsession that is narrated in detail is that of Macário, whose story—we are informed in the very first line—is "a simple one." A disingenuous announcement, to be sure, for it is anything but "simple." It is the exploration of a young man whose soul is blinded by love, a youth whose near instantaneous love for the blonde girl named Luísa prompts him to ignore her past, and because all restraint is absent, he soon finds himself between wind and water. And it will take a shattering occurrence to wake him to a reality that is anything but "peculiar," anything but "simple."

• If the modernity of nineteenth-century city life becomes a complex of inventions that ought to facilitate the way one lives, the other side of that dubious coin is the simplicity of country life, where the ways of the telegraph and théâtrophone—and other inventions in "Civilization" (1892)—are unknown. The thread that runs through this story speaks to nostalgia for a rustic life free from hectic minutiae, and the rapid pace quickly gets to the heart of the meaning of the sight of an unobstructed, star-spangled sky. And that twinkling sky will be but one example that prompts Eça to depict the wonders of nature with poetic inspiration and show himself to be a writer of refined sensibilities.

• Not all Portuguese editions (Lello & Irmão, Livros do Brasil, Aguilar, Porto Editora) include Eça's foreword and afterword to "The Wet Nurse," and therefore do not explain that he had titled it "A Topic for Verse" [*Tema para Versos*] when he submitted it to the *Gazeta de Notícias* in Rio de Janeiro in 1893. It was his friend Luís de Magalhães who invented this title for a story about a wet nurse" [A Aia] for a collection of Eça's short stories—*Contos*, which he put together shortly after the author's death. However, after the publication of *Contos* the title "The Wet Nurse" took hold, with subsequent editions and publishers following suit. The foreword as setting for this story matters because of what Eça "offers" to poets as material: dark, daring, and dramatic deeds, which together constitute the stuff of legend, along the lines of the traditional "Once upon a time...."

• The twin themes of greed and betrayal quickly bring to the fore the insidious designs of the three noblemen brothers who are the protagonists of "The Treasure" (1894). If, as the cliché has it, money is the root of all evil, a chance find becomes the driving force to pursue it; and if extreme measures are taken to acquire it, then extreme consequences will result. It is a dark tale in that Eça sees no good in his creations, only total "darkness" of character in them. And, as they are in "The Falling Snow" and will be in "The Dead Man," crows figure as birds of ill omen.

• Obsession in various forms takes us through other powerful emotions in "The Dead Man" (1895): love begets jealousy begets vengeance begets judgment. The action of this twelfth-century tale begins at the door of a church in Spain when a dashing young man—a single young man—fixes his eyes on a beautiful young woman who, we will learn in short order, is married to a possessive, elderly man. This husband's jealousy and the young man's love will trigger a series of fantastic events that can only be explained as not of this world. And given the pervasiveness of religion and belief, then some other powerful force must explain the unexplainable. Is it faith? Is it love? And if it is love, what kind, or kinds, of love? And what effect must the young man's encounters with the fantastic occurrences have on the sanity of more than one person?

• Through Ulysses, being held captive by Calypso on the island of Ogygia, Eça invites us in "Perfection" (1897) to consider what may, at first, seem an imponderable: What is perfection? Can it be defined? Is it, as the common phrase would have it, in the eye of the beholder? With its cast of familiar characters from Greek mythology, "Perfection" asks these questions as well as others, chief among them the effect that perfection could have on us if we were sated by it. Would life become humdrum? Would it become mere routine? Would it become mechanical? Would it erase the thrill of emotion? Would it deprive us of the resolution of conflict that enriches life? Calypso, being a goddess, does not understand Ulysses's response to perfection. Will we, mere mortals like him, understand it?

• "José Matias" (1897), published thirteen years after the appearance of "The Peculiarities of a Blonde Girl," examines once again the obsession of love. A tale of keen psychological insight, it may well be Eça's most lauded short story, this one viewing the obsession of love through the roseate lens of idealism and—given that a garden separates the lovers—an ongoing, detailed examination of emotional responses to furtive smiles, stolen glances, peeks from behind drawn curtains, and the flutter of roses and dahlias. The love of this eponymous protagonist for the beautiful Elisa Miranda is nurtured at a remove, and it spans years and years and years, and his eventual torment will be his unwillingness to sully their love. But sully it how? Alexander Coleman has written of this consummate story: "'José Matias' affords us an oblique and highly restricted version of the theme common to it and *The Maias*—the obstruction of feeling, love, and passion."[2] Upon publication, "José Matias" was immediately judged a masterpiece. That judgment has endured, for this story—like very few others—would have us fathom what can be wrought by the intensity of love.

• In a faraway time, a young Rabbi named Jesus began to teach the coming of the kingdom of God, and with a magic that had never been seen before, he cured all manner of human ills. Word spread. Many clamored. Powerful and powerless alike sought him. A vintner; a Roman centurion; the rich; the poor: all who had heard of his magic desperately wished for him to intercede on their behalf. But a crippled little boy had faith, a crippled little boy implored his mother to search for Jesus because he knew that Jesus loved all children, even a pitiful, crippled little boy who slept on a ragged bed of straw. But if that gentle Rabbi were to cure his and his mother's sorrows with magic, how would He make himself known in "The Gentle Miracle" (1898)?

• Of the eleven stories included in this volume, "The Catastrophe" is the only one that was not published in Eça's lifetime.[3] We can only wonder why not, for this powerful story engages us with its naked intensity, its aroused passion, and its blunt honesty. As the first-person narrator deals with the dread, the horror of a foreign invasion (by Spain?), he simultaneously describes, in unsparing detail, the pathetic state of the Portuguese military—its training, its uniforms, its arms, its

2. Alexander Coleman, *Eça de Queirós and European Realism* (New York: New York University Press, 1980), 240.

3. Maria Filomena Mónica (*Contos Escolhidos*, Selection and Introduction [Lisbon: Relógio D'Agua Editores, 2004], 25) believes that it was written sometime in the 1890s.

barracks, its morale. And when war comes and he goes off with his national militia, he again deals with … the dread, the horror of combat. And what ensues is a ringing endorsement of the exalted meaning of patriotism: a passionate, honest outcry that heralds a clear-eyed vision of loyalty to one's country. And the reader will come to understand what Eça understood—that catastrophes come in several guises if we are not alert to threats from within and from without.

In the original Portuguese, this story is almost always published in one volume with *The Count of Abranhos* [*O Conde de Abranhos*], Eça's posthumous novel/memoir about a conniving, cowardly, self-serving politician. No one knows the reason. Perhaps it is because both are posthumous publications; then too, perhaps it is because the character of the story's protagonist stands in direct contrast to the character of the novel's protagonist.

Translation Sources

For the ten stories published in Eça's lifetime, I used *Contos I* (Lisbon: Imprensa Nacional-Casa da Moeda, 2009), Edição Crítica das Obras de Eça de Queirós: preface, Carlos Reis, edition, Marie-Hélène Piwnik. For "Master Devil" (which contains the original [1867] *Gazeta de Portugal* version), I used: *Prosas Bárbaras*, 6th ed. (Lisbon: Livros do Brasil, n.d).

For "The Catastrophe," I used *Contos II* (Lisbon: Imprensa Nacional-Casa de Moeda, 2003), Edição Crítica das Obras de Eça de Queirós: preface, Carlos Reis; edition, Marie-Hélène Piwnik; *Contos Escolhidos de Eça de Queirós* (Lisbon, Relógio D'Agua, 2004); edition and introductory study, Maria Filomena Mónica.

Works Cited and Consulted

Coleman, Alexander. *Eça de Queirós and European Realism*. New York: New York University Press, 1980.

Eça de Queirós, José Maria. *Prosas Bárbaras*. 6th ed. Text and notes, Helena Cidade Moura. Lisbon: Livros do Brasil, n.d. Introduction, Jaime Batalha Reis.

Machado da Rosa, Alberto. *Eça, Discípulo de Machado?* Lisbon: Editorial Presença, n.d.

Mónica, Maria Filomena. *Eça de Queirós*. 6th ed. Lisbon: Quetzal Editores, 2018. Invaluable biography as well as critical study, with numerous photographs chronicling Eça's life. It is also available in English: *Eça de Queiroz*. Translated by Alice Aiken. Woodbridge, U.K., and Rochester, N.Y.: Tamesis [Boydell and Brewer], 2005. Foreword, Sir Raymond Carr.

———. *Contos Escolhidos de Eça de Queirós*. Selection and Introduction. Lisbon: Relógio D'Agua Editores, 2004. Introductory study.

Pinheiro, Magda. *Lisbon: A Biography*. Translated by Mario Pereira. North Dartmouth, Mass.: Tagus Press, 2018.

Piwnik, Marie-Hélène: *Contos I*: introductory study; *Contos II*: introductory study.

Silva, João. *Entertaining Lisbon: Music, Theater, and Modern Life in the Late 19th Century*. Oxford: Oxford University Press, 2016.

Simões, João Gaspar. *Vida e Obra de Eça de Queirós*. 2nd ed. Lisbon: Livraria Bertrand, 1973.

Tavares Dias, Marina. *A Lisboa de Eça de Queiroz*. 2nd ed. Lisbon: Quimera Editores, 2003.

Publication Notes:
Editions of Eça de Queirós's Short Stories

In addition to the half dozen or so extant unabridged editions of Eça's short stories, further evidence of their ongoing popularity in Portugal is seen in two large-format books of a different kind:

• *Contos de Eça de Queiroz: O Tesouro, O Suave Milagre, O Defunto*, 3rd ed. Lisbon: Assírio Bacelar, 1993. An adaptation of "The Treasure," "The Gentle Miracle," and "The Dead Man," by José Carlos Teixeira, all three depicted in illustrations by E. T. Coelho.

• *Seis Contos de Eça de Queirós*. Porto: Porto Editora, 2016. For children ("*os mais novos*"): An adaption in simplified form of "The Wet Nurse [A Topic for Verse]," "The Treasure," "The Dead Man," "Civilization," and "The Gentle Miracle," by Luísa Ducla Soares with illustrations by Rafaello Bergonse.[4] The cover, interestingly, features a full-scale color drawing of a man, a boy, and a girl seated on a garden bench, the man reading to the children as they look at pages of the book with him. It is a rendition based on a photograph of Eça reading to his son, José Maria, and to his daughter, Maria, in the garden of their home in Neuilly [France]. The photograph is reproduced in the photos section, between pages 384 and 385 [no. 50], of Maria Filomena Mónica's *Eça de Queirós*, Portuguese edition, and between pages 272 and 273 [no. 30], English translation.

• For original graphics: *Adão e Eva no Paraíso seguido de O Senhor Diabo e Outros Contos*. Lisbon: Guerra e Paz Editores, 2018, edition prepared by Ana Salgado, has the added attraction of reproducing the illustrations for three stories that appeared in *Revista Moderna* in 1897: four [pages 193, 198, 201, 208] in "Perfection," three [pages 218, 227, 230] in "José Matias," and one [242] in "The Gentle Miracle."

✳

Dr. Trevor Lipscombe, director of the Catholic University of America Press, enthusiastically embraced my efforts to promote the writings of José Maria Eça de Queirós, this great

---

4. The book also includes a story titled "Frei [Brother] Genebro."

nineteenth-century Portuguese author who is still not as well known as he deserves to be. I extend many thanks to Theresa Walker, the Press's managing editor, for patiently shepherding me through the multiple steps that make a manuscript into a book. And I am grateful to Aldene Fredenburg, who always strikes the right chord as a copy editor.

I am greatly indebted to the noted scholar and Eça biographer Dr. Maria Filomena Mónica for permission to reproduce her condensed introduction to José Maria Eça de Queirós, which first appeared in *Portuguese Studies* 18 (2002): 50–63. Professor Paulo de Medeiros of the University of Warwick helpfully led me to Gerard Lowe, who granted authorization on behalf of the Modern Humanities Research Association, the journal's publisher, to reprint the introduction with this translation of a selection of Eça's short stories.

The great majority of the readers of the journal would have been familiar with the people and events that she cites, but for the ease of those readers unfamiliar with Portuguese history and culture, I have provided a Glossary after Dr. Monica's introduction and at the end of each of the stories in this selection, with the exception of "The Falling Snow" and "[The Wet Nurse] A Topic for Verse."

Introduction

Maria Filomena Mónica
Instituto de Ciências Sociais, Universidade de Lisboa

José Maria Eça de Queirós
(1845–1900)

*

In 1908, at the age of eighty-two, Eça's mother, Carolina Augusta Eça de Queirós, descended the Chiado, dressed in gray, with a little dark hat decorated with white *aigrettes*. In spite of the recent death of her husband and her eldest son, she appeared serene. She was on her way to lunch with a relative. When this lady expressed concern over the grief suffered by Aurora, the only one of her seven children still surviving, Carolina Augusta retorted, "Why wouldn't she be depressed? What with one heartbreak after another! Her father and two brothers having died!" It was as if none of this—neither the death of her husband nor her children—had anything to do with her. This woman, so chic and self-contained, is one of the great mysteries of Eça's life.[1]

It is a mystery that, unfortunately, cannot be solved. There is nothing about Carolina Augusta in the archives; Eça's books

---

1. M. D'Eça de Alpoim, *Os Eças* (Viana do Castelo: 1992).

make little reference to her, and the son never spoke of her. The claim that Eça's personality was affected by his relationship with his mother lacks supporting evidence.[2] It is possible that Eça was traumatized by his illegitimacy, but the opposite is just as likely to be true. Considering the high incidence of births outside marriage at the time, he may have viewed his situation with indifference. In such circumstances the researcher can only adopt the attitude that some questions must be left unanswered.

It is known that Eça was registered in 1845 as the child of an "unknown mother." Much has been made of this fact, but his mother's coolness may have been more traumatic for the child than the words of a priest. What is known for certain is that Eça's upbringing took place mainly behind closed doors, without the company of anyone his own age. Eça's character was formed at his elderly grandmother's knee, listening to the poetry of Mendes Leal, and in the company of black servants who told him stories of Charlemagne. In the cloistered life of Verdemilho the old folks loved the little boy, but the grandson of Judge Queirós was not allowed to play with the barefoot boys who loitered about the manor house. The reserve that marked Eça until his death may be in part attributed to this limbo.

For it was a sort of limbo. Eça knew from the time he was a very small boy that aside from his nurse, who had breast-fed him, and his grandparents, to whom he had been entrusted, he had a father and a mother. He knew that they had married when he was about four years old. He had heard that he had brothers and sisters in Oporto. He alone, for reasons he did not understand, had remained in Verdemilho. Like all children who are faced with a mystery that adults prefer not to explain, he tried to forget about it. He spent days looking at the books in his grandfather's library. As a frail child he avoided the chal-

2. J. Gaspar Simões, *Vida e Obra de Eça de Queirós*, 4 vols (Lisbon: Bertrand, 1980).

lenge of physical adventures. He did not know if he was unhappy or not. He knew only that he lived in a bell jar.

At ten he was sent to school in Oporto as a half-boarder. At weekends, rather than going to his parents' house, he stayed with an uncle and aunt. Nineteenth-century families were often oddly composed, but this was an unusual solution, even for the period. Eça reacted by being an excellent student. He continued to read everything he could get his hands on. The serialized fiction of the *Nacional*—for which Camilo, Arnaldo Gama, and Evaristo Basto were writing—was greedily consumed. At fifteen he was writing romantic poems. Shortly thereafter he fell in love with a cousin. The girl's father, who had received him in his house, put an end to the fantasy. Thin, with a large nose and sunken eyes (Eça resembled his mother), he probably did not greatly attract the girls. But this was not the reason he did not marry his cousin: more important than his physical appearance was the lack of a fortune. The uncle claimed that their being first cousins was justification for his refusal, yet shortly afterward the girl was to marry another first cousin, João Pedro Schalwach, a lieutenant colonel and fifty-year-old widower. In 1861, Eça left for Coimbra. It was not after all with his cousin Albuquerque that he would discover sex, but in a brothel. And he enjoyed it.

At university he continued to lack self-confidence. In the first year he lived not in a *república* [dormitory for university students], but in the house of a family friend, which hardly helped him to bloom. He remained solitary. During the day he attended classes; at night he planned the writing of poems that would immortalize humanity. He was diligent and passed his exams. And eventually he left Dr. Dória's house and went to live in a *república*. He at once became an atheist, learned to despise the classics, and began to read the French poets. Eça did not miss a single new book that arrived in Coimbra. Victor Hugo was his hero, Proudhon and Balzac his mentors. By this time politics interested him infinitely less than literature. Had he wished to be a militant he did not lack for opportunity: while at Coimbra he witnessed the forced resignation of the rector, the agitation around the question of *Bom Senso e Bom Gusto* [Good Sense and Good Taste], and the flight of students to Oporto. Yet, although he knew Antero de Quental, he preferred the company of bohemians such as João Penha.

With his bachelor's diploma in hand, he arrived in the capital in 1866. His father, Judge Teixeira de Queirós, had been transferred to Lisbon, where he lived in a splendid house in the Rossio. For the first time Eça went to live with his parents. He did not enjoy it. He scarcely knew his brothers and sisters; his father wore him down with advice about a career; his mother alarmed him with her severity. Quite by chance, in the office of the periodical *Gazeta de Portugal*, which was publishing some of his short stories, he met a very different soul, the gregarious Jaime Batalha Reis. Eça began virtually to live in his house. In a room where Reis lived in the Bairro Alto, he continued to read: Flaubert, Poe, Renan, and Nerval. He visited the Grémio Literário [Literary Circle], where, along with Batalha Reis, he delighted in consulting the poetry of Baudelaire in old French magazines.[3] It was at this point that he realized that he wanted to be a writer.

His father, however, was not inclined to support him much longer and went to speak with a friend, the well-known landowner José Maria Eugénio de Almeida, who arranged a job for Eça as editor of a newspaper with headquarters in Évora. The idea of moving to the provinces did not appeal to Eça, but the salary would amply make up for the inconvenience. In December of 1866, Eça departed. Once in Évora, he confined himself

---

3. J. Batalha Reis, Introduction to "*Prosas Bárbaras*," in *Obras de Eça de Queirós*, 4 vols. (Porto: Lello, n.d.), 1:556.

to reciting the "radical" primer, which consisted of speaking ill of all politicians and protesting against all taxes. He stayed in Évora until August 1867, at which point, sick to death of landowners, dust, and heat, he returned to the capital. He knew that it was in the city and not the plains of the Alentejo that he might become known.

After a lull (Batalha was on holiday), he resumed the life he most enjoyed: conversations with friends, suppers, and strolls about the city until dawn. Eça alternated talks with Oliveira Martins, whom he met at this time, with revelries with Luís de Resende, his schoolmate from the college in Lapa, who visited Lisbon from time to time. Surprisingly, after the journalism of Évora, he returned to the romantic prose of the *Gazeta de Portugal*.

One of his most striking traits—eternal dissatisfaction with the places he lived in—began to emerge. Just a few months after his arrival in Lisbon, the capital had already begun to elicit feelings of frustration. With his head teeming with the heroes of the French novels he was reading, the Lisbon of the Fusão (the coalition government that lasted from 1865 to 1868) looked to him like a provincial prison. It was at this time that, together with Antero and Batalha Reis, he invented a *persona*, Carlos Fradique Mendes, under whose name he wrote his sole poem, "Serenata de Satã às Estrelas" [Satan's Serenade to the Stars]. As the title implies, it was intended to shock the bourgeoisie.

The bourgeoisie was the chief enemy of the "*geração de* [generation of] 1870," all of whom detested its complacency, its opulence, its joyfulness. The group to which Eça belonged was utopian, fighting the "civilization" that Prime Minister Fontes Pereira de Melo was trying to import into Portugal. The so-called material improvements, the railways, the telegraph, the machinery, seemed meaningless to them. Some, like Antero de Quental, turned nostalgically to an age when their grandfathers had taken up arms in the struggle for liberty. Others, like Oliveira Martins, looked to the radiant future of socialism. Eça decided to travel.

At twenty-four, he departed by ship for Palestine, as a tourist, along with his friend Luís de Resende. The excuse for the trip was to witness the opening of the Suez Canal (1867). Eça adored everything he saw: Turkish baths, hashish, and the women he passed in the street. Influenced by the descriptions and comments of famous writers about the place, he, too, admired the smells, the light, the sounds of the Orient. In the bazaar his timidity vanished. He even lost his physical fear: he rode horseback, crossed crags and cliffs, lost himself in the mountains of Upper Syria. What he had always suspected was true: Portugal smothered him.

When he arrived back in Lisbon his friends were open-mouthed. The trip had turned him into a dandy. Eça appeared in light-colored trousers, rolled up high, and straw-colored gloves. He carried little bags of hashish in his pockets. For once, he felt superior to his companions. But his father spoiled the occasion, once again insisting on the need for a job. Eça resisted the idea of embarking on a career as a magistrate. Instead, he published a short story entitled, "A Morte de Jesus" [The Death of Jesus] and an article about the festivities that had taken place around the inauguration of the Suez Canal. But in Portugal it was not possible to live from writing alone. In desperation he applied for the diplomatic service. His father got him a position as district councilor in Leiria.[4]

When he reencountered Ramalho, who had been his teacher in the *liceu*, Eça arranged for them to write something together—anything that would make money. Thus were born the satirical pamphlets *As Farpas* [The Barbs] and the novel

---

4. Ambassadorial posts were reserved for aristocrats and politicians. Eça applied, therefore, for the consular service.

O Mistério da Estrada de Sintra [The Mystery of the Sintra Road]. Eça's work as a bureaucrat in Leiria, and especially anything concerned with local elections, was neglected. He preferred to examine life close-up. Every day he passed the local cathedral and then added another scene to the novel in which he hoped to reveal the hypocrisy of priests. Politicians sickened him; priests were repellent; the bourgeoisie, uncouth.

Once the apprenticeship in Leiria was over, Eça returned to Lisbon. Though not a militant by nature, he then participated in the Conferencias do Casino [Casino Lectures]. On one hand, he saw the gesture as a favor to his friends; on the other, he fancied shocking the established critics with the concept of Realism in literature. The government prohibited the continuation of the talks, owing in great part to the climate that then prevailed in Europe, with the Commune in Paris and the monarchy overthrown in Spain. Even in Lisbon the times favored insurrection. Eça was only an observer, but he knew that Antero and Batalha Reis were conspiring with the Spanish "internationalists" who had sought refuge in Lisbon.

On November 9, 1872, he left for Cuba. He had taken first place in the Foreign Ministry examination but had to wait some months, since the post earmarked for him in Brazil was given to another candidate who had important connections. Once in Havana he could not get used to the heat, the bad manners, the harshness of daily life. He loathed the Spanish colonial elite and much preferred the Americans who came to Cuba on holiday. It was among this community that he met two women, Mollie and Anna, whom he proceeded to woo, both at the same time. Mollie was wealthy and single, Anna cultivated and married. When both left for the United States, Eça followed them. After requesting leave from the Foreign Ministry, Eça spent several months in America. Here the relationship with Anna deepened. She wanted to leave her husband, but Eça was afraid of the consequences. He left New York in haste and went to Pittsburgh, where, unexpectedly, he proposed marriage to Mollie. This rather insignificant girl refused him, at which point Eça turned to the beautiful Anna. But not for long. He learned by letter that she had left her husband. At this point he refused to see her. Whatever may have occurred between them, if Eça was later capable of writing in *Os Maias* [The Maias] of Carlos Eduardo's passion as he did, it was no doubt because of this affair. Without Anna, Eça would have left us only the little *burguesas* of the Chiado, like Luísa of *O Primo Basílio* [Cousin Bazilio], or prostitutes, such as Colombe of *A Cidade e as Serras* [The City and the Mountains].

Eça's next post was in Newcastle. It was a harsh city, but at least it was in Europe. And after the adventures of the past months Eça was in need of peace and quiet. He had not forgotten Anna, but knowing that she was on another continent calmed him. What he now wanted above all was to write. Little by little, Eça forgot Anna. For a writer, the single life was infinitely superior to the domesticity that marriage would demand. Eça took advantage of his free time, and in Newcastle it was abundant, to recreate Leiria: its squares, its pious women, its priests.

Before leaving for England, Eça had shown the manuscript of *O Crime do Padre Amaro* [The Crime of Father Amaro] to Batalha Reis. Yet, at this point, considering it only a rough draft, he did not want to publish it. His friend, who was on the point of launching a new magazine with Antero de Quental, promised him he would have plenty of time to introduce any changes he wanted to the typographer's proofs. After considerable hesitation, Eça yielded. But it all went wrong. In the midst of much haste, Eça's serialized episodes came out in the *Revista Ocidental*, in February 1875, without any amendments. Predictably, Eça was furious. Although he did not yet feel secure as a writer, he knew he had produced something exceptional. He avenged himself by immediately publishing *O Crime do Padre Amaro* as a book.

He would have been grateful for some encouragement, but there was none. Though they did not tell him so, both Antero and Ramalho thought the book immoral. Only Batalha Reis liked it. Had it not been for him there is no telling if *O Crime* would have come out. Doubly isolated, Eça's situation was not pleasant: in England no one could read his book; in Portugal no one understood it. Alberto de Oliveira tells a revealing story. After Luís de Resende had read *O Crime do Padre Amaro*, he told Eça, "How could you have devoted five hundred pages to describe life in Leiria, where nothing that happens in one year could interest me for one half hour?"[5] Resende was not the only one who failed to understand *O Crime do Padre Amaro*. In a letter to Oliveira Martins in March 1875, Antero wrote, "I'm much more afraid of *Father Amaro* (which is Pigault-Lebrun decked out in Flaubert, as you'll see to your amazement) than I am of socialism; but Batalha has fixed ideas and some rather peculiar ones. He says that *Father Amaro* is *revolutionary* and stands by it."[6] That the work is extremely daring, no one can deny. It is equally undeniable that it is one of the most astonishing literary debuts of its time.

Only when the third edition appeared did Antero praise Eça. Though aware that Eça did not greatly prize his opinions, Antero wrote him a letter that ended with words that were bound to stroke his ego: "As for artistic merit, you don't need for me to point it out to you. You are a conscientious artist and know full well what you're doing. Your style—aside from an

5. Alberto de Oliveira, *Eça de Queiroz: Páginas de Memória* (Lisbon: Portugália, [n.d.]), 87.

6. Pigault-Lebrun was a writer famous for the pornographic nature of his novels. For the letter, see *Obras Completas/Antero de Quental/Cartas*, ed. Ana Maria Almeida Martins, 2 vols. (Lisbon: Comunicação, 1989), 1:270.

occasional lapse in usage and a certain deficiency of vocabulary (you never wanted to read the classics!)—is admirable." And the highest praise: "For some time now I've noticed that you are the only one of us who's never banal. In your sentences there is never a word to fill in, to round out, inserted there from what you've heard and not from what you've imagined. Each word in them is there because it should be: it depicts, it describes, it explains. That is the ideal of style."[7]

Meanwhile, full of energy, Eça had a thousand plans. Like Zola, he dreamed of writing a series of short works in which he would portray "*a sociedade portuguesa tal qual a fez o Constitucionalismo*" [Portuguese society exactly as Constitutionalism has made it]. He thought rather disingenuously that he could reform Portugal through laughter: like all satirists he was a moralist. In 1878, *O Primo Basílio* appeared. Once again Ramalho thought it indecorous, while Teófilo Braga, who was committed to destroying the monarchy, praised it. Although it caused more scandal than *O Crime*—owing to a daring sex scene—the book is less violent than the first. It is proof that Eça was a good judge of his own work that he always preferred *O Crime*.

Far away in Newcastle, he continued thinking of the book he would write next. He was now reading English authors and regretting that he had come to them so late. By the end of the 1870s, when he was transferred to Bristol, Eça could take pride in being famous. In Brazil, Machado de Assis had taken the trouble to review his work. In spite of misplaced moralism, Machado de Assis's reservations touched Eça. A work of art, as he now perceived it, did not need to justify itself or serve a social purpose.

Lost in the north of England, he continued to work. It is remarkable what he managed to produce in 1878 and 1879.

7. Almeida Martins, *Obras Completas*, 499–500.

Aside from the sketch for the future short story *A Catástrofe* [The Catastrophe] (about a possible Spanish invasion), Eça wrote *A Capital* [The Capital], in which he attacked the republicans, *O Conde de Abranhos* [The Count of Abranhos] (this time it was the turn of monarchist politicians), and *A Tragédia da Rua das Flores* [The Tragedy of the Street of Flowers] (a work whose central theme was incest). Yet on rereading what he had written, Eça felt a kind of panic. He was convinced that if he were to publish these books he would never be able to set foot again in Lisbon.

What followed was a painful phase of intellectual reconversion. Conscious of the limitations of realism, Eça did not want to fall into spiritualism, which was beginning to be fashionable. The success of *O Primo Basílio* had labeled him a naturalist, a designation he now despised. It was difficult for him to abandon what he did best—caricature. He would have liked to let his imagination wander in the universe. A beautiful woman with whom he spent holidays at Anjou—and whom we know only from photographs—must have helped in his liberation. In 1880 he published *O Mandarim* [The Mandarin], an oriental fantasy, while he thought about his greatest novel, *Os Maias*.

In the middle of writing *Os Maias*, Eça produced another book, *A Relíquia* [The Relic]. It was, once again, an attack on sanctimonious churchy women (*beatas*). It is far inferior to *O Crime do Padre Amaro*. Eça's greatest pleasure—aside from including a scene of the Passion of Christ—was entering it in a competition organized by the Academy of Sciences. As he had expected, he failed to win the prize, but the rejection caused Pinheiro Chagas, who was in charge of writing the final report, many sleepless nights. Eça was delighted with the controversy.

In 1886, Eça married. It is not correct to say, as Gaspar Simões has done, that the marriage was little more than a step up the social ladder for Eça. The decisive motive was certainly not passion, although reading the love letters, especially Eça's, one could believe that he had been overcome by a storm of emotions. Eça was one who knew how to manipulate words. In this case he needed to convince Emília that the marriage would be right for her. Initially she had resisted, either because she considered herself to be dishonored on account of an earlier entanglement with Luís de Soveral or because she was still emotionally attached to the man. Emília was then twenty-eight and resigning herself to spinsterhood. Eça's superb letters dissuaded her from that.

At forty, Eça had experienced all the passions, love, and adventures he expected to have. He wanted a companion. He chose Emília because she was the sister of friends, because she had some aptitude for managing a household, and because she was capable of bringing up children. By the standards of the time she had received a reasonable education: she spoke foreign languages, read books, could maintain a conversation. And she was not a *petite bourgeoise* who was likely to fall in love with a Basílio at the first opportunity. These were the reasons, all of them eminently serious, that led Eça to the altar.

Marriage at first hand, however, was rather different from what Eça had imagined. It did not take him long to realize that he had lost the silence to which he had become accustomed. Emília soon became pregnant, and less than a year after the wedding a daughter, Maria, was born. Three boys then followed in succession. For the first time Eça had to furnish a house (up until then he had always lived in furnished houses). His expenses increased: there were nannies to hire, summer holidays to organize. Even if Eça could isolate himself in the pavilion at the end of the garden, his life had changed. No one knows if this was what he wanted: it was what he got.

In 1888, after eight years' gestation, his masterpiece, *Os Maias*, was published. By now it was no longer a work of realism but a novel of manners with a tragedy at its core. There were many other innovations. Under the influence of English literature, the time element was treated in a new way, and, for the first time, Eça admitted the possibility of extraordinary coincidences. Various reasons could account for the long gestation period of the work, but what most delayed its publication was the intellectual crisis through which Eça had passed. He had come in contact with writers—Dickens, George Eliot, Thackeray, Carlyle—very different from those who had been the delight of his youth. Although he continued to like Flaubert, he acknowledged that he had rivals. Eça wrote and rewrote, endlessly, the same pages.[8] In *Os Maias* there are no longer social ideals; there is only a country that cannot renew itself and someone who loves a goddess.

Os Maias is the most autobiographical of his works. To a certain extent, one can see the Eça of the 1880s in Carlos da Maia and in João da Ega. There is an obvious risk of reading too much into the novel, but surely it is not wrong to say that the hatred of politicians, the panic brought on by the stultifying life in Lisbon, the desire to publish a magazine, the decrying of imported fashions, the awareness of the difficulty of literary creation, the contempt for a Portugal that mimicked France were all things that Eça transposed from himself into his fiction.

Had Eça stayed in Portugal, he might not have lived a life very different from that adopted by Ega. Ega is an Eça who did not go away and in not doing so made himself the court jester. Carlos da Maia also has many of the author's traits. In the realm of love, Carlos is even closer to Eça than Ega. When Car-

---

8. Some modern critics have tried to identify the dates on which various parts of the novel were written. A. Freeland contends that chapters 1–4 and part of chapter 7 must have been written in the period 1880–83; the rest, chapters 11–18, cannot be dated precisely. Nonetheless, Eça would have had a clear concept of the work by 1883; see Freeland, *O Leitor e a Verdade Oculta: Ensaio sobre Os Maias* (Lisbon: Imprensa Nacional, 1989).

los speaks of his inability to form a relationship with a woman without feeling overcome by tedium—or by fear?—soon afterward, it is Eça who speaks. Carlos's on-again, off-again liaison with the Countess of Gouvarinho must not have been so very different from the amorous incidents with Anna. Maria Eduarda, the distant goddess, is perhaps the object that symbolizes his incapacity to love. Many of Carlos da Maia's reactions to the country are those that Eça expressed on various occasions. Consider the sadness with which Carlos comments on the physical characteristics of the population of Lisbon or the joy he feels on some luminous January mornings. It is also Carlos who best mirrors Eça's hesitation about a possible return to the *patria*. In 1888, Eça imagines a destiny for Carlos—residence in Paris—that was to become his own.

In *Os Maias*, Eça has replaced the anger expressed in his first work with a gentle discouragement. In some passages he even evinces compassion for his compatriots. Eça is now less critical of politicians. And the priest who appears on the farm in the Beira is a good man. Only with regard to the *bourgeoisie*, illustrated by the horrendous Eusèbiozinho and Dâmaso Salcede, does he maintain his rage.

With the exception of a rabid critique by Fialho de Almeida, the book that was Eça's masterpiece was viewed with indifference. It is regrettable that the only debate, inspired incidentally by Pinheiro Chagas, centered on the attempt to determine who was behind the figure of the poet Alencar. Instead of commenting on the book, the critics became indignant, or pretended to, that Eça had supposedly mocked an old poet. Some intellectuals must have felt they had been targeted in the scene in *Os Maias* set in the Trindade theatre. Apart from the arrogance with which Eça treated the *literati*, why did *Os Maias* matter?[9]

9. Aside from "O Grande Maia," published in *Hoje*, Bulhão Pato also edited three editions of the pamphlet *Lázaro Consul* (Lisbon: 1889). In fifteen pages, in verse, the poet

As far as the public was concerned, *O Primo Basílio* was still preferred.

In the year in which *Os Maias* was published, Eça was appointed consul in Paris. He was later to die in the city on which he had long set his heart. And die in more than one sense: *Os Maias* was the last book published in his lifetime. After 1888, Eça felt unable not to write, but to publish. And yet, when he arrived in Paris he had been full of plans. Some were even put into practice. In 1889 the magazine *Revista de Portugal* appeared. It was to be the vehicle through which he hoped to form an elite. Oliveira Martins, deeply involved in politics, wanted nothing better and would become Eça's great collaborator. But the publication was excessively pretentious, and it failed in 1892.

During the 1890s, Eça went to Lisbon a number of times in connection with the settlement of the Resende estate. A group of his friends, known as the Vencidos da Vida (those defeated by life), had been meeting regularly for dinner. To a certain extent they were the light-hearted side of the "Vida Nova" [New Life], the political movement led by Oliveira Martins. Eça attended only two of the eleven dinners but lent his support to the group. The sight of this bunch of snobs dining sumptuously in a country of starving people infuriated the petite bourgeoisie, but Eça paid little attention to their criticism. Besides, he took little interest in Oliveira Martins's projects. Soon he was to return to Paris.

Over the years Eça had spoken on occasion of the need for a purifying crisis as a means of awakening the decadent *patria*. In 1890, he got his crisis, in the form of a threat from the British government. But the Ultimatum, as it came to be called,

---

attacked Eça. Antero later justified Bulhão Pato; see A. Quental, *Cartas*, 2 vols. (Lisbon: Editorial Comunicação, 1989), vol. 2, letter no. 562, August 14, 1888. See also Eça's reply, in *Tempo*, February 8, 1889. In this article Eça refers to Pinheiro Chagas as "sempre este homen fatal [always this fatal man]," and denies that Alencar could have been inspired by Bulhão Pato.

brought nothing good to the fore. During this period Eça witnessed exhibitions of political romanticism that left him even more depressed. He turned inward. In Paris he did not seek the company of a single intellectual. The new aesthetic fashions irritated him. He did not like the Parnassians, and of the Symbolists he tolerated only Verlaine. If he understood the reaction of the young to Positivism, he still considered the idolatry of the form to be unseemly.

Before leaving England, Eça resuscitated Fradique Mendes as a kind of alter ego. When Oliveira Martins asked him to collaborate on a magazine, he wrote articles under the old satanic pseudonym, but his friend did not last long in the editorship of *O Repórter*. Fradique was laid to rest until *Revista de Portugal* was revived. *Correspondência de Fradique Mendes* is a difficult work to interpret. To what degree is Eça serious when, in a positive tone, he presents us with an unbearably petulant creature? Since the articles were never collected in a book during his lifetime (he went on correcting the proofs until the day of his death), we have only what appeared in the magazines, where Eça gives us not one view of Fradique, but several. He puts into the mouths of some of his friends—Ramalho, Batalha Reis, Carlos Mayer—a variety of opinions about the character of his hero. Fradique has some qualities, among which are physical beauty, money, cosmopolitanism, that Eça would like to have had. But he also had many ridiculous facets.

During these years Eça led a more bourgeois life, going on holidays with his wife and children, consorting with ambassadors, conversing with expatriates. In Portugal his friends were members of the establishment. But this did not lead him, as has been claimed in certain circles on the Left, to write reactionary things. The suggestion that Eça had "betrayed" the ideals of his youth is based on several fallacies, the main one being that in his youth Eça had been a revolutionary. Antero de Quental and

Batalha Reis had unquestionably been, but not Eça. None of this prevented him from changing his opinions, however, like anyone else. In his youth Eça had believed it possible to improve man's lot. With time, this belief disappeared. This did not make him a reactionary but a skeptic—or, as he himself put it, in 1898, a "vague, saddened anarchist."[10]

In 1892, Eça had written a short story, "Civilização" [Civilization], for the *Gazeta de Notícias* of Rio de Janeiro. It was to be the basis of *A Cidade e as Serras*. What is generally forgotten when the work is discussed is the fact that Jacinto, the hero who stays in the mountains, is not the only central character.[11] At least as pivotal is the narrator, Zé Fernandes. In the end, no one knows if Zé Fernandes chooses the city or the mountains. The ambiguity deepens if one adds that when Eça died he still had not revised the whole of the second part, later committed to the care of Ramalho, who was a far more conservative writer.

Meanwhile, Eça was also writing—and being published in serial form— *A Ilustre Casa de Ramires* [The Illustrious House of Ramires]. Contrary to orthodoxy, the aristocracy is not favorably portrayed. Gonçalo is a weak, cowardly, uncultivated person. The plot that concerns his ancestors does not serve to point up the hero's strength but rather his weakness. Tructesindo may have the soul of a barbarian, but he is a man who is true to his word. By contrast, Gonçalo is a liar. *A Ilustre Casa de Ramires* is not an apology for Gonçalo, much less for the *patria*.[12] On February 14, 1896, in a letter to Oliveira Martins,

---

10. "A Rainha," *Revista Moderna*, January 15, 1898; also in "Notas Contemporáneas," in *Obras de Eça de Queiroz*, 2:615.

11. Frank F. de Sousa called attention to this fact in *O Segredo de Eça: Ideologia e Ambiguidade em A Cidade e as Serras* (Lisbon: Cosmos, 1996).

12. "An Interpretation of "The Illustrious House of Ramires," in A. J. Costa Pimpão, *Escritos Diversos* (Coimbra: Universidade de Coimbra, 1972). In the part that is a historical novel, Eça amuses himself using heroic language, archaic rhetoric, medieval dialogue. As an ironic imitation of Herculano it is peerless. Through the figure of Castanheiro, Eça

Eça informs him that he is at work on *A Ilustre Casa de Ramires* with a view to its serialization in *O Serão*, a magazine that was in fact never published. In November 1897, *A Ilustre Casa de Ramires* began to appear in installments in *Revista Moderna*, but when the magazine folded, the serialization of the novel was interrupted.[13] The struggle between Eça and his editors over the delivery of the manuscript continued. Eça acknowledged his fault in the matter but did nothing to complete the work. In July 1899, he was still reviewing the proofs. When he died, he had yet to write the conclusion.

After Eça's death, the publisher asked Ramalho to correct the proofs, but the task was finally completed by Júlio Brandão. Since the original manuscript has disappeared, it is impossible to know what the editor may have changed, but it is plausible to think the changes were fewer than they would have been if made by Ramalho or by Eça's eldest son.[14] Strictly speaking, from the middle of chapter 10 on, or rather from the dawn that preceded the thrashing that Ramires gives Ernesto de Narcejas until the end, the text was revised after Eça's death.

Eça's last years were marked by sadness, despondency, and physical debility. In the French spas to which he went on

---

also targets young writers such as Alberto de Oliveira, who were going about preaching the need for a return to tradition.

13. This Brazilian version was never published. In essence, if not in detail, it is almost identical to the published version. Da Cal believes that the idea of taking the protagonist to Africa must have arisen after Eça had finished the installments, since the possibility had never been raised before; see Ernesto da Cal, *Lengua y estilo de Eça de Queiroz* (Coimbra: Universidade de Coimbra, 1975, 84). See also the edition of *A Ilustre Casa de Ramires*, ed. Elena Losada Soler (Lisbon: I.N., 1999). Since the manuscript no longer exists, the editor used the edition that was partially published in *Revista Moderna*, along with the first edition of the novel (1900).

14. In *In Memoriam de Eça de Queiroz*, ed. Eloy do Amaral and M. Cardoso Martha (1922), Júlio Brandão explains (158–64) that he left "intact" the pages by Eça that had been entrusted to him, although it is not clear what this means. H. Cidade Moura, who edited the text for [the publisher] Livros do Brasil, says that she used the first edition because "não tivemos possibilidades de consultar os manuscritos [we were unable to consult the manuscripts]"; see *A Ilustre Casa de Ramires* (Lisbon: Livros do Brasil, n.d.), 364.

pilgrimage, the doctors were not able to diagnose his illness. He strolled on the banks of the Seine at close of day, where he bought old Portuguese books from the secondhand dealers. The idea of death, which had never been far from his spirit, tormented him. He gazed in the mirror at the haggard creature that Columbano had painted.[15] At fifty, he looked like an old man.

In the summer of 1900, following his doctors' advice, he left for Switzerland. Ramalho, who was in Paris en route to Italy, accompanied him as far as Geneva. Eduardo Prado, a Brazilian friend of Eça's, also spent some days with him before leaving for the Alps. On August 13, feeling no improvement, Eça decided to return to Paris. He still planned to go to Heidelberg to see a specialist, but in Basel he felt so ill that he took the train for home. When his wife met him at the station, she understood at once how grave his condition was. Indeed, he had only three days to live. On the sixteenth he died.

His body arrived in Lisbon a month later. There was discussion on whether he should be buried beside his grandfather in the cemetery at Outeirinho, which was his expressed wish, but Emília decided against it. Eça was to stay in the tomb of the Resendes in the cemetery of the Alto de São João in Lisbon. As the years passed, the Resendes family took possession of his image, his books, his memory. The unpublished works were mutilated, rewritten, and reinterpreted. Today, his body lies in Tormes, near the mountains where he never wished to live.

Eça was a cosmopolite, but a cosmopolite who suffered because of what went on in the place where he was born. He was not a patriot, if by that is meant someone who has an imperial vision of his country. But he was one, if the term can be applied

15. Columbano painted three portraits of Eça, all of which have disappeared. A reproduction exists of the third and last painting, the original having been lost in the sinking of the ship St. André.

to one who is touched by the disasters that befall his country and feels joy at its glories, one who is indignant about its meanness and who yearns for a better life for its people. With *Os Maias* in the bookshops, Eça had left England in glory. He might compare himself (and he was aware of this) to the great European novelists. If he was not universally recognized, this was not for lack of merit but because he wrote in a language that no one read.

It is difficult, because the causes are so diverse, to explain why *Os Maias* was the last book by Eça to be published in his lifetime. His realist phase, which had given him the energy to write *O Crime do Padre Amaro*, was outgrown. The short fantasies, like *O Mandarim*, were the fruit of a single summer. *Os Maias* is his testament. And a sad testament it is. The scope of the work exhausted him. Perhaps, if the world in the last years of the century had not been moving on so fast, he might have recovered. But nothing turned out as he would have liked. Suddenly, Eça found himself without a voice. Would it have made sense to return to the realism of *O Primo Basílio*? To the satire of *A Relíquia*? To the tragedy of *Os Maias*? Eça realized that the 1890s had destroyed everything he had believed in. To cite only the best, there was applause for decadent novels, such as *A Rebours*, for epigrammatic plays, like *The Importance of Being Earnest*, and for symbolist poets, such as Mallarmé. But these did not inspire him. Eça felt he belonged to another, happier world. Still, he tried not to give up. *Fradique* is obviously a response to the new challenges. Nonetheless, Eça was not happy enough to publish what he was writing—neither *Fradique*, nor *A Cidade e as Serras*, nor *A Ilustre Casa de Ramires*.

The idea that Eça spent the last days of his life sighing for a return to his native country is a myth promoted by the Salazar regime. According to this version Eça, an alter ego of Jacinto, would have been reconciled at death's door with Portugal. One of the first people to pave the way for this idea, as it happens, was Eça's young admirer Alberto de Oliveira. In 1918, in the memoirs that he dedicated to him, he wrote,

> Nonetheless, I am absolutely convinced that Eça de Queiroz *never lived abroad*. He resided there, and he anchored his literary and consular vessel in sundry parts of the world, but he never settled on terra firma. His home and his life were always, throughout his long exile, an island surrounded by Portugal on all sides.[16]

The truth was precisely the opposite. The fascination that Paris had inspired in Eça had passed, but this did not make him long for Lisbon, much less for the mountains. The city was his element, the land abroad a refuge.

Glossary
(in order of appearance)

CHIADO: a district of shops, cafés, theaters, and bookstores in the center of Lisbon with the fashionable Rua Garrett running through it.

JOSÉ DA SILVA MENDES LEAL (1818–86): Portuguese poet, dramatist, and politician.

VERDEMILHO: small town in the Aveiro district (central coastal region of Portugal).

OPORTO: Porto, coastal city in northwest Portugal; the country's second largest.

CAMILO CASTELO BRANCO (1825–90): prolific Portuguese writer said to have produced more than 260 books.

ARNALDO GAMA (1828–69): Portuguese novelist, primarily historical fiction.

---

16. A. de Oliveira, *Eça de Queiroz, Páginas de Memórias* (Lisbon: Portugália, n.d., 63).

EVARISTO BASTO (1821–65): Portuguese writer of serial pieces [*feuilletons*].

COIMBRA: riverfront city in central Portugal, site of the University of Coimbra, the oldest in the Portuguese-speaking world (founded in 1290).

PIERRE-JOSEPH PROUDHON (1809–65): French politician, socialist, and professed anarchist whose writings had considerable influence on Eça.

BOM SENSO E BOM GOSTO: a response written in the form of a letter by Antero de Quental in 1865 to refute an attack on modernist poets by the traditionalist Feliciano de Castilho. Antero de Quental (1842–91): one of the great Portuguese poets, often spoken of as being in the company of Luís de Camões and Fernando Pessoa; António Feliciano de Castilho (1800–75): a Romantic poet whose exchange with Antero led to the controversy that became known as the *Questão Coimbrã* ("Coimbra Question").

JOÃO PENHA (1838–1919): Portuguese poet credited with introducing Parnassianism to Portugal.

ROSSIO: for centuries the principal square of the Baixa (downtown Lisbon).

JAIME BATALHA REIS (1847–1935): Portuguese agronomist and diplomat, a friend of Eça's, and an integral member of the Antero de Quental-Eça de Queirós circle.

BAIRRO ALTO (LITERALLY, "UPPER NEIGHBORHOOD OR QUARTER"): a maze of streets with shops, cafés, secondhand bookstores, and *fado* houses; site of the Jardim de São Pedro de Alcântara, famous not only for its garden but also for the *miradouro* or lookout with its magnificent, sweeping views of the Avenida da Liberdade, the Baixa, and the Tagus River.

GUSTAVE FLAUBERT (1821–80): known for his novel *Madame Bovary* and always searching for *le mot juste* ("the right word") as the basis for the reality of his fiction. He was the writer that Eça admired the most.

INTRODUCTION

JOSEPH ERNEST RENAN (1823–92): French philosopher and historian of Christianity.

GÉRARD DE NERVAL (1808–55): French writer, poet, and translator.

CHARLES BAUDELAIRE (1821–67): French poet known for his *Fleurs du mal* and for his influence on Paul Verlaine, Arthur Rimbaud, and Stéphane Mallarmé.

ÉVORA: a city in south-central Portugal.

ALENTEJO: the region that covers nearly all of the southern half of Portugal.

JOAQUIM PEDRO DE OLIVEIRA MARTINS (1845–94): Portuguese politician and social scientist; part of the '70s generation together with Eça, Antero de Quental, and Ramalho Ortigão.

ANTÓNIO MARIA DE FONTES PEREIRA DE MELO (1819–87): Portuguese statesman who served three times as prime minister of Portugal.

LEIRIA: a city in the Centro Region of Portugal, approximately eighty miles north of Lisbon; locale of *O Crime do Padre Amaro*.

JOSÉ DUARTE RAMALHO ORTIGÃO (1836–1915): Eça's instructor of French at the lycée and lifelong friend; he was another member of the Vencidos da Vida.

JOAQUIM TEÓFILO FERNANDES BRAGA (1843–1924): Portuguese writer, playwright, and politician.

JOAQUIM MARIA MACHADO DE ASSIS (1839–1908): considered the greatest writer of Brazilian literature, novels, and short stories; he took Eça to task for [the content] of *O Crime do Padre Amaro* and *O Primo Basílio*.

MANUEL JOAQUIM PINHEIRO CHAGAS (1842–95): Portuguese author of historical novels, journalist, and politician; he was Eça's bête noire.

JOSÉ VALENTIM FIALHO DE ALMEIDA (1857–1911): Portuguese writer, journalist, and translator; an early admirer of Eça's who subsequently became his most vitriolic critic.

RAIMUNDO ANTÓNIO DE BULHÃO PATO (1828–1912):
Portuguese poet, essayist, and memoirist.

ULTIMATUM [BY THE BRITISH GOVERNMENT, JANUARY 11,
1890]: it demanded the retreat of Portuguese military forces from
areas in Africa that had been claimed by Portugal on the basis of
historical discovery, but that the United Kingdom claimed on the
basis of occupation.

PARNASSIANS: a group of nineteenth-century French poets who
stressed technical perfection and precise description.

SYMBOLISTS: proponents of a nineteenth-century reaction (especially by French poets) against naturalism and realism in favor of
spirituality, imagination, and dreams. Important figures were
Paul Verlaine (1844–96) and Stéphane Mallarmé (1842–98).

POSITIVISM: a theory that every rationally justifiable assertion can
be verified scientifically.

O REPÓRTER: a magazine headed by Oliveira Martins on which Eça
collaborated with pieces from time to time.

CARLOS MAYER: a wealthy friend of Eça's from the time of their
student days at the University of Coimbra; integral member of the
Vencidos de Vida group.

OUTERINHO: south of Outeiro and northeast of the city of Viana de
Castelo (which borders the Atlantic in northwest Portugal).

A REBOURS: a novel by the French writer Joris-Karl Huysmans
(1848–1907) published in 1884.

ANTÓNIO DE OLIVEIRA SALAZAR (1889–1970): prime minister of
the so-called *Estado Novo* (New State) and strong man of Portugal
for thirty-six years, from 1932 to 1968. His rule was influenced by
Catholic, papal thought, with political freedoms curtailed and
dissidents repressed by military police. He suffered a stroke in
1968 at the age of seventy-nine and was never cognizant of having
lost power. Marcello Caetano (1906–80) succeeded him and was
overthrown in the Carnation Revolution of 1974.

Stories

The Falling Snow

THE WOODCUTTER ROSE from his shabby bed at daybreak and lit the oil lamp.

Next to the fireplace, gaunt and shriveled from the cold, a little boy slept wound in the tattered remains of a blanket. The hapless woodcutter was weak with fever; until nightfall the day before he had tramped the black underbrush, and upon his return not even a meager broth awaited him in the drowsy atmosphere of the fireplace.

It was snowing heavily in the mountains, and the poor man had thin, small children who, when they prayed at night, shivering all over and huddled around their mother, choked on tears of hunger, which was why he rose at that early hour to make his way through the thick, soft fog and trudge along hills and pine groves to split, cut, and prune in the harsh winds, in the deep, silent snow.

The little boy slept with his feet stiff and white from dried mud; white, too, were his chest and feet, and his thick hair lay disheveled. In one corner, on muddy mats covered with their mother's petticoat, the two younger children, their elbows purplish, slept the sleep of cold and hunger. The woodcutter took the jacket that he wore to the mountains, wrapped their hardened feet, frozen from long bouts of cold, and with the oil lamp went to lean over the miserable bed where his wife slept. Her body was glued to the little warmth the straw provided, as it would to a loved bosom, her arms loose and limp like those of a barren woman; her black hair spilled bleakly over the bed like a sign of mourning; and the blanket riddled with holes outlined the chaste, fertile shape of her breasts.

The woodcutter then grasped his black ax and the stiff bundle of rope, covered himself with a coarse wool hood, and set out slowly, starved and skeletal, along the deep, rugged paths that were livid and blanketed with patches of fog.

His hovel stood alone at the foot of the mountains, far from villages, among a few trees that raised their stripped, bare, and supplicant black arms to the heavens.

That family lived there, numbed by the cold and emaciated from hunger, face to face with snow and winters, their breasts full of the religion of the sun, of harvests, and of rich, bright abundance like divine, flaming possessions that are inaccessible in the dust of light, and as distant as God in paradise. The father went off every day to the great mountains to struggle amid the branches; the mother, at home, sewed tatters at the foot of the unlit fireplace, and at nightfall she stood next to the door that had been disjointed by the wind and cracked by the cold to see whether she would catch a glimpse of the arrival of her husband, stooped over under the heavy bundles of wood, as he moved slowly along the fog-filled shortcuts.

The woodcutter continued to walk toward the mountain slopes.

Dawn weighed heavily on him in the midst of fog and cold, sporadic showers.

Snow was falling, lightly. His soul huddled itself inside his body like a clothed saint, frightened by the supernatural harshness of things. Because all of that nature was possessed of strange cruelties.

The morning was dark, and slow, and mournful, like a widow at the moment of burial. In the little tenuous light, bits of ice suspended from thistle and heather had the appearance of shreds of shrouds, while at the tops of the motionless trees, birds—still and silent—ruffled their feathers in the biting wind.

The clouds, barren and dew-heavy, dissipated as the cold woodcutter, pale like the trees, walked on and on—blue, disconsolate, serene, scratched by brambles and drenched by raindrops dripping from the trees.

As he slowly tramped the hard, snow-covered ground, he thought about peasants who at that hour in warm lands come out whistling under the bright, religious morning, amid pale plants and the fertile splendor of the ubiquitous dew, to guide their strong, slow-moving oxen through furrows while swallows sing gaily and gloriously. He had a wife and children who were starving in the hovel, and although he struggled, working feverishly and driving himself constantly, he didn't always see their beloved faces fill with the colors of life. His poor family was always yellowish, and it was because of the cold, because of the hunger. They didn't even have a new blanket, not even a little wool! The good God, up there above, seems so well sheltered in the warmth of his paradises and his stars that he doesn't remember the poor people in the country and mountains who shiver from the cold. And there were people who always saw their children nice and warm with good, ruddy color!

Thus did the doleful woodcutter think as he trudged on, wet and full of sorrowful, morbid ideas. Now the snow was coming down like an immense dispersal of fluffs of wool.

And he thought that he could be a well-to-do rustic and see at night, gathered around his blazing, peaceful fireplace, a hardy group of harvesters and sowers, their hair loose, in the midst of lots of good laughter, a big bowl of broth, and the cracking of roasting chestnuts ... an atmosphere of good, simple-hearted people.

The snow continued to fall, nonstop and erratic, and you

could hear the sound—undefined like from a sea, labored like from a beehive—of the diseased multitudes of pine trees.

The poor woodcutter glanced around at the immense pockets of snow that were entangled in dim, barren rocks overlaid with thistle; and from time to time a crow, passing by silently in the dark, would beat the air around him with a wild flapping of its wings.

Day was beginning to dawn. He felt alone in the midst of that barbaric, inimical nature, and now and then his arm, weakened by fever, sagged under the ax and the moist length of rope.

Slowly, he made his way into the pine grove. It was dense, and the night still held fast in the thick growth of the livid foliage. The snow falling on the branches turned into dew from the heat of the sap.

The trees looked as if they had been seized by a religious scare.

When he exited the pine grove to head for the mountains, it reminded him of when he used to frequent the corn huskings of a village in the south and, beneath the melodic, passionate light of the constellations, sing to guitar accompaniment beside a sweet girl with a saintly brow and mulberry-colored hair; and he, the lost one, would soften his eyes on glimpsing the whiteness of her neck through the opening in his handkerchief!

Today, he thought, at that hour that poor woman wailed in her soul seeing her children without a morsel of bread as they paced their damp hovel in ragged clothes, clutching her skirts and crying out, *Mother! Mother!* And the wretched man's eyes quivered in the swell of his tears.

The woodcutter gripped his ax and penetrated the forest.

The aged oaks, violent and prophetic; the weary poplars; the noisy chestnuts; the gigantic elms; and the foliage and bristly brier patches where the wind howls in distress: all of that hearty, living greenery that sings to the sun in the dustiness of the stark light, all of that shadowy, disheveled Diana that is called a forest, slept beneath the burden of the snow, all of it silent, stoic, and magnificent.

The woodcutter, ax held high, continued on through the forest. He knew those strange configurations, those snowy escarpments, the pensive faces of the cliffs, all the entanglement of branches and of leaves, where drops fall like an echo of past rains; and nonetheless, upon straightening up against an aged oak, he blanched, as if standing before a profanation.

His good, simple heart did not understand, but it felt those immovable, quiet, and sonorous lives that are trees, shrubs, plants, efflorescent growths; he had compassion for the moans of trunks, for crushed shells, for torn bushes, and he felt there that he was sacrificing immense lives of trees to the hunger of his children.

The woodcutter sank his black ax into the trunk of an oak, and the whole immense tree shook with grievous shudders, and its branches spread out all along the trunk—fallen, lifeless, and sapped of strength—as if to watch themselves die without complaint in a wild, magnificent silence.

The sun came through, dull, drab, weak. Devoid of strength, devoid of vitality. Devoid of a sacred, brilliant ascent, amid drifting pockets of fog, amid lugubrious, fleeting clouds.

The birds, chirping forlornly, were beginning to flutter about him.

And the woodcutter, drenched through and through, red and fierce-looking, his hair disheveled, his chest arched and his ax raised in his hands, struggled with just and tragic frenzy against the trunks, against the branches, against the budding roots, against the hard bark and the tenacious fiber; and he filled the forest floor with black boughs, dead tree limbs, all fallen and inert like so many conquered suits of armor.

Those trees that took so long to grow and strengthen, and

to become accustomed to tumultuous winds, and to know how to cling to the sheets of rain, and to embrace the soft nakedness of fog and steam ... those trees dotted with November's bites, full of legend and the smell of tempests, shrank their branches in a fearful tremor when the ax glittered lugubriously in the air.

The woodcutter's shirt was loose, his jacket torn, and his wooden clogs made deep prints in the snow. Starved, distressed, short of breath, he took long steps through the forest, hacking brambles, crushing roots, finding himself covered with flying chips and bits of vines, while with tragic gestures he waved his ax to shoo away the flight of crows; and full of love for his children, he tortured the trees with fiery blows, screaming at them: *Cowards*!

Thus did the woodcutter do battle with the snow, and the wind, and the rain, and the dampness, and the fog, and the fever, and the pain, until nightfall.

He already had a pile of branches and firewood, so he bound it all together with rope as hard as his arms and stuck his ax inside. He propped the enormous bundle against a mountain of snow, and the two ends of the rope by which he had to pick it up were black and wet. He then stooped in order to hoist it onto his broad back, but when he started to stand up, slowly, wearily, he felt his muscles go slack, his hands turn cold, and, overcome with weakness, the woodcutter fell, his hair sweaty and pasted to his forehead, as his stiff fingers clawed at the snow.

Thus was he lost in the soft aura of a gradual fade until he opened his sluggish eyes—and he lay alongside the bundle, silent and filled with tenderness.

Night drew near as ripples of mist descended. The atmosphere took on a severe, opaque pallor, and as a sporadic, vaporized rain fell, all the ground became heavy with snow.

Next to the woodcutter's feet lay a big, withered trunk,

dead, without roots, without branches, without sap; on one side rot was starting the process of decay.

All around him there rose the profusion of trees covered with snow, all of them lean, in the midst of the transparency of the mist, all of them sad and nocturnal like white monks.

In the distance a clearing opened, and through it could be seen far off a great light that was fading, serene and weak.

The woodcutter's neck was bare and exposed to the snow, but with his chest aching and soaked, he still grasped the two ends of the rope to secure the bundle. And although his muscles were stiff, his face flushed, his temple swollen, his great veins bulging like cordage, and his legs rigid, he exerted himself to stand up. But he fell on the snow, weakened, dislocated, smothered, and enveloped in the damp coldness of fever.

Then he stared at the stripped, bare, snow-covered trunk, and he thought that his body was going to waste away there and die amid the putrefaction of the trunks.

And all his flesh was seized by a terrible shudder. His wife and children had come to mind, as had the poor shepherd who would shake the snow from his hair and the brambly thorns from his jacket when he entered their hovel.

The snow was falling, sadly. At that hour his wife would be waiting next to the door if she spotted him far off, bent over under his bundles as he trudged the paths white with snow.

She would be leaning against the doorjamb with one hand, the other wrapping the children in the folds of her skirt to shield them from the nighttime cold.

And the woodcutter was there alone, crushed beneath the implacable snow!

And when they didn't see him? And he tried to recall whether he had already one time or another spent the night in the mountains. Never.

If they didn't see him coming, they would all go, crying and wailing and protecting the oil lamp from the wind, to search for him among the sinister heaths.

From time to time hallucination gripped him, and he saw shadowy figures rise up on the trunks like a terrible vapor; and that spiraled shape of human similarities always rose and rose until getting lost in the livid transparency of the air.

The snow continued to fall as if dripping from the clouds.

And he thought, disconsolately, that his wife and children would learn of his death in the snow, beneath the furious entanglement of foliage and the prolonged, biting wind, with him silent and solitary like a wolf!

Then that body—crushed by the snow, in smudged, wet clothes and gone flaccid in the softness of the fog—stiffened; with blazing eyes, chattering teeth, and seized by laughter, his skin torn by prickly shrubs, the woodcutter straightened up and, suffocated, disheveled, stiff, and livid, he screamed in the night.

There was a startled scattering of birds throughout all the dark foliage. And the wind blew and carried off clusters of leaves in its violent spirals. And all the daylight vanished in the clearing. There was no one on the mountain. He was alone. Alone! Neither shepherds, nor cowherds, nor lost wayfarers. Alone! And the birds were disappearing, the leaves were disappearing, and the light was disappearing. He found himself alone.

Then, seeing all around the solitary, black forest; the angry accumulation of shadows; the livid faintness of the lowest branches; the tenebrous shapes; the nocturnal curvatures of the roots; hearing the ululation of wolves in the distance and overhead the fluttering of crows, he stretched out, prostrate, and shouted in the night, under the falling snow and the creaking branches: Jesus!

And the entire forest became silent, indifferent, imposing;

the crows flew off, cawing; he felt weak, dispirited, broken, emaciated, moribund; and from above, the great sky, the serene sky, the sacred sky, the consoling sky spewed snow over that wretched flesh.

And the woodcutter lay inert. The snow continued to fall, fragmented and white. He was stretched out, seeing overhead the great immobility of the forest, the mists, which caused droplets to brush his face, and the spectral shadow of the bundle of wood.

He felt his body numbed with pain brought on by the cold, an acute burning sensation on his brow and his eyes; and it seemed to him that an immense wound chafed his back, that he suffered awful burns on contact with the snow beneath his body.

From time to time he sobbed. And when he did, he saw great shadows hovering above his head, and they would flee cawing in distress, with a terrible racket of wings whitened by the snow, frightened and ferocious.

It was the crows. He trembled all over. He glimpsed them now when they came to alight on his chest, bent down and flapping their wings, half suspended, to sink their black beaks into his poor flesh.

Then he painfully moved his numb arm and fumbled about. Grasping a loose branch, a black and thorny one, he threw it at the black shadows of the crows. His hand, though, was nearly insensible from the cold, and the branch, feebly pitched, snapped back on his face and tore his flesh with its thorns. But by then his inert hands lacked the strength to fling it off him.

And he started to weep. The terrifying crows were flying about, and he buried his feet in the snow, which he drew up to himself as if to pelt them. The crows swooped down.

The snow continued to fall and already covered his stiff legs. Then, seeing the forest that drenched him with water, the ground that sapped him of life, the wind that bit him, the snow that buried him, the crows that were coming to peck him, all the savage hostilities of things—he was overcome with anger and, silent, of fierce mien, his eyes luminous in the night, he laid his head firmly on the bundle of wood, and readied himself to die.

Then a blast of wind blew all of a sudden, and it seemed to the poor woodcutter that he heard in that gust the sound of crying and a voice calling out in distress.

The wind redoubled its fury, scattering the crows that teetered on their wings amid the whirling currents of the ferocious blast.

The snow continued falling. The crows, frightened by the wind that had arisen, hovered over the last branches.

The snow continued falling, and the woodcutter's arms and entire chest were covered. The crows fled, and the whole flock looked like an unwieldy, ill-defined shadow.

The snow continued falling. And the man's throat was covered, and his mouth was covered.

The crows were vanishing in the transparency of the night.

The snow continued to fall, indomitable and barren. The poor woodcutter's forehead was covered, and only his thick, dark hair still stirred slowly in the wind.

The snow obliterated the night with white. Wolves howled in the distance.

And the snow kept falling. The shadows of the crows vanished beyond the black branches.

His hair disappeared. Only the snow remained!

Master Devil

DO YOU KNOW the Devil? I'll not be the one to relate his life to you. And nevertheless, I know by heart his pleasant, grotesque, celestial, luminous, and tragic legend.

The Devil is the most dramatic figure in the history of the Soul.

His life is the great adventure of Evil. It was he who invented the fripperies that weaken the soul and weapons that bloody the body. And yet at certain moments in history, the Devil is the consummate representative of human rights. He wants freedom, fertility, power, law.

He is, then, a kind of sinister Pan in whom roar deep-rooted rebellions of Nature. He combats priesthood and virginity; he counsels Christ to live and mystics to enter into humanity.

He is incomprehensible: he tortures saints but defends the church. In the sixteenth century he is the biggest overseer of the collection of tithes.

He is a poisoner and a strangler. He is an impostor, a tyrant, and is vain and treacherous.

And yet he conspires against the emperors of Germany: he consults Aristotle and Saint Augustine, and he torments Judas who sold Christ, and Brutus who stabbed Caesar.

At the same time the Devil suffers a sweet, tremendous sadness. Perhaps he feels a nostalgia for Heaven!

While still young, when the stars call him Lucifer, *he who brings light*, he rebels against Jehovah and commands a great battle amid the clouds.

Afterward he tempts Eve, dupes the prophet Daniel, taunts Job, and tortures Sara, and in Babylon he's a gambler, a clown, a slanderer, a libertine, and a hangman.

When the gods are exiled, he camps with them in the damp forests of Gaul, and he readies majestic expeditions on the ships of the emperor Constantine.

Full of fear before the sad eyes of Jesus, he still tortures the monks of the West.

He would mock Saint Macarius, sing psalms in the church of Alexandria, offer bouquets of carnations to Saint Pelagia, steal the abbot of Cluny's chickens, peck the eyes of Saint Sulpice, and at night, tired and dusty, knock on the door of the Dominicans' monastery in Florence and go to sleep in Savonarola's cell.

He studied Hebrew, argued with Luther, read the Bible closely, and at nightfall came to the crossroads of Germany to desport with mendicant friars, sitting on the grass or on the saddle of his horse.

He preferred charges against the Virgin; and he was the pontiff of the black Mass, after having inspired Socrates's judges.

In his old age, he, who had discussed battle plans with Attila, indulged in the sin of gluttony.

And Rabelais, when seeing him like that—fatigued, wrinkled, bald, fat, and somnolent—jeers him. Then the demographer Wier lampoons him with bloody pamphlets and Voltaire bombards him with epigrams.

The Devil smiles, glances all around at the deserted calvaries, writes his memoirs, and, on a foggy day, after having said goodbye to his old comrades—the stars—dies, weary and silent.

Béranger then writes his epitaph.

The Devil was celebrated at his death by sages and poets: Proclus showed his substance, Presul his nocturnal adventures; Saint Thomas revealed his destiny; Torquemada described his wickedness; and Pierre de Lancre his jovial inconstancy. John Dick wrote about his eloquence, and James I of England did the chorography of his States. Milton sang of his beauty and Dante of his tragedy. The monks erected statues of him. His sepulcher is Nature.

The Devil loved very much.

He was a gallant inamorato, husband, father of sinister generations.

He was esteemed, in Antiquity, by Caesar's mother, and in the Middle Ages he was loved by the beautiful Olympia. In Brabant he married the daughter of a merchant. He had voluptuous encounters with Fredegunda, who assassinated two generations.

He was the inamorato of cheeky serenades sung to the wives of the merchants of Venice.

He wrote wistfully to the nuns of the convents in Germany. *Feminae in illius amore delectantur*, Abbot Caesar of Hellenbach says tragically. In the twelfth century he tempted the melodramatic mothers of the Burgaves with sun-filled looks. In Scotland there was great hardship on the mountains: for fifteen "shillings" he bought the love of the wives of the "highlanders" and paid them with the counterfeit money that he minted in the company of Philip I, Louis VI, Louis VII, Philip the Fair, King John, Louis XI, and Henry II, and with the same copper that was used to fabricate the cauldrons in which the counterfeiters were boiled alive.

*

BUT I ONLY want to tell the story of an unhappy love of the Devil's in the lands of the North.

Oh women, you who harbor in your hearts the grief that nothing cures—neither simples, nor balms, nor dewdrops, nor prayers, nor tears, nor sunshine, nor death ... come to hear this flowery story!

It was in Germany, where the absinthe flower grows. The house was made of wood, adorned and finished with tracery that was faultless, like the surplice of the archbishop of Ulm. Maria, fair and blonde, was spinning on the balcony, which overflowed with flowerpots, climbers, doves, foliage, and sunshine. At the back of the balcony there was an ivory Christ. With their leaves become hands, the plants piously cleansed the blood from his wounds, and the doves, with the heat of their breasts, warmed his painful feet. Inside the house, her father— the old man—drank beer from Heidelberg, wine from Italy, and cider from Denmark. He was vain, fat, lethargic, and mean.

And the girl spun continuously. Attached to the distaff by a fine white thread, the spindle turned continuously; and attached to her heart by sorrow, a desire teemed continuously.

And she spent the livelong day spinning.

Now, there chanced to pass below the balcony a handsome, delicate, and timid youth who stopped to lean against the pillar opposite the girl.

Seated alongside the crucifix, she covered Jesus's feet with her blonde tresses.

The plants and branches above enveloped the head of the image with freshness and shade. It seemed that all of Christ's spirit was there: above, consoling in the form of a plant; below, loving in the form of a woman.

He, the fair youth, was the pilgrim of that sweet, saintly girl. His look always sought her heart; and her look, always serious and pure, sought the soul of her cherished pilgrim.

Their eyes scrutinized their souls. And youth and girl were radiant, like messengers of light, keen to relate what they had seen. It was enchantment!

"If you knew," said one look, "her soul is immaculate."

"If you saw," said the other look, "his heart is serene, strong, and red."

"It's consoling, that chest where there are stars!"
"It's purifying, that bosom where there are blessings!"
And they both looked—silent, ecstatic, perfect.

And the city lived: trees creaked beneath the balconies of the electors; hunting horns blew in towers; songs of pilgrims rose on roads; saints read in their niches; devils mocked atop the weathervanes of churches; almond trees blossomed; and the current of the Rhine River carried the singing of harvest women.

And girl and youth beheld each other: the branches nested their dreams, and Christ nested their souls.

Now, one afternoon the ogives were radiant, like the miters of archbishops. The air was warm, the sun was going down, and the stone saints were florid, either from reflections of light or from desires for life. On the balcony, Maria was spinning her skein of flax; reclined against the pillar, Jusel was spinning his dreams.

Then, in the distant silence, they heard the lament of an Innsbruck guitar wound with ivy by the shepherds of Heidelberg, and a hearty voice singing:

> Your eyes, my beloved,
> Are like two dark nights.
> But your lips are made of light
> And sing of bright dawns.
>
> Your breasts, my beauty,
> Are two wax doors,
> And were my mouth a sun,
> Like it would I melt them!
>
> Your lips, flowers of flesh,
> Are gates to Paradise:

And Saint Peter's bench
Rests on your wisdom tooth.[1]

I would like to have a shirt
Of a finely spun fabric,
Made from all the *Ohs* that
Your chest has already exclaimed.

When we get married
The nightingale will say Mass.
And your bridal dress
Will be woven by the sun!

The blessing will leave us
Some old oak tree!
And for wedding gifts
We shall have dewdrops!

And a robust young man with a beautiful, marmoreal pallor appeared at the end of the street. His black eyes were akin to the two legendary suns of the land of Evil. Black, too, and potent-looking and resplendent, was his hair. Attached to the blouse that he wore was a red cactus flower.

Behind him, walking unsteadily as if he were injuring his feet on the pavement, came a perfect page like one of the ancient statues that in Greece created the legend of beauty. His attire exuded an aroma of ambrosia, and he had the inert, fixed eyes of marble Apollos. His melancholy, serene brow was like that of exiles who bear the immortal nostalgia of a lost homeland. And he was carrying an amphora of the kind sculpted in Miletus, on which one could feel the smoothness of Olympian nectars.

1. The original Portuguese of these four lines is as follows: "Os teus lábios, flor de carne / São portas do Paraíso: / *E o banquinho de S. Pedro/É no teu dente de siso.*" (The italics are mine.) No native Portuguese speaker that I've consulted sees an idiomatic sense in the last two lines.

The man with the marmoreal pallor approached the balcony, and in between the mournful entreaties of the guitar, said in a resonant voice, "Oh genteel maiden, oh pretty Isolde of the balcony! Like two pilgrims flushed by the sun, allow these lips of man to advance on a sweet pilgrimage of love, from your hands to your neck!"

And looking at Jusel, who was stripping the petals of a daisy, he sang slowly, his great peals of laughter cold and metallic.

> Whoever plucks a nightingale
> And rips a poor flower,
> Shows that in his heart
> He has but tatters of love.

And he raised to the balcony his terrifying, desolate eyes that were like blasphemies of light. Maria had removed the distaff, and only the birds, flowers, and Jesus remained on the balcony!

"The warbler has flown away," he said jovially. And then turning to Jusel, "Perhaps it felt the proximity of a vulture. What say you, Bachelor?"

With serene eyes, Jusel continued to strip the daisy.

"In my time, Master Sigh," said the man with black eyes while slowly crossing his arms, "there would already have been two swords here, sprays of sparks flying in the shade. But heroes are disappearing and men are increasingly born of the pain of women. Look at this one! It's a heart that has a jerkin with a collar. But a pale, gray, whitish heart, of all colors except red and firm. So! That girl has blonde hair, which goes nicely with my black hair. Slim figures call for strong arms. Red lips of desire fancy red weapons of blood. The lady is mine, Bachelor!"

Jusel had lowered his great plaintive eyelids, and he saw the petals plucked from the daisy falling like murdered wishes detached from his bosom.

The man with the resplendent eyes grasped him roughly by the hand.

"Bachelor Tenderness," said he, "close by here is a place where gillyflowers sprout expressly for the innocents who die. If you have some possessions to leave, I recommend to you this excellent Rabil." It was the page. "We must protect the nocturnal birds. The vultures have been yawning since the war ended. I'm going to give them tender bones. If you wish to leave your heart to your beloved in the way of the troubadours, I'll undertake to deliver it to her well saturated with mire, on the point of a sword. You are beautiful, loved, fair, delicate, perfect. Just imagine, Rabil. It's a well-considered farce to snatch this beauty away from the fellow high above the suns. If you were in love with some star, I would send it your final goodbyes via a reliable messenger. As for the sacraments, that's futile. I'll see about purifying you with fire. Rabil, play on the guitar the rondo of the deceased: announce Bachelor Sigh in hell! Get a move on, my sons! Ah! But in a secret duel with honorable weapons!" And, thumping heroically the hilt of his sword, "I have this weakness here. Where is your strength?"

"There," replied Jusel, pointing to the Christ that stood on the balcony full of plants and doves, illuminated by the setting sun, which was white amid the foliage, dying amid the fluttering of wings.

"Ah!" the man of the cactus flower said in a cavernous voice. "Listen, Rabil! Do you remember Actaeon, Apollo, Derceto, Inachus, and Mars?"

"They were my brothers," the page said slowly, rigid, like a stone figure.

"All right, Rabil. Onward, through the night! I'm getting a whiff of Jerusalem here!"

And they vanished beneath arcades and sinister pilasters, sobbing.

*

THE FOLLOWING NIGHT there was a great purifying moon throughout Germany. Maria lay prone on the balcony: it was the celestial hour during which jasmines pollinate.

Down below, Jusel was leaning against the pillar, and his eyes sighed for that white, feminine form as the water in the gardens that rises in a jet sighs with a bubbling murmur toward the blue of the sky.

Maria said with longing, "Come."

A radiant Jusel climbed the balcony, and they sat at the foot of the image. The air was as serene as it was in the country of souls.

The two bodies turned and came together, as if they were approaching God's arms.

The dark foliage that enveloped Christ extended over the two blond heads with signs of blessing.

In the softness of the shadows there was a nuptial mystery.

Jusel held her hands closely, like captive birds, and said with the humble voice of primitive hearts, "I've wanted to see you like this, so near to me! If only you knew! I have infinite misgivings. You are so blonde and so fair! I had a dream that frightened me. It was out in the country. You were right next to me, perfectly still, and a choir could be heard singing inside your heart. A nebulous dance of spirits swirled all around, and some said, 'That choir is of the dead; they are the unhappy lovers who cry in the heart of that woman.' Others said, 'They are the sorrows of the ardent *Minnesänger* who sob there.' Still others said, 'Yes, that choir is of the dead; they are our beloved gods who cry there in exile.' And then I stepped forward, saying, 'Yes, yes, that choir is of the dead; they are the desires that she felt for me, that are remembered and mourned.' What an awful, awful dream!"

"Why," she asked, "do you lean against the pillar every day with your hands nearly crossed?"

"I'm reading the letters of light that your eyes write to me."

They fell silent.

At that moment they were the flowering soul of night.

"Which ones are my eyes, which are your eyes!" exclaimed Jusel. "I don't even know!"

And silence reigned again.

She felt the desires projected by his eyes, saw them coming to fall in the depths of her soul like the loud cry of injured birds.

And, inclining her body, she asked, "Do you know my father?"

"No. What does that matter?"

"Ah, if you knew...."

"What does that matter? I'm here. If he truly loves you, he'll be pleased with this love of mine, always at your feet, like a dog. You are a saint: the essence of Christ dwells in your heart. What do I want? To hold your heart captive, close, like a bird. Forget all of this passion, keep yourself so immaculate that if you were to die, you could be buried in the transparency of the blue. Desires are akin to a vine of ivy: you want me to root them out. You are the reason of my soul. If you didn't love me, I would be shattered. For me to enter your heart, remove nothing from it, do you hear? In it you have the faith of Jesus and longing for your mother—let them be. We are all of us content here inside it, contemplating the brilliance of your gaze like a starry sky. What do I want from you? Your sorrows. When you cry, come to me. I'll tear my soul into shreds for you to dry your eyes. Do you want to get married? Let us do so in the heart of Jesus. Give me the bodkin that fastens your hair: it'll be our stole."

Transfigured and celestial, standing in front of the image and pushing away branches, with the point of the bodkin he carved on Christ's chest the entwined first letters of their two names, J and M.

"It's our betrothal," he said. "Heaven is sending us the stars sweetened with light. Christ will not forget this love that weeps at his feet. The divine exhalations that escape from his chest will appear on high with the shape of our letters. God will know this secret. What does it matter? I have already told Him, the stars, the birds, the plants, and the blooming flowers, because—do you see?—the flowers, the constellations, the doves, the grace, all of that … all of that effusion of goodness, of innocence, of grace, was simply, oh my adored one, an eternal billet-doux that I was writing to you!"

And on their knees, ecstatic and quiet, they felt mixing in their hearts, in their secrets, in their desires, all the vague and immense goodness of the religion of grace.

And their souls spoke, full of mystery.

"Do you see?" asked her soul. "When I see you, it seems that God is diminished and shrinks and comes to nest in your heart; when I think about you, it seems to me that your heart expands, spreads, embraces the sky and all the universes, and encompasses God everywhere!"

"My heart," his soul sighed, "is a shell. Your love is the sea. For a long time this shell will live, drowned and lost in that sea. But if you expel me from inside you, as in an abandoned shell the sound of the sea is still heard, so in my abandoned heart will the whisper of my love always be heard!"

"Look," said her soul, "I am like open country. I have trees and grass. What there is of maternity in me is a tree to give you cover; what there is of passion in me is grass for you to walk on!"

"Do you know?" asked his soul. "In heaven there is an invisible forest in which are scarcely seen the tips of the roots that are the stars. You were the warbler of those woods. My wishes injured you. For a long time I've watched you tumbling through the air, crying resplendently if the sun illuminates you; sadly if rain soaks you. For a long time I've watched you descending. When will you fall into my arms?"

And the voice said, "Hush."

They did not speak.

And the two souls, detached from cherished bodies, rose: dazzled, ineffable, tender, confused. They had the sky for their element; their smiles were the stars; their sadness, night; their hope, dawn; their love, life; and always more tender and more vast, their souls enveloped everything that rises from the world as just, perfect, and chaste—prayers, tears, ideas—and spread throughout the whole of the heavens, united and immense, for God to pass overhead!

And then at the balcony gate there erupted a resounding, metallic guffaw. The two arose: resplendent, pure, clothed in Grace. At the gate stood Maria's stiff, fat, sinister father. Behind him, the man with marmoreal pallor vainly waved the scarlet feather of war while the page laughed, bringing brightness into the shade.

The father slowly approached Jusel and scoffingly asked, "Where do you wish to be hanged, you scoundrel?"

"Father, Father," exclaimed an anguished Maria in a convulsion of tears as she clung to the old man's body. "No! He's my husband! Our souls were married. See, there it is. Look at it! There, on the image…."

"The what?"

"There on the chest. Look. Our names are joined, like on a deed. Look. He's my husband. He loves me so very much. But look. Below Jesus's chest, where the heart is. Right below the heart. And he, the sweet Jesus, allowed this other wound to be made on him!"

The old man looked at the entwined letters like divine espousals that had taken refuge in Christ's bosom.

"Scrape them off, old man, because that's ivory," shouted the one with black eyes.

The old man stepped toward the image, the knife from his

belt in hand. He was trembling. He was going to scratch out the roots of that love even from the immaculate heart of Jesus!

And then the image, under the just and incorruptible gaze of light, pulled out the nail from one of its wounded hands, and with that hand covered the betrothal letters on its chest.

"It's him, Rabil!" shouted the man with the cactus flower.

The old man was sobbing.

And then the pale man who had played the guitar at Innsbruck, where the shepherds of Heidelberg make wreaths of ivy, came sadly beside the image, linked the lovers' arms as depicted on old German prints, and said to the father, "Bless them, old man." And he departed, vigorously thumping the hilt of his sword.

"But who is he?" asked the scared old man.

"Not so loud," said the page of the amphora of Miletus. "That's Master Devil.... All good wishes, my newlyweds!"

*

IN THE EARLY MORNING HOURS—on the road to Neckar, where cherry trees stand out—the man with the thick black hair said to the page as white as marble Apollos, "I have aged. Life is slipping away from me. I'm the last of those who battled the stars. Vultures already hiss me. It's odd: I feel growing in my chest a sound of forgiveness. I liked that girl. Pretty blonde locks.... Would that such had been given to me during my time in heaven! I am no longer up to adventures of love! The lovely Imperia says that I have sold myself out to God!"

"The lovely Imperia!" exclaimed the page. "Women! Vanities, vanities! The lovely women went off with the lovely gods. Nowadays men are mystics, friars, saints, lovers, troubadours. Women are ugly, avaricious, gaunt, bourgeois, dressed in sackcloth, wasted away by cilices, with a little bit of inconvenient soul, and flesh so diaphanous that you can glimpse our primitive clay through it! Naught but misfortunes! Ah, Athens! Corinth! Miletus! Tenedos! Abydos!"

"I'm finding the labor of Six Days laughable. The stars tremble with fear and distress. The moon is a sun struck by lightning. Blood is beginning to decrease in the world and dye greatly increase. I have squandered evil. I was prodigal. If, at the end of my life, I had to amuse myself by forgiving and consoling … so as not to die of boredom! Be at peace, world! Be infamous, slimy, putrid, vile, and squalid, and nevertheless be a star in the heavens, you impostor! And yet man has not changed: he's the same. Have you not seen him? In order to love, that one wounded the chest of the image with a bodkin. As in ancient times, man does not begin to enjoy something good without first piercing the flesh of a God! This is my last adventure. I'm off to the center of nature, out by the open sea, to calmly set about dying."

"Devils also go away! Good-bye, Satan."

"Good-bye, Ganymede."

And the man and the page separated in the night.

After a short distance, the man came across a stone crucifix. "You're also deserted," he said, staring at it. "The villains nailed you and turned their backs on you! You were greater than me! You suffered in silence."

And sitting on the steps at the foot of the cross while awaiting dawn, he played the guitar and sang in the stillness:

> Who, stars, stripped you
> Of the trees of light?

And with a great melancholy peal of laughter:

> Will Autumn reach the Devil?
> Will Winter come to Jesus?

Glossary to "Master Devil"
(in order of appearance)

PAN: the ancient Greek god of forests, pastures, flocks, and shepherds, and companion of nymphs. He has the head, chest, and arms of a man and the legs, horns, and ears of a goat, like a faun or a satyr.

DANIEL: eponymous prophet of the book of Daniel who lived in Babylon during the Captivity; the tales are in chapters 1–6 and the visions in chapters 7–12.

JOB: eponymous figure of the book of Job; he suffers and anguishes without God's protection until he is rewarded by God for acceptance of his will.

SARA: the wife of Abraham and mother of Isaac.

CONSTANTINE THE GREAT: Roman emperor from 306 to 337; noted for the many reforms that he enacted and for being the first Roman emperor to convert to Christianity.

SAINT MACARIUS: Christian monk and hermit, 300–91, known for his wisdom and virtue.

SAINT PELAGIA: Christian saint and hermit in the fourth or fifth century.

SULPITIUS THE PIOUS [SAINT SULPICE]: a seventh-century bishop and saint who devoted himself to the study of scripture and relief of the poor.

GIROLAMO SAVONAROLA (1452–98): Italian Dominican friar and preacher in Renaissance Florence.

JOHANNES WEIR (1515–88): Dutch physician, occultist, and demonologist.

PIERRE-JEAN DE BÉRANGER (1780–1857): French poet and songwriter.

PROCLUS LYCEUS (412–85 CE): Greek philosopher.

PRESUL: failed to identify.

TOMÁS TORQUEMADA (1420–98): Castilian Dominican friar and first Grand Inquisitor of the infamous Spanish Inquisition.

PIERRE DE LANCRE (1553–1631): French judge who conducted a witch hunt and wrote books on witchcraft and Satan in sexual intercourse.

JOHN DICK [DIQUE, IN EÇA'S PORTUGUESE]: a Scottish witch hunter prosecuted in 1661–62.

CHOROGRAPHY: the systematic description and mapping of regions or districts.

OLYMPIA: possibly Saint Olympia (c. 361–408), a Christian Roman noblewoman of Greek descent.

BRABANT: a state of the Holy Roman Empire.

FREDEGUNDA: sixth-century queen consort of Chilperic I, Frankish king of Soissons; she is said to have been murderous and cruel.

FEMINAE IN ILLIUS AMORE DELECTANTUR: Women delight in that love.

HELLENBACH: in the region of Bavaria, in Germany.

BURGRAVES: governors or rulers of a German town or castle.

PHILIP THE FAIR: Philip IV (1268–1314), king of France from 1285 until his death.

SIMPLES: herbs or plants used for medicinal purposes.

ULM: a city in the south German state of Baden-Württemberg, founded in medieval times.

OGIVES: the diagonal arches across Gothic vaults.

MILETUS: once considered the greatest and wealthiest of ancient Greek cities.

ISOLDA [ISEULT]: daughter of the king of Ireland and lover of Tristan—the main characters of the "Tristan" poems and Richard Wagner's opera.

TENDER BONES (MY EMPHASIS): This usage—"tender bones" for *ossos tenros*—is in the Livros do Brasil edition, and the choice here is mine. The *Contos I* and *Adão e Eva no Paraíso* editions have it as *essas terras*—i.e., *those lands*. Marie-Hélène Piwnik (*Contos* I:87, line 218) states that the *Gazeta de Portugal* edition in [Livros do Brasil] "*parece mais adequada,*" and in context "tender bones" does clearly *seem more appropriate* than "those lands."

ACTAEON: in Greek mythology, a Theban hero. He happened upon a naked Artemis bathing in the woods, and as punishment he was transformed by her into a stag, which was subsequently torn to pieces by his own hounds.

DERCETO: chief goddess of northern Syria in Classical antiquity.

INACHUS: the first king of the city of Argos in Greek mythology; he was one of the three judges in a dispute between Poseidon and Hera.

MARS: the Roman god of war.

MINNESÄNGER: people who wrote and performed *Minnesang*, German "love song."

NECKAR: possibly the Neckar River in Germany, a major tributary of the Rhine.

TENEDOS: a Turkish island in the Aegean Sea, mentioned in both the *Iliad* and the *Aeneid*.

ABYDOS: one of the oldest cities of ancient Egypt and sacred site of many temples.

GANYMEDE: described by Homer (*Iliad*, book XX) as the most beautiful of mortals. Zeus fell in love with his beauty and abducted him in the form of an eagle to serve as a cup bearer on Olympus.

The Peculiarities of a Blonde Girl

HE BEGAN BY TELLING ME that his story was a simple one and that his name was Macário.

I should mention at the outset that I met this man at an inn in Minho. He was tall and heavyset, with a few strands of white hair bristling around his shiny, smooth, and ample bald pate. His black eyes—which were surrounded by wrinkled, sallow skin and dark, puffy circles—exuded a singular clarity and rectitude from behind his round tortoiseshell glasses. Clean-shaven, with a prominent, resolute chin, he wore a black satin cravat secured at the back by a clasp and a long ivory-colored coat that featured narrow, tight-fitting sleeves and velveteen cuffs. And along the lengthy opening of his silk vest, on which glittered a heavy antique gold watch chain, the soft pleats of an embroidered shirt peeked through.

This was in September, and night already fell much sooner, with a sharp, dry chilliness and spectacular darkness. I had stepped down from the diligence exhausted, starved, and shivering under a scarlet-striped horse blanket.

I had just journeyed across the mountain with its dun-colored, desolate expanses. It was eight o'clock at night, the skies dank and murky. And, whether it stemmed from a certain cerebral drowsiness caused by the monotonous motion of the diligence or from the nervous debility of fatigue, or the influence of the steep, dull landscape coupled with the deep nocturnal silence, or the oppressive electric air that filled the heavens, the fact is that I, naturally positive and realistic, had come all that way tyrannized by imagination and chimeras. For certain, in each of us there exists at bottom, no matter how objectively educated one may be, a vestige of mysticism; and sometimes we need only to glimpse a gloomy landscape, or the old wall of a cemetery, or an ascetic wilderness, or the assuasive whiteness of moonlight for that mystical vestige to rise up, to disperse like fog, to fill our souls, our feelings, and our thoughts, and thus become the most mathematical or the most critical of beings, as sad, as visionary, as idealistic as an old poet monk. What had plunged me into chimeras and dreams was the appearance of Rostelo Monastery, which I had seen on its gentle hill in the soft autumnal light of early evening. Then, as night fell and the diligence continued to clatter to the anemic trot of its emaciated white horses, and as the coachman, with the hood of his cloak pulled down on his head, was ruminating while smoking his pipe, I began, plaintively and ridiculously, to ponder the sterility of life. And I wished to be a monk, to be in a monastery, tranquil, in the midst of trees, or in the murmuring hollow of a valley, and while the stream there sang harmoniously in its stone bed, to read *The Imitation*, and, listening to the nightingales in the laurel groves, feel a longing for heaven. A person can't be more stupid. But such was my state of mind, and I attribute to this visionary disposition the lack of enthusiasm, the impression made on me by the story of that man with the velveteen cuffs.

Nonetheless, it piqued my curiosity at supper. I was cutting a chicken breast smothered with white rice and scarlet slivers of sausage, while the chubby, freckle-faced maid was causing a young wine to foam by pouring it into my glass from a glazed pitcher held high. The man, seated across from me, was calmly eating his jelly. With my mouth full and my Guimarães linen napkin between my fingers, I asked him if he was from Vila Real.

"I live there, and have for many years," he replied.

"According to some, it's the land of pretty women," I said.

The man didn't respond. "Hmm. What do *you* say?" I pressed him.

The man withdrew into a conspicuous silence. Until that moment, he had been gay, talkative, full of bonhomie, laughing frequently. But then his refined smile froze.

I realized that I had inadvertently touched the raw nerve of something remembered. In the fate of that old man there was, for certain, "a woman." And in that fate would be his melodrama or his farce, because unconsciously I had supposed that the man's "fact" or "story" would be grotesque and would evoke derision.

So I said to him, "I've been told that the women of Vila Real are the prettiest in Minho province. For those with black eyes, Guimarães; for fine figures, Santo Aleixo; for hair, Arcos, for it's there that you see light hair the golden color of wheat."

The man kept silent, eating with his eyes cast down.

"For waistlines, Viana; for good skin, Amarante; and for all these attributes in one woman, Vila Real. I have a friend who went to Vila Real to get married. Maybe you know him. Peixoto is his name. A tall fellow with a blond beard, a graduate."

"Peixoto, yes," he said, regarding me gravely.

"He went to Vila Real to get married as people formerly went to Andalusia to get married—a matter of obtaining the pick of perfection. To your health."

I was clearly making him ill at ease, because he stood up and slowly stepped over to the window, which was when I noticed his big cassimere shoes with their thick soles and leather laces. And he left.

When I asked for my candlestick, the maid brought me a shiny antique brass oil lamp and said, "You're with another guest. In number 3."

At the inns of Minho every bedroom is an inconvenient dormitory.

"Very well," I said.

Number 3 was at the end of the hallway. On either side of the doors the passengers had placed their footwear to be cleaned: big, muddied riding boots, with leather spurs; a hunter's white shoes; a propertied man's boots with high, red legs; a priest's boots, high ones, with silk tassels; a student's shabby calfskin ankle boots; and at one of the doors, number 15, there were a woman's small, fancy ankle boots with uppers of lasting, and next to them a child's tiny boots, all beat-up and worn-out, the kidskin legs with their loose laces sagging to one side. Everybody was asleep. In front of number 3 were the cassimere shoes with leather laces, and when I opened the door I saw the man with velveteen cuffs tying a silk kerchief around his head. He was wearing a short floral-patterned jacket, coarse, high woolen hose, and rustic cloth slippers.

"Don't mind me," he said.

"Not at all." And I took off my coat to bring about a friendly atmosphere.

I'll not explain why he told me his story shortly afterward, when he was already lying down. There is a Slavic proverb from Galicia that says, "What you won't tell your wife, what you won't tell your friend, tell to a stranger at an inn." But he underwent unexpected and overpowering moments of rage in the telling of his long, troubled confidence. It was with respect to my friend Peixoto, who had gone to Vila Real to get married. I saw that old man of nearly sixty shed tears. Perhaps his story will be regarded as trivial; however, that night I was nervous and impressionable, and it seemed shocking. Nonetheless,

I shall relate it merely like a peculiar incident in a person's love life.

So he began by telling me that his story was a simple one, and that his name was Macário.

I asked him then whether he was from a family that I had known with the surname Macário. And since he told me that he was a cousin of theirs, I warmed up to him quickly, because the Macários were an old, old family, practically a dynasty of merchants who adhered to their longstanding tradition of honor and scrupulousness with religious severity. Macário informed me that back in his youth, in 1832 or 1833, his uncle Francisco owned a dry goods store in Lisbon, and he was one of the clerks. The uncle soon recognized certain intelligent instincts in Macário, besides his practical and arithmetical abilities, and consequently entrusted him with the accounts. Macário became his bookkeeper.

He told me that, being by nature apathetic and even timid, he lived a very reclusive life at that time. All his interest was confined to faithful and scrupulous work, a country lunch now and then, and great care with his suits and underclothes. It was an austere, domestic existence. A great social simplicity cleared up a person's habits, thereby making spirits more carefree and feelings less complicated. To have an enjoyable supper beneath the grape trellises of a garden; to watch the water of a flowing stream; to be in tears over the rousing melodramas performed by candlelight in the wings of the Salitre: such were the pleasures that sufficed to content the discreet bourgeoisie. Besides, the times were confusing and revolutionary, and nothing like war makes a man withdrawn, snug by a fireplace, humble, and easily gratified; it is peace that, providing idleness for the imagination, occasions the impatience of desire.

At the age of twenty-two Macário had yet to "experience Venus," to quote the expression spoken to him by an elderly aunt who had been the mistress of Judge Curvo Semedo of the Arcádia.

But around that time there came to live on the third floor across from the Macários's dry goods store a forty-year-old woman dressed in mourning. Pallid and dark-complexioned, she had a shapely, rounded bust and a desirable appearance. Macário's desk was on the first floor above the store, next to a balcony, and from that vantage point one morning he spotted that woman with her curly black hair. Wearing a white negligee, her arms bare, and her tresses hanging loose, she approached a small window to shake a dress outside. Macário took in the sight, and, involuntarily, he thought to himself that at the age of twenty that woman doubtless had been a most captivating and domineering creature, because her coarse, unruly hair, thick eyebrows, prominent lips, and firm, aquiline profile betrayed an active temperament and a passionate imagination. Nevertheless, he calmly continued aligning his figures. But that evening he sat smoking by the window of his room, which opened onto the courtyard. It was July, and the atmosphere was seductive, electric, and a neighbor was playing an emotive Moorish song from a melodrama on his rebec. A sweet, mystery-filled penumbra enveloped the room, and Macário, in his slippers, began to picture that wild, black hair and those pale, marmoreal arms; he stretched, like sensitive cats rubbing themselves, and languidly swayed back and forth against the wicker chair, deciding with a yawn that he led a humdrum existence. And the following day, still affected by the previous one, he sat down at his desk with the window wide open, and, watching the building opposite where all that black hair lived, he set about leisurely sharpening his quill. But nobody approached the window framed in green. Macário was bored, out of sorts, and his work dragged on. It occurred to him that in the street it would be pleasantly sunny and that one could enjoy being in the agreeable shade of the country while butterflies fluttered about honeysuckles. And when he closed his desk, he heard the window across from him open; for certain it was black hair. But blonde hair appeared. Oh! And Macário, immediately and conspicuously, went to the balcony to trim a pencil. It was a girl of perhaps twenty—refined-looking, fresh, gilded like an English tableau. The whiteness of her skin had something of the transparency of old porcelain, while in her profile there was a pure line reminiscent of ones seen on antique medals: the picturesque poets of bygone days would have called her dovelike, ermine, snowy, and golden.

Macário said to himself, *It's her daughter.* The other woman wore the black of mourning, but this one, the blonde girl, had on a blue-flecked muslin dress with lacy sleeves and a chambray kerchief wrapped around her bosom, and her entire person spoke of what was clean and youthful, and fresh, supple, and tender.

Back then Macário had curly blond hair and a short beard. And I imagine that he would have carried himself with that laconic, nervous air that after the eighteenth century and the Revolution was so common in plebeian peoples.

The blonde girl, naturally, noticed Macário, but, naturally, she closed the window, drawing behind it an embroidered muslin curtain. These small curtains date from the time of Goethe, and they have an interesting function in one's love life: revelation. Raising one corner, pulling it back, and peeking out reveal an intention; drawing the curtain, fastening a flower to it, and shaking it signals that an attentive face is stirring and waiting there behind it: such are time-honored ways in which a romance can begin, in reality as well as in art. The curtain rose ever so slowly, and the fair face peeked out.

Macário did not relate to me chapter and verse the story of his love affair. He simply said that inside of five days he "was crazy about her." His work quickly deteriorated, becoming slow and inexact, and his beautiful cursive handwriting acquired loops, hooks, and scrawls wherein lay all the impatient romance of his nerves. He couldn't see her in the mornings due to the burning July sun that scorched and beat down on the small window. Only in the afternoons was the curtain pulled back and the window raised, and she, laying a cushion on the sill, would lean on it daintily and pertly, her fan in hand. That fan concerned Macário: it was a round Chinese palm fan made of white silk with painstakingly embroidered scarlet dragons, an edging of blue plumage as fine and tremulous as down, and an ivory handle—from which hung two tassels of gold threads—inlaid with mother-of-pearl in the attractive Persian style.

It was a magnificent fan, and in those days not what one would expect in the plebeian hands of a girl dressed in muslin. However, since she was blonde and her mother so dark-complexioned, Macário, with this interpretive intuition of a man in love, said to his curious self, *She must be the daughter of an Englishman.* Englishmen travel to China, Persia, Hormuz, and Australia, and they return loaded with those gems of exotic luxuries, and although Macário didn't even know why that Mandarin fan concerned him to such an extent, he did, as he said to me, "find it odd."

A week had gone by when one day Macário saw from his desk that the blonde girl was leaving with her mother, because he had become accustomed to considering that magnificent person her mother, a woman magnificently pale and dressed in the black of mourning.

Macário stepped over to the window and saw them cross the street to enter the store. His store! He went down immediately—shaking, anxious, passionate, his heart pounding. Both were already leaning on the counter as a clerk unrolled a bolt of black cashmere for them. This affected Macário. He himself told me so.

"Because, after all, my good man, it didn't make sense for them to come and buy black cashmere for themselves."

Of course not. They didn't wear riding habits, they certainly wouldn't want to upholster chairs in black cashmere, there were no men at their home; therefore, that call at the store was a delicate way of seeing him up close, of speaking to him, and it had the ingrained charm of a sentimental lie. I said to Macário that were this the case, he should have found that amorous ploy strange, inasmuch as it signified a likely complicity on the mother's part. He admitted to me that he hadn't thought of such a notion. What he did was approach the counter and say stupidly, "A very good choice, ladies, a very good choice. And this cashmere does not shrink."

And the blonde girl raised her blue eyes up to him, and it was as if Macário felt himself enveloped in the sweetness of a kind of heaven.

However, when he was about to speak a revealing, passionate word, his uncle Francisco appeared at the back of the store in his long, ivory-colored coat with yellow buttons. Since it was peculiar and unusual to find the bookkeeper making a sale at the counter, and because Uncle Francisco with his narrow, celibate judgment would be scandalized, Macário started slowly up the spiral stairway that led to the office, but he still heard the girl saying softly in her charming voice, "Now I would like to see some Indian scarves."

And the clerk went in search of a small parcel of those scarves, layered and bound in a strip of gilded paper.

Macário, who had seen in that visit a revelation of love, almost a *declaration*, was absorbed all day long in the bitter impatience of passion. He went around absent-minded, preoccupied, in puerile fashion, and did not attend to his accounts; he ate dinner without speaking and without listening to Uncle Francisco as he praised the meatballs; he hardly glanced at his earnings, which were paid to him in silver coins at three o'clock sharp; and he did not fully understand his uncle's advice or the clerks' concern over the disappearance of a parcel of Indian scarves.

"It's customary to allow the poor to enter the store," Uncle Francisco had said with his majestic brevity. "That's twelve thousand *réis* in scarves. Enter the loss on my account."

Macário, meanwhile, was secretly contemplating a letter, but it so happened the following day—while he stood on the balcony—that the mother, she of the black hair, came to lean on the windowsill; and at that very moment Macário spotted a friend of his passing along the street, and when the latter caught a glimpse of that lady he nodded and doffed his straw hat to her with a smile. Macário was delighted. That night, wasting no time, he looked his friend up and put it to him abruptly, not beating around the bush.

"Who's that woman you greeted today, the one across from the store?"

"That is Senhora Vilaça. Beautiful woman."

"And the daughter?"

"The daughter?"

"Yes, a blonde with a fair complexion who has a Chinese fan."

"Oh, right! The daughter."

"That's what I've said."

"Yes. And so?"

"She's pretty."

"Yes, pretty she is."

"And they're respectable people, aren't they?"

"Yes, that they are."

"Fine! Do you know them well?"

"I know them, yes, but not all that well. I used to see them at Dona Claudia's house."

"Good. Listen to this."

And Macário, giving an account of his demanding, awakened heart and telling of his love in the impassioned speech of the times, begged him as if it were the glorious apex of his life "to find a way of introducing him there." It wasn't difficult. On Saturdays, the Vilaças frequented the home of a very wealthy notary on Rua dos Calafates, where the gatherings were quiet, simple affairs that consisted of singing motets to harpsichord accompaniment, solving riddles, and playing games of forfeits from the days of Queen Dona Maria I, with the maid serving orgeat at nine o'clock. Well. The very first Saturday after chatting with his friend, Macário—sporting a blue coat, twilled cotton pants with metal fasteners, and a purple satin cravat—was bowing to the notary's wife, Senhora Dona Maria da Graça, a curt, brusque woman who wore a dress embroidered in a mélange of colors and had an enormous tortoiseshell pince-nez perched on her aquiline nose, as well as a marabou feather in her gray hair. In one corner of the room, in the midst of a frou-frou of voluminous dresses, sat the blonde Vilaça girl wearing white, innocent and fresh-looking with her air of a colored engraving, while her pale, haughty mother spoke softly to a judge of apoplectic mien. The notary was a learned man, a Latinist, and a friend of the muses. He wrote in a contemporary journal, *The Ladies' Go-Between*, because he was, above all else, a gallant, and he even dubbed himself in a picturesque ode "Venus's pageboy." As a result, his gatherings were given over to the fine arts, and one night a poet of his acquaintance was to come and read a short poem titled "Elmira or the Venetian's Revenge." The first instances of Romantic boldness started to appear at that time, while the revolutions in Greece began to attract Romanesque spirits versed in mythology to the lands of the East. People everywhere were talking about Janina's pasha and voraciously embracing the virginal new world of minarets, harems, amber-hued sultanas, pirates from the Aegean Sea, and lavish rooms redolent of aloe where decrepit pashas petted lions. Consequently, the curiosity was great, and when the poet showed up with his long hair, his disastrous hooked nose, his neck shrunk in the high collar of his tailcoat (in style during the Restoration), and with his sheepskin in a tin tube, he made no impression whatsoever on Senhor Macário, who was totally engrossed in sweet talk with the Vilaça girl.

Speaking to her solicitously, Macario asked, "So, did you like the cashmere that you saw the other day?"

"Very much," said she in a quiet voice.

And from that moment their marriage was written in the stars.

Meanwhile, an animated evening was spent in the spacious parlor. Macário could not recall all the characteristic historical particulars of that gathering. He only remembered that a magistrate from Leiria recited the "Madrigal to Lídia." The man read it standing up, his right leg ahead of the left, one hand holding a round magnifying glass over the text while keeping the other inside the vee of his high white vest with its high collar. The ladies who formed a circle around him wore floral-motif dresses embellished with feathers, the sleeves of which ended in a fluff of lace and black silk gloves, their fingers aglitter with rings. Smiling warmly, murmuring sweetly, chuckling quietly, gossiping incessantly, and gently flicking fans bedecked with sequins, they all said, "Very nice, very nice!" And the magistrate, turning the magnifying glass aside, bowed with a smile, which exposed a rotten tooth.

Then dear Dona Jerónima da Piedade e Sande, deeply affected, sat down at the harpsichord and sang the old aria by Sully in her nasal voice:[1]

---

1. "Sande" and "Sully" can both be called into question; see the Glossary.

Oh Richard, oh my king,
The world is abandoning you.

Which prompted the fierce Gaudêncio, a democrat from the year 1820 and an admirer of Robespierre, to snarl hatefully to Macário, "Kings! They're vipers!"

Afterward, Canon Saavedra sang "Pretty Girls, Pretty Girls," a song from Pernambuco that was very popular during the reign of Senhor Dom João VI. And thus did the night go—a slow-paced, literary, erudite, refined night enthralled by muses.

Eight days later—on a Sunday—Macário was received in the Vilaças's home. The mother had invited him, saying, "I hope you will honor our poor excuse for an abode." And even the apoplectic judge standing at her side exclaimed, "*Poor excuse*! Say, rather, that it's a palace, beautiful lady!"

Also invited that night were Macário's straw-hatted friend; an old Knight of Malta, infirm, tiresome, and deaf; an ecclesiastic from the cathedral, celebrated for his treble voice; and the Hilária sisters, the oldest of whom had been present—as the companion of a lady from Casa da Mina—at the Salvaterra bullfight at which the Count of Arcos lost his life. And this lady recounted one picturesque episode after another of that afternoon: the figure of the clean-shaven Count of Arcos, a scarlet satin ribbon tied to his pigtail; the sonnet recited by a skinny poet—a hanger-on from Casa de Vimioso—when the count entered the ring riding his sidestepping black horse saddled Spanish style, his silver-embroidered coat of arms on the trapping; the tumble taken at that moment by a Franciscan friar in the upper rows, and the hilarity of the court, such that even the Countess of Pavolide burst out laughing; King Dom José I, attired in scarlet velvet adorned with gold, leaning against the edge of the viewing stand while fingering his gem-studded snuff box with his physician, Dr. Lourenço, and his friar confessor motionless behind him; the imposing appearance of the bullring crowded with people from Salvaterra, town leaders together with area beggars, friars, and lackeys; and the chorus of exclamations that rose when King Dom José I entered: "Long live the king, our lord!" And the people knelt, and the king sat, eating bonbons from a velvet bag held by a servant standing behind him. Then followed the death of the Count of Arcos, fainting spells, and even the king leaning over the parapet, beating on it with his hand and shouting in all the confusion, and the chaplain of the Casa dos Arcos hurrying to administer extreme unction. And Hilária, who had been terror-stricken, heard the moos of the oxen, the shrill cries of the women, and the screams brought on by hysteria; and then she had seen an old man dressed from head to toe in black velvet brandishing a rapier, struggling with the noblemen and ladies who prevented him from jumping into the bullring as he bellowed with rage! It was the count's father. Afterward she fainted in the arms of a Congregation priest. When she came to, she found herself next to the bullring. The royal berlin stood at the exit, its coachman in feathered headgear, the mules fitted with bells, and the outriders equipped with goads. The king was already inside, hunched in a corner, pale, feverishly inhaling snuff, huddling with his confessor; and across from him sat the powerful, broad-shouldered Marquis of Pombal, one of his hands atop a high cane, looking grim and speaking slowly and imperiously as he gesticulated with his pince-nez. But outriders goaded the mules, postilions cracked whips, and the berlin set out at a gallop while the public shouted, "Long live the king, our lord!" And the bell of the palace's chapel door tolled the knell! It was an honor bestowed by the king on Casa dos Arcos.

When Dona Hilária finished relating these past misfortunes with a sigh, the table games began. It was peculiar that Macário did not remember the one he had played on that radiant night.

He remembered only that he had stayed at the side of the blonde Vilaça girl, whose name was Luísa, and that he had taken considerable notice of her fair, rosy skin touched by light, as well as the gentle, lovable petiteness of her hands with fingernails more polished than Dieppe ivory. And he also remembered an odd mishap that, from that day on, engendered in him great hostility toward the clergy of the cathedral. Macário was sitting at the table, and next to him was Luísa, who had positioned herself to face him, one hand propping up her pretty and lovable blonde head and the other forgotten in her lap. Across from them sat the beneficiary with his black biretta, his glasses settled on the pointed tip of his nose, his close-shaven cheeks with a bluish tinge, and his big, complicated, hirsute ears, which looked like two open peepholes detached from his skull. Now, since at the end of the game a few tokens had to be paid to the Knight of Malta, who was sitting alongside the beneficiary, Macário took a coin from his pocket, and while the knight—bending over, with one eye blinking—was adding the sums on the back of an ace, Macário continued to talk to Luísa while spinning his gold coin on the green felt like a bobbin or a toy top. It was a new coin that glittered and sparkled, giving the appearance of a ball of golden mist as it spun round and round. Luísa smiled as she watched it, and Macário thought that all of heaven, purity, and the goodness of flowers and the chasteness of stars were to be found in that bright, unaware, spiritual, seraphic smile with which she followed the spinning and spinning of that new gold coin. But all of a sudden the coin, rolling over to the edge of the table, fell off toward Luísa's lap and disappeared, without the metallic sound of the coin hitting the wood floor. The beneficiary quickly and politely bent down to look; Macário pushed his chair back to search under the table; Senhora Vilaça provided illumination with a candlestick; and Luísa stood up and gave a little shake to her muslin dress. The coin did not turn up.

"That's strange," said the friend with the straw hat. "I didn't hear it clink on the floor."

"Neither did I, neither did I," they all said.

The beneficiary, his back arched, was searching tenaciously, and the Hilária girl was muttering a prayer to Saint Anthony.

"Well, there are no holes in the house," said Senhora Vilaça.

"A disappearance like that," grumbled the beneficiary.

Meanwhile, Macário was venting his emotion with dispassionate exclamations: "For the love of God! Really now! It'll turn up tomorrow! Please! I do beg you! Truly, Dona Luísa! For the love of God! It's not worth it."

However, mentally he said to himself that there had been a subterfuge—a theft—and he attributed it to the beneficiary. No doubt the coin had rolled right by him, not making a sound, and he had covered it with his big, stained, ecclesiastic shoe; and then, under the pretense of his brief, brusque move to look, had snatched it up. And when the two were leaving the Vilaças's home, the beneficiary, wrapped in his great camlet capote, said to Macário on the stairway, "A coin like that disappearing! What a turn of events!"

"You think so, Father Beneficiary?" Macário stopped to ask, astounded by such impudence.

"Why, of course I do! And you! A seven thousand five hundred *réis* gold coin! Do you grow them? Good grief! I'd go crazy!"

Macário found that cool astuteness tedious and did not respond.

The beneficiary then added, "Tomorrow morning, my good man. Send someone tomorrow morning. What the devil.... God forgive me! What the devil! A gold coin doesn't simply vanish like that! What a big pot at that game, huh!"

And Macário felt like smacking him.

It was at this point that Macário told me, in a deeply affected voice, "At all events, my friend, to go straight to the heart of the matter: I had decided to marry her."

"What about the gold coin?"

"I thought no more about it. *Why* think about it? I had decided to marry her!"

II

MACÁRIO told me more precisely what had motivated him to make that profound, enduring decision. It was a kiss. But I will keep to myself that simple, chaste moment, particularly because the only witness was an image of the Virgin hanging in her blackwood frame in the dark parlor that gave onto the stairway. An ephemeral, superficial, fleeting kiss. Yet it sufficed for Macário's severe, honorable spirit to obligate him to take her as his wife, to always be true to her, and to give her possession of his life. Such was their betrothal. The welcome shadow cast by their neighboring windows had become his destiny, the moral end of his life, and the pervasive, dominant thought in his work. And this story, naturally, assumes an elevated character of sanctity and sadness.

Macário spoke to me at length about the makeup and appearance of Uncle Francisco: his stately stature; his gold eyeglasses; his grayish beard a ribbon of growth from ear to ear below the chin, in the so-called "necklace style"; a nervous tic that he had in one nostril; the harshness of his voice; his austere and majestic calmness; his old-school authoritarian, tyrannical principles; and the telegraphic brevity of his words.

When Macário said to him one morning at breakfast, abruptly, without smoothing the way, "I ask your permission to get married," Uncle Francisco, who was pouring sugar into his coffee, said not a word, slowly stirring it with his spoon, and looking majestic, formidable. When he finished noisily drinking the coffee from the saucer, he slipped the napkin from around his neck, folded it, sharpened his toothpick with the knife, put it between his teeth, and took his leave. However, at the door of the room he stopped; turning around to Macário, who was standing next to the table, he said curtly, "No."

"Excuse me, Uncle Francisco!"

"No."

"But listen, Uncle Francisco—"

"No."

Macário became incensed. "In that case I'll do it without your permission."

"Thrown out on your ear."

"I'll leave first. Make no mistake."

"Today."

"Today."

About to close the door, Uncle Francisco turned around again, exclaiming, "Oh!"

Macário, who was exasperated, apoplectic, digging his fingernails on the window, also turned around, with a glimmer of hope.

"Hand me my snuff box," said Uncle Francisco.

He had forgotten his snuff box! Only that distressed him!

"Uncle Francisco—" Macário began.

"Enough said. Today is the twelfth, but you'll be paid for the entire month. So leave."

The old ways of doing things brought about these senseless situations. It was brutal and idiotic. Macário confirmed that for me.

That very evening Macário found himself in the room of a boardinghouse on Praça da Figueira with six gold coins, his trunk of underclothes, and his passion. However, he was calm. Although he foresaw troubles ahead, he had friends and acquaintances in the business world. Known for his good name, the neatness of his work, his ironclad integrity, his family connection, his business acumen, and his beautiful cursive hand-writing … all these traits gave him, respectfully, open entrée into all offices. The following day he went in high spirits to look up Faleiro, an old acquaintance from his former firm.

"I'd be happy to give you a position, my friend," he said to me. "I really would, but if I do, I'll be on the outs with your uncle, my old friend of twenty years. He told me so in no uncertain terms. You understand. Force majeure. I'm sorry, but…."

And all the contacts that Macário went to see, banking on his solid relationship with them, feared "being on the outs with your uncle, my old friend of twenty years."

And they all said, "Sorry, but…."

Macário then turned to young merchants—men who were strangers to his old firm and family—and especially to foreigners, because he hoped to meet people unencumbered by a twenty-year friendship with his uncle. But for them Macário was an unknown, and as a consequence equally unknown were his dignity and his expert work. If they made inquiries they learned that he had been let go posthaste from his uncle's business on account of a blonde girl dressed in muslin. This circumstance deprived him of any sympathy. Business eschews a lovesick bookkeeper. As a result Macário reached a crisis point, and while seeking, asking, and searching again and again, time passed, swallowing his six gold coins piece by piece.

Macário moved to a cheap boardinghouse and continued making inquiries. But having always been a person of reserved manner, he hadn't made friends; he felt helpless and alone, and life looked bleak.

He went through all of his money. With no other choice he gradually settled into the age-old tradition of indigence, which decrees inevitable, established steps, and the first one was to pawn his belongings. Then he sold them. Watch, rings, chain, blue tailcoat, braided jacket—all those possessions carried off item by item and wrapped in a shawl by a withered old woman afflicted with asthma.

Meanwhile, he saw Luísa at night in the small, dark room that gave onto the landing. A faint oil lamp burned on the table, and he was happy there in that dimness, sitting chastely at Luísa's side in a corner of an old wicker settee. He didn't see her during the day because now he wore secondhand clothes and beat-up boots and didn't want to reveal to Luisa—who looked so fresh and dainty in her clean chambray—his seedy, mended appearance. There in that feeble, subdued light he gave vent to his growing passion and hid his down-at-the-heels dress. According to what Macário told me, Luísa's temperament was most peculiar. Her character was as blonde as her hair … if it's true that blonde is a weak, lackluster color. She spoke infrequently, yet always smiled when she did, her small white teeth on display, and said, "Yes, of course" to everything; and she was, moreover, simple, almost nonchalant, and given to acquiescence. She unquestionably loved Macário, but with all the love that her frail, tearful, inept nature could offer. She was like a skein of flax that you could spin however you wished, and sometimes during those nights together she would doze off.

One day, though, Macário found her ill at ease, and in a hurry, her shawl haphazardly wrapped, continuously glancing at the door.

"Mamá has caught on," she said.

And she proceeded to tell him that her mother suspected something, that she was even curt and morose, and might have guessed that they had a marriage plan afoot, a plan hatched like a conspiracy.

"Why don't you come to ask Mamá for my hand?"

"But I can't, my love! I have no position yet. We'd starve. Maybe in a month or so, because I have something in the works now."

Twisting one end of her shawl, her eyes cast down, Luísa kept silent for a moment. "At least wait," she then said, "until I signal you from the window before you come up again. All right?"

Macário burst into tears, his sobs violent, desperate.

"Shh!" uttered Luísa. "Not so loud!"

Macário told me about that night. He wandered the streets while feverishly contemplating his grief and contending with the stark, frigid January weather in his short jacket. He did not sleep, and early the following morning he stormed into Uncle Francisco's room and spoke to him abruptly, hoarsely.

"Look." He showed him three coins worth but a pittance. "It's all I have. My clothes are gone. I've sold everything. Soon I'll die of hunger."

Uncle Francisco, who was shaving by the window with an Indian scarf tied around his head, turned to stare at Macário while putting his glasses on.

"Your desk is still there." Then, with a decisive gesture, he added, "But stay single."

"Uncle Francisco, listen to me—!"

"Single, I said," continued Uncle Francisco, sharpening his razor with a swipe on the leather strop.

"I can't."

"Then get out!"

Macário left, stunned. He went back to his living quarters, lay down, wept, and fell asleep. He went out early evening, completely at a loss, and like a saturated sponge, unable to absorb more disappointment, so once again he tramped the streets aimlessly.

At one point, all of a sudden, a voice from inside a store called out to him. "Hey! Hello!"

It was his straw-hatted friend, who, struck with amazement, opened his big arms to Macário. "What the devil! I've been looking for you since this morning."

He told Macário that he had just arrived from the country, learned of his predicament, and proposed to him a way out.

"Do you want to hear it?"

"Of course!"

A business establishment wanted an able, determined, and hardy man to undertake a difficult, although profitable, mission to Cape Verde.

"I'm ready!" exclaimed Macário. "I'm ready! Tomorrow!"

And he immediately went to write to Luísa, asking her for a farewell visit, a final meeting, the kind in which desolate, passionate arms anguish over separation. He arrived and found her wrapped in a shawl, shivering with cold. Macário wept. She, with her passive, blonde sweetness, said to him, "You're doing the right thing. Maybe you'll get rich."

The next day Macário set off for Cape Verde.

He underwent difficult voyages on hostile seas, monotonous seasickness in stuffy berths, the unforgiving sun in the colonies, the tyrannical brutality of wealthy plantation owners, the weight of humiliating burdens, the emotional angst of absence, treks into the interior of ominous lands, and the melancholy of caravans that follow—through tempestuous nights and never-ending days—calm rivers that exude death.

Macário returned.

And that very evening he saw Luísa—fair, fresh, rested, serene, and leaning against the windowsill with her Chinese fan. The next day he went, eagerly, to ask her mother for her hand in marriage. Macário had earned a tidy sum, and Senhora Vilaça opened her big, welcoming arms to him with profuse exclamations. It was decided that the wedding would take place in one year.

"Why?" I asked Macário.

So he told me that his Cape Verde profits didn't constitute all the necessary capital to establish himself; it was only start-up capital. Having brought back from Cape Verde the bases of powerful business dealings, he would work like a dog for a year, and then he would be able to raise a family free from worry.

And work he did. He put into that labor all the creative force of his passion. He rose at dawn, ate in a hurry, and didn't waste time on talk. Evenings he visited Luísa, and then anxiously sped back to the grind like a miser to his coffer. He had a solid, strong build and was hale and hearty; he made use of ideas and muscles with the same drive; and he lived in a maelstrom of figures. Sometimes Luísa stopped at his store for a bit, and to have that fugitive bird alight there gave him the joy, courage, faith, and consolation for an entire work-filled month.

Around that time Macário's straw-hatted friend came to ask that he stand surety for a sizable loan that he had taken out in order to start a big hardware store. Macário, who now enjoyed an excellent credit rating, guaranteed it with pleasure. His straw-hatted friend was the one who had made possible that providential business deal in Cape Verde. His marriage would take place in two months, and at times Macário already felt feverish blushes of hope color his face as he began to have the banns proclaimed. However, one day the straw-hatted friend disappeared with the wife of an army lieutenant. With his own establishment just getting started, it was a confusing matter to straighten out and well-nigh impossible for Macário to come up with a clear account of that painful imbroglio. What was clear, though, was Macário's status as the guarantor: he was obligated to repay the loan. When that dawned on him, he turned as white as a sheet and said simply, "I'll liquidate and pay it in full!"

And when he liquidated, he ended up poor again. But that same day, since the disaster had generated much publicity and his honor was deemed sacrosanct by all, Peres & Co., the firm that had sent him to Cape Verde, came to propose to him another voyage and another profitable outcome.

"Go to Cape Verde again!"

"Make a fortune again! You're devilishly good at it!" said Senhor Eleutério Peres.

When he realized with stark awareness that he was alone and poor, Macário burst into tears. Everything was lost, finished, over and done with: he needed, patiently, to begin his life anew; to return to the prolonged miseries of Cape Verde; to dread once more episodes of despair like those of the past; and to sweat the selfsame blood and sweat. And Luísa? Macário wrote to her. Then he tore the letter into pieces. He made his way to her house and saw light in the windows. He climbed the steps up to the first floor, but paused there because he was overcome by grief, by a cowardly fear to reveal the disaster to her, by the awful panic of a separation, by the terror of her begging off, refusing, hesitating! Would she agree to wait much longer? He didn't dare to speak, explain, or ask, and went back down on tiptoe. It was nighttime. He then wandered the streets beneath a serene, silent moon, and it was while walking aimlessly that he heard out of the blue, at an illuminated window, a Moorish ballad being played on a rebec. He remembered the time he had caught his first glimpse of Luísa, and he also remembered the bright sunshine, as well as her blue-flecked muslin dress! Continuing to roam, he found himself on the street of his uncle's store, and he paused to glance up at his erstwhile home. The office window was closed. How many times from there had he seen Luísa and the easy back-and-forth movement of her Chinese fan! But light shone in one window on the second floor; it was his uncle's room. And even from a distance Macário discerned that the figure leaning against the framework was Uncle Francisco. A wave of nostalgia washed over him, nostalgia for all of the placid, secluded, solitary, simple past. He remembered his room, and the old desk with the silver lock, and the miniature of his mother that he kept on top of the headboard of his bed; and he remembered, too, the dining room and its old African blackwood sideboard, and the big water jug with its handle shaped like a hissing serpent. Driven by an inexplicable instinct, he decided on the spot and knocked on the door. He knocked again. He heard the window opening and his uncle's voice.

"Who's there?" asked Uncle Francisco.

"It's me, Uncle, it's me. I've come to say goodbye."

The window closed. Shortly afterward the door opened with a loud clank of locks, and standing there was Uncle Francisco, an oil lamp in one hand. Macário thought him thin, older-looking, and kissed his free hand.

"Come on up," said his uncle.

Macário followed him without a word, clinging to the handrail.

When he reached the room, Uncle Francisco set the lamp down on an enormous blackwood table, and, still on his feet with his hands in his pockets, waited.

A quiet Macário just stood there, too, stroking his beard.

"What do you want?" asked his uncle in a loud voice.

"I've come to say goodbye. I'm going back to Cape Verde."

"Bon voyage." And turning his back on his nephew, Uncle Francisco went over to the window and started tapping his fingers on it.

At first, Macário didn't move; then, having become indignant, he took several steps to leave.

"Where are you going, you numbskull?" shouted his uncle.

"Away from here."

"Sit down!" And an agitated Uncle Francisco spoke while pacing the floor with long strides. "Your friend is a scoundrel! A hardware store! Sure it was! You are a good man. Stupid, but a good man. Sit down there! Sit down! Your friend is a scoundrel! You are a good man! You went to Cape Verde! I know that! You paid the loan in full. Of course you did, and I know that, too! Tomorrow please go back down to your desk. I've ordered a new wicker seat for it. And from now on, please put *Macário & Nephew* on the invoices. And get married. Get married. I hope it works out for you. Withdraw some money. You need personal items of clothing as well as furnishings. And put it all on my account. The bed in your room is made."

With tears in his eyes, a stunned and radiant Macário wanted to embrace him.

"All right, all right." Macário was going to leave.

"Oh you nitwit! You want to leave your own home!"

And opening a small cupboard, Uncle Francisco brought out jelly, a dish of marmalade, an old bottle of Port, and biscuits. "Eat."

And he sat down alongside his nephew and again called him a nincompoop. A tear could be seen trickling down his wrinkled cheek.

So it was decided that the marriage would take place in one month. And Luísa began to prepare her trousseau.

It was a time when Macário knew love and happiness to the full. He envisioned the end of his life fulfilled, complete, joyful. He was almost always at his fiancée's house, and one day he accompanied her on a shopping excursion to various stores. He wanted to buy her a little present, and that very afternoon. They had left Luísa's mother with a dressmaker on the first floor of a shop on Rua do Ouro, and the two of them had gone down, gaily and laughing, to a goldsmith's shop on the ground floor of the same building.

It was a fine winter day, bright and clear, with a brilliant, boundless, comforting royal-blue sky.

"What a beautiful day!" said Macário.

And with his fiancée on his arm, he walked a short stretch along the sidewalk.

"It is," agreed Luísa. "But we could be seen … the two of us alone."

"Don't worry. It's all right."

"No, no."

And Luísa gently pulled him toward the goldsmith's shop. There was only one clerk, a man with a swarthy complexion and shaggy hair.

"I'd like to see women's rings," Macário said to him.

"With gemstones," added Luísa. "The prettiest ones you have."

"Yes, with gemstones," said Macário. "Amethysts, garnets … you know, the best that you have."

Meanwhile, Luísa was examining the blue velvet-lined display cases in which glittered wide bracelets inlaid with jewels, chains, cameo necklaces, armorial rings, thin wedding bands as fragile as love, and all the scintillating pieces of gold work.

"Look, Luísa," said Macário.

The clerk had laid out—on top of the glass at the far end of the counter—a dazzling arrangement of gold rings, some set with gemstones, others chased or enameled; and Luísa, picking them up and putting them down with her fingertips, considered each one, saying, "It's ugly. It's heavy. It's big."

"Look at this one," Macário said to her.

It was a ring set with small pearls.

"It's pretty," she said. "Exquisite."

"Here. Try it on," said Macário. And taking her hand, he very slowly and sweetly slipped the ring on her finger; and she laughed, revealing her small white teeth, all of them with fine enamel. "It's too big," he said. "What a shame!"

"We can make it smaller, if you wish. Tell me the size and we'll have it ready for you tomorrow."

"Good idea," said Macário. "Yes, a good idea. Because it is pretty, isn't it? The pearls are uniform in size, and they all have the same luster. Very pretty indeed! And those earrings in the shape of a shell?" he asked, going to the other end of the counter, to another display. "How much are they?"

"Ten *moedas*," said the clerk.

Meanwhile, Luísa continued examining the laid-out arrangement of rings, trying each one on all of her fingers, scrutinizing that precious, brilliant, refined display.

All of a sudden, though, the clerk turned very pale and stared at Luísa as he slowly ran a hand over his face.

"Good," said Macário, stepping toward the clerk. "Then tomorrow we can pick up the ring. What time?"

The clerk didn't answer and began to stare at Macário.

"What time?"

"At noon."

"All right. Until then," said Macário. And they were going to leave. Luísa was wearing a blue woolen dress that dragged somewhat, lending a melodious lilt to her walk as the hem swept the floor, and she had her small hands hidden in a white muff.

"Excuse me!" the clerk suddenly blurted out. Macário turned around. "You haven't paid."

Macário looked at him gravely. "Of course not. Tomorrow, when I come for the ring. I'll pay you tomorrow."

"Excuse me!" the clerk said again. "I'm referring to the other one."

"What other one?" asked Macário, his surprise showing in his tone as he turned back toward the counter.

"That lady knows," replied the clerk. "That lady knows."

Macário slowly reached for his wallet. "I beg your pardon. If it's an old bill—"

The clerk opened the countertop, speaking resolutely. "Nothing of the sort, my dear sir. It's from right now. It's a ring with two diamonds, a ring taken by that lady."

"Me!" said Luísa in a low voice, her cheeks flushed.

"What? What are you saying?"

Macário—tense, pale, his teeth clenched—glared at the clerk.

"That lady," the clerk then said, "took a ring from the display case there." Macário, perfectly still, was staring straight at him. "A ring with two diamonds. I clearly saw her." So disturbed was the clerk that he stammered in a voice charged with concern. "I don't know who that lady is, but she took it from there."

Without thinking, Macário gripped the clerk's arm and turned to Luísa; wan, at a loss for words, and with beads of perspiration on his forehead, he asked her to say something. "Luísa, speak up...." But his voice broke.

"I ...," she uttered, but having blanched, she was upset, tremulous, disconcerted, frightened. And she had dropped her muff on the floor.

Macário went and grabbed her wrist, his eyes riveted on her. And his expression was so determined, so imperious, that it frightened her, and she abruptly thrust her hand into her pocket and showed him the ring.

"Don't hurt me," she said, flinching.

Macário didn't move; his arms were limp, his lips colorless, and he had an abstracted air about him. Then he suddenly tugged at his coat and, recovering his presence of mind, spoke to the clerk.

"You're right. A lapse, of course. The lady had forgotten. And the ring. Yes. Obviously, Senhor. If you would be so kind.... Look, my dear, let me have the ring and this gentleman will wrap it. How much is it?"

Macário opened his wallet and paid.

Then he picked up the muff, shook it gently, dabbed his lips with a handkerchief, gave his arm to Luísa, and, saying to the clerk, "My apologies, my apologies," he led her outside—an inert, passive, numbed, and terrified Luísa.

They started walking along the street. A far-off sun shone on the happy tableau: carriages hurried by, rolling to the crack of a whip; smiling individuals passed by, chatting animatedly; street vendors cried out gaily, their voices loud and clear; and a man on horseback, wearing tapir-hide breeches, was making his rosette-bedecked horse sidestep. The street was crowded and noisy, and alive, happy, and sun-drenched.

Macário was walking mechanically, like a somnambulist. He stopped at a corner. He had Luísa's arm linked with his, and he saw her hand hanging down; it looked waxen now, her veins a soft blue, her fingers slender and lovely. It was her right hand, and that hand was the hand of his fiancée. And, instinctively, he read a playbill for that night, *Palafox in Saragossa*.

All of a sudden, letting go of Luísa's arm, he quietly said to her, "Go away."

"Listen," she said, leaning toward him.

"Go away." And in a terrible, hollow voice, "Go away. Look, I'll call the authorities and have you sent to Aljube. So get away from me."

"But listen, for heaven's sake," she implored him.

"Go, go!" And he made a threatening gesture with his clenched fist.

"For the love of God, don't hit me here," she said, choked up.

"Get away from me. People might wonder. And don't cry because you could be seen. So go!" And leaning in close to her, he said softly, "You are a thief."

And turning his back on her, Macário slowly withdrew, his walking stick tap-tapping the pavement.

From a short distance he looked back: he still caught sight of her blue dress in the midst of the crowds.

Since Macário left for the country that very afternoon, he never learned another thing about that blonde girl.

Glossary to
"The Peculiarities of a Blonde Girl"
(in order of appearance)

MINHO: a province in northwestern Portugal, bordering the Atlantic.

THE APPEARANCE OF ROSTELO MONASTERY: If it is real, I have failed to identify this monastery after a search of sites in the Minho.

THE IMITATION: *The Imitation of Christ* [*De Imitatione Christi*] by Thomas à Kempis, 1418–27; a Christian devotional book for spiritual life.

VILA REAL: a city in the historical province Trás-os-Montes, in the northeastern corner of Portugal.

GUIMARÃES: a city in northern Portugal, in the district of Braga (Minho province).

SANTO ALEIXO: a city in the Vila Real region.

ARCOS (DE VALDEVEZ): a municipality along the northern border of Portugal and Galicia [Spain], in the Viana do Castelo district of the Minho.

AMARANTE: a small town in the northern Portuguese district of Porto.

SLAVIC PROVERB FROM GALICIA: This Galicia would be the historical and geographic region between Central and Eastern Europe.

SALITRE: a theater, mainly for drama and comic opera, that dated back to the late 1700s. After undergoing a name change to Teatro das Variedades in 1858, it was eventually razed to make way for the Avenida da Liberdade, Lisbon's Champs-Élysées. All that remains of it is the street name Rua do Salitre; see Silva, *Entertaining Lisbon*, 67–72.

JUDGE CURVO SEMEDO OF THE ARCÁDIA: The [New] Arcádia was a literary society cofounded by the Count of Pombeiro in

Lisbon in 1790; Belchior Manuel Curvo Semedo Torres de Sequeira (1766–1838), Portuguese poet of note.

QUEEN DONA MARIA I (1734–1816): A troubled queen who suffered from religious mania and melancholia, she was judged mentally insane in February 1792.

DONA JERÓNIMA DA PIEDADE E SANDE: Richard Franko Goldman (trans. Eça de Queiroz, *The Mandarin and Other Stories* [Athens: Ohio University Press, 1965], viii) makes the case for a misprint here in names. He argues that the "Sande" of Dona Jerónima's surname ought to be "Saúde," which would make the meaning of her full name Dona Jerónima of Piety and *Health*, not Dona Jerónima of Piety and *Sandwich* (an example of Eça's humor?).

He further believes that "Sully" is "Lully." Jean-Baptiste Lully? However, this aria leads us to André Grétry (1741–1813) and his comic opera titled *Richard Coeur-de-lion* and Blondel's aria: *Ô Richard, ô mon roi! / L'univers t'abandonne*. The two lines appear in Balzac's *Père Goriot*.

KING DOM JOÃO VI (1767–1826): Son of Maria I, called *o Clemente* (the Clement One), he presided over a turbulent time in Portuguese history, having to live through the interventions of Spain, France, and Great Britain and a difficult marriage to Carlota Joaquina of Spain, as well as a forced voyage to Brazil when troops of Napoleon I invaded Portugal. He remained in Brazil for years, helping to create a modern state before returning to Portugal.

KING DOM JOSÉ I (1714–77): father of Maria I; he turned over effective control of power to the Marquis of Pombal.

MARQUIS OF POMBAL, SEBASTIÃO JOSÉ DE CARVALHO E MELO, FIRST MARQUIS OF POMBAL (1699–1782): A statesman and prominent minister in the government, he introduced numerous fundamental reforms, but he is most notably known for his re-building of the central downtown area [Baixa] of Lisbon after the violent earthquake (9 on the Richter scale) of November 1, 1755.

"NECKLACE STYLE BEARD": in his novel *The Count of Abranhos*, Eça—apropos of the Portuguese poet Almeida Garrett—cites a lithograph by Pedro Augusto Guglielmi that clearly shows the "necklace," a half moon of ears-to-below-the-chin growth of beard that appears to be approximately one inch wide.

FORCE MAJEURE: a superior or overpowering force.

PALAFOX IN SARAGOSSA: José Antonio de Palafox y Melci (1776–1847), the Spanish general who, in the first siege of Saragossa [Zaragoza] during the Peninsular War in 1808, spearheaded the city's resistance and fight against the French and Polish troops. If there is indeed a play titled *Palafox in Saragossa*, I have been unable to find it.

Goya's portrait of Palafox—on horseback, sword in hand—hangs in Madrid's Prado Museum.

The historical fact is that Napoleon's troops laid siege to the Spanish city, and the clear literary fact is that Macário "lays siege" to Luísa in "The Peculiarities of a Blonde Girl." Marie-Hélène Piwnik (*Contos* I:192, footnote) writes apropos of *Palafox in Saragossa*, "It's very likely that [said] work, related to the siege of Saragossa and Palafox's feats, is of a Romantic tenor to serve as counterpoint to Macário's disillusionment" [*É bem provável que a obra, relacionada com o sítio de Saragoça e os feitos de Palafox, seja de tenor romântico, em contraponto com a desilusão de Macário*].

Civilization

I

I HAVE A DEAR FRIEND (his name is Jacinto) who was born in a palace and lived on forty *contos* of income from fertile lands of grain, olive oil, and livestock.

Since infancy, when his mother—a stout, gullible lady from Trás-os-Montes—scattered fennel and amber in order to stay in the good graces of the Beneficial Fairies, Jacinto had always been more hale and hearty than a pine tree on sand dunes. A pretty, murmurous, limpid river, with a very smooth bed of very white sand barely reflecting glossy snippets of a summer sky or aromatic, evergreen foliage, would not offer to one who has cruised such a river, on a bark laden with cushions and chilled champagne, more comfort and ease than life offered to my comrade Jacinto. He never had measles and he never had worms. He never suffered, even at the age in which one reads Balzac and Musset, the torments of sensibility. In his friendships he was always as fortunate as the classical Orestes. Of love he had only known the honey—that honey which love invariably grants to those who, like bees, practice it with nimbleness and mobility. As for ambition, he had only experienced good comprehension of general ideas, and the "peak of his intellect" (as the old medieval chronicler puts it) was still neither dull nor rusty. And yet, from the age of twenty-eight, Jacinto was already feasting on Schopenhauer, the book of Ecclesiastes, and other lesser pessimists, and three or four times a day, he would yawn—a slow, deep yawn while running his slender fingers over his cheeks, as if he were palpating pallor and ruin. Why?

He was, of the men I had met, the most completely civilized, or rather the one who had supplied himself with the greatest sum of intellectual, ornamental, and material civilization. In that palace (called in flowery language the Jessamine)—which his father, also a Jacinto, had built over an honorable seventeenth-century house with pine-laid floors and a whitewashed exterior—there existed, I believe, everything for the good of the spirit or of substance that man had created through uncertainty and pain since abandoning the happy valley of Septa-Sindu, the Land of Easy Waters, the sweet Arian country. The library consisted of two rooms as spacious and bright as public squares, and it featured rugs from Caramania and completely covered walls from floor to ceiling, where by turns the sunlight that penetrated through windowpanes and the illumination provided by electricity diffused a calm light conducive to study. It housed, on shelves of ebony, twenty-five thousand volumes magnificently bound in scarlet morocco leather; and of the philosophical systems alone there were 1,817, as with sound prudence—that is, to save space, the bibliophile had only collected the ones that irreconcilably contradict one another!

One afternoon that I wished to copy a legal opinion by Adam Smith, I ended up scouring the length of the bookcases in search of this economist—eight meters of political economy! Thus did my friend Jacinto find himself well-provided with all the essential works of intelligence, and even of stupidity. The only drawback to this monumental storehouse of knowledge was that everyone who entered there inevitably fell asleep there on account of the armchairs, which conveniently had fine adjustable supports to hold a book, a cigar, or a pencil to take notes; and they offered, besides, a flaccid, oscillating combination of cushions on which the body soon discovered, to the detriment of the spirit, sweetness, profundity, and peace, as though laid out on a bed.

At the rear, like a high altar, was Jacinto's workroom. His austere and abbatial leather chair with escutcheons dated from the fourteenth century, and all around it hung numerous acoustic tubes, which, against the backdrop of the moss- and ivy-colored silk drapery, looked like serpents that were asleep and hanging from an old farm wall. I never think about his desk without amazement, as it was littered with clever and ingenious instruments to cut paper, number pages, glue stamps, sharpen pencils, erase mistakes, print dates, melt sealing wax, bind documents, and emboss accounts. A few made from nickel, others from steel, all were resplendent and slow and difficult to manage; and some, with stiff springs and sharp points, could pinch and hurt fingers. And on the large Whatman sheets of paper that he used for writing, and that cost five hundred *réis*, I was occasionally surprised by drops of my friend's blood. But he deemed all those instruments indispensable to compose his letters (Jacinto did not compose works), as he also deemed indispensable the thirty-five dictionaries, as well as the manuals and encyclopedias, and the guides and directories, all of which filled a tall, isolated bookcase shaped like a tower that silently revolved on its pedestal, and that I had christened the Lighthouse. Nevertheless, what totally imparted to that study a portentous character of civilization were—atop their own bases—the great trappings, the facilitators of thought: the typewriter, the copiers, the Morse telegraph, the phonograph, the telephone, the théâtrophone, and still others, all of them with shiny metals, all of them with long wires. Dull, staccato sounds constantly rang out in the tepid atmosphere of that sanctuary. Click, click, click! Clang, clang, clang! Jingle, jingle, jingle! Jangle, jangle, jangle! It was my friend, communicating. All those wires sunk in universal forces, transmitted universal forces. And, unfortunately, they did not always remain disciplined and in check! Jacinto had captured on the phonograph the voice of Councilor Pinto Porto, a rotund, oracular voice at the moment of his exclaiming respectfully, authoritatively:

"Amazing invention! Who wouldn't marvel at the advances of this century?"

Well, then, desirous of having a few ladies, relatives of Pinto Porto (the amiable Gouveias), marvel at the phonograph on a sweet Saint John's Eve, my overcivilized friend caused the well-known rotund, oracular voice to blare through the instrument's wide tube, which resembles a flaring horn:

"Who wouldn't marvel at the advances of this century?"

But inexplicably or abruptly, some vital part or spring certainly malfunctioned, because all of a sudden the phonograph began to repeat over and over, nonstop, endlessly, in a more and more rotund voice the councilor's maxim:

"Who wouldn't marvel at the advances of this century?"

In vain did a pale Jacinto pounce on the instrument with trembling fingers. The exclamation kept recurring, and rolled on, oracular and majestic:

"Who wouldn't marvel at the advances of this century?"

We withdrew, on edge, to a distant room decorated in excess with fabrics from Arras. In vain! Pinto Porto's voice carried there, too, and was in the fabrics of Arras, implacable and rotund:

"Who wouldn't marvel at the advances of this century?"

Furious now, we buried a cushion in the phonograph's mouth, and piled on blankets and heavy quilts to suffocate the abominable voice. In vain! Beneath the thick woolen throws, the voice, muffled but oracular, roared:

"Who wouldn't marvel at the advances of this century?"

The amiable Gouveias had become agitated, desperately tightening their shawls around their heads. Even in the kitchen —where we sought refuge—the voice followed, stifled and smothered:

"Who wouldn't marvel at the advances of this century?"

We fled to the street, petrified.

It was early morning. A jovial group of girls, on the way back from the fountains with armfuls of flowers, passed by singing:

> All the herbs are blessed
> The morning of Saint John....

Jacinto, breathing that fresh air, wiped away slow drops of perspiration, and we returned to Jessamine, the sun already high and already hot. We opened the doors gingerly, as if fearful of awakening someone. Horrors! At the hall entrance we heard muzzled, strident sounds: *"wouldn't marvel at ... advances ... century...!"* Only in the afternoon was an electrician able to silence that phonograph.

Considerably more gratifying (for me) than that study dreadfully cluttered with civilization was the dining room, for its intimate, clear, and comprehensible layout. The table sat only six friends whom Jacinto chose on the criteria of literature, art, and metaphysics, and there, amid the tapestries of Arras depicting hills, orchards, and porticos of Attica, replete with classicism and light, they repeatedly renewed banquets that, for their intellectuality, recalled those of Plato. Each forkful crossed with a thought or words adeptly arranged in the form of a thought.

And matching each place setting were six forks, all of them of artful, dissimilar shapes: one for oysters, another for fish, another for meats, another for vegetables, another for fruit, another for cheese. The glasses, for the diversity of shapes and colors on a tablecloth more glittering than enamel, looked like sylvan posies scattered on pristine snow. But Jacinto and his philosophers, recalling what the experienced Solomon teaches about the ruin and bitterness brought on by wine, scarcely drank—in three drops of water—one drop of Bordeaux (Chateaubriand, 1860). Thus is it recommended by Hesiod in his *Nereus*, and Diocles in his *Bees*. And of sundry waters there was always a redundant luxury at Jessamine: ice-cold water, carbonated water, sterilized water, soda water, salt water, mineral water, and still others, in serious bottles with therapeutic treatises printed on the label. The cook, Master Sardão, was the sort that Anaxagoras equated with the Rhetoricians, with the Orators, with all those who know the divine art of "tempering and serving the Idea." And in Sybaris, the City of Excellent Living, the magistrates would have voted Master Sardão, at the festival of Juno Lacinia, the crown of gold leaves and the Milesian tunic that was owed to civic benefactors. His artichoke soup and roes of carp; his fillets of venison macerated in aged madeira with a purée of walnuts; mulberries iced in ether; and still other hors d'oeuvres, numerous and profound (and the only ones tolerated by my Jacinto) were works of an artist made superior by the abundance of new ideas that always coupled the rarity of taste with the magnificence of form. Such a dish from that incomparable master resembled—by its presentation, its elaborate elegance, its arrangement of fresh, harmonious colors—an enameled gem crafted by Cellini or chased by Meurice. How many afternoons did I wish to photograph those compositions of excellent fantasy before the carver cut them up! And this excess of refinement in eating harmonized delightfully with the serving.

Five servants and one Black page, uniformed like shadows in white, glided, in the ostentatious manner of the eighteenth century, over a rug that was softer and smoother than the moss of Brocéliande. The (silver) platters rose from the kitchen and the butler's pantry in two elevators: one for the hot dishes, lined with tubes of boiling water, and another for the cold dishes, this one lined with zinc, ammonia, and salt, and both festooned in such a profusion of lush flowers that it was as if even the soup emerged, steaming, from the romantic gardens of Armida. And well indeed do I remember one May Sunday when a bishop—the erudite bishop of Chorazin—was dining with Jacinto and the fish got stuck in the middle of the elevator, making it necessary to summon masons with levers to remove it.

II

THE AFTERNOONS that there was a "Plato banquet" (for thus did we designate those feasts of truffles and general ideas), I, as a neighbor and intimate friend, would arrive at sundown and familiarly go up to Jacinto's rooms, where I always found him indecisive about which dress coat to wear, because he alternately wore one of silk, of linen, of Jaeger flannels, and of *foulard* from the Indies. The room drank in the freshness and aroma of the garden through two huge windows, magnificently hung with (besides the Louis XV-style silk curtains) a single pane of glass on the exterior and one consisting of small sections of crystal on the interior; an awning, suspended from the cyma, comprised a silken blind that pleated and rolled like movable clouds within a jalousie of Moorish grating. All these measures (wise inventions of Holland & Co., of London) served to gauge light and air according to the readings on thermometers, barometers, and hygrometers mounted on ebony, instruments that a meteorologist (Cunha Guedes) came every week to verify for accuracy.

Positioned between these two balcony windows, and resplendent with light, stood the dressing table for Jacinto to make his *toilette*—an enormous glass table, *entirely* of glass, to render it impenetrable by germs, and covered with all the essentials of personal hygiene and neatness that a man of the nineteenth century needs in a capital so as not to detract from the sumptuous whole of civilization. When our Jacinto, dragging his ingenious silk and kidskin slippers, stepped over to this altar, I, comfortably settled on a couch, would idly open a journal, usually the *Electropathic Review* or an issue of *Psychic Investigations*. And Jacinto would begin…. Each one of those essentials of steel, of ivory, of silver, imposed on my friend—by the all-powerful influence that things exert on the owner (*sunt tyrannae rerum*)—the obligations to use it appropriately and deferentially. And thus did Jacinto's embellishment operations attest to the prolixity, both reverent and insuppressible, of the rites of a sacrifice. He began with his hair. With a hard, round, flat brush he layered his straight blond hair on top and both sides of the part; with a narrow, recurved brush that looked like a scimitar he curled his hair over his ears; with a concave brush in the shape of a roofing tile he applied pomade to his hair at the back and on the nape of his neck. He would then take a deep breath and smile. Next, with a long-bristle brush, he groomed his mustache; with a light, flexible brush he frizzled his eyebrows; with a brush fashioned from very fine feathers, he smoothed his eyelashes. And in this way Jacinto would remain in front of the mirror, running hairs over his hair for fourteen minutes.

Combed and tired, he moved on to purifying his hands. Two servants stood at the back to manipulate the washroom's devices energetically and adroitly—devices that were merely a small-scale assemblage of the monumental mechanisms in the bathroom. On the green and rose-colored marble of the washroom there were only two faucets (hot and cold) for his head; four jets graduated from *zero* to *one hundred degrees*; the vaporizer for perfumes; the cock of sterilized water (for his teeth); the spout for his beard; and even taps that sparkled and ebony knobs that, when touched lightly, unleashed the roar and rumble of torrents in the Alps. Never, to wet my fingers, did I approach that washroom without dread, as I had been made wary by the one bitter January afternoon when, unexpectedly, the tap's solder having become undone, the hot water jet burst at *one hundred degrees*, whistling and steaming, furious and devastating. We all fled, terrified. An outcry shook Jessamine. Old Grilo, who had been Jacinto's father's valet, ended up with blisters all over his face and faithful hands.

When Jacinto laboriously finished drying himself with Turkish and linen towels, and even with a braided rope (to reestablish circulation), he would yawn—a deep, slow yawn.

And it was this yawn, perpetual and vague, that troubled us, his friends and philosophers. What did this excellent man lack? He had his steadfast health, like a wild pine tree growing in the dunes; a light of intelligence able to illuminate everything resolutely and clearly, with nary a tremor or waver; forty magnificent *contos* of income; all the sympathies of a city given to mockery and skepticism; a life purged of shadows, freer and smoother than a summer sky. And nevertheless, he yawned constantly, and with his slender fingers was always touching the pallor and wrinkles on his face. At the age of thirty, Jacinto was becoming hunchbacked, as if weighed down by an unfair burden! And because of the melancholy slowness of all his movements he seemed bound, from his fingers to his will power, by the tight mail of an invisible suit of armor that held him in check. It was painful to witness the boredom with which he grasped his mechanical pencil or his electric pen to point out an address or picked up the speaking tube to notify the coachman! In this slow movement of a thin arm, in the creases that wrinkled his nose, even in his long, worn-out silences, one sensed the constant shout that went directly to his soul: *What tedium! What tedium!* Clearly, life for Jacinto was weariness, either because it was onerous and difficult or because it was uninteresting and hollow. That's why my poor friend continually sought to integrate new interests, new facilities into his life. Two inventors, men of considerable zeal and inquisitiveness, were charged—one in England, one in America—with informing him of all the inventions, even the very smallest, that might contribute to improving Jessamine's comfort. Moreover, he himself corresponded with Edison. As for ideas, Jacinto did not stop searching for interests and emotions that would reconcile him with life; he had, in fact, immersed his entire being in a quest for those emotions and those interests by the most remote paths of knowledge, on the verge of devouring—from January to March—seventy-seven volumes on the *evolution of moral ideas among Negroid races!* Ah! Never did a man of this century do battle more vigorously against the drought of life! To no avail! Even from explorations as captivating as that one, through the morals of the Negroids, Jacinto returned more gloomy, with more cavernous yawns.

And it was then that he sought, intensely, refuge in reading Schopenhauer and Ecclesiastes. Why? Without doubt because both of those pessimists confirmed for him the conclusion that he drew from rigorous, patient experience: "that everything is vanity or pain, that the more you know the more you agonize, and that having been king of Jerusalem and obtained all the pleasures in life only leads to greater bitterness." But why had the healthy, wealthy, serene, and intellectual Jacinto arrived in this way at such gloomy disillusionment? The old valet Grilo claimed that "His Excellency suffered from affluence!"

III

NOW, right after that winter during which he had become absorbed in the morals of Negroids and installed electric lighting among the trees in the garden, it so happened that Jacinto was faced with the unavoidable moral necessity of journeying to the North, to his old ancestral home in Torges. He had no knowledge of Torges, and it was with uncommon tedium that he readied himself for seven weeks to make that rural trip. The farm is in the mountains, and the rugged family seat, where there still stands a tower from the fifteenth century, had been occupied for thirty years by the caretakers—good, hard-working people who ate their soup around the smoke of the fireplace and spread the wheat to dry in the seignorial rooms. At the very beginning of March, Jacinto had taken care to write to Sousa, his agent, who lived in the village of Torges, instructing him to have the roofs repaired, the walls whitewashed, and the glass of the windows replaced. Afterward he ordered the shipment—by fast trains, in crates that only with difficulty managed to slip through Jessamine's large doors—of all the necessary comforts for two weeks in the mountains: feather beds, easy chairs, divans, Carcel lamps, nickel bathtubs, acoustic tubes to summon retainers, and Persian rugs to soften the floors. One of the coachmen departed with a coupé, a victoria, a brake carriage, mules, and bells.

Then the cook left—with kitchen utensils, jars of truffles, huge cases of mineral water, and the icebox. From daybreak on, they nailed and hammered in the mansion's broad courtyards, like in the construction of a city. And the baggage, piling up piece by piece, recalled a page from Herodotus as he narrated the Persian invasion. Jacinto had become emaciated over the concerns of that Exodus, but we finally set out on a June morning with Grilo and thirty-seven trunks.

I accompanied Jacinto on my way to Guiães where my aunt

lives, a good league away from Torges, and we traveled in a re-served car, amid vast cushions, with partridges and champagne in a basket. Halfway through the journey we were supposed to change trains at the station that had a sonorous name ending in *ola* and a very pleasant, immaculate garden of white roses. It was a bright Sunday, but with an immense dust cloud, and we encountered there—filling the narrow platform—a festive multitude of people coming from a pilgrimage to Saint Gregory of the Mountain.

For that change, on the afternoon of a popular fete, the timetable allowed only three miserly minutes. The other train was already waiting alongside the sheds, impatient and whis-tling, while a small bell pealed furiously. And even without paying much attention to the pretty girls who cavorted there in groups, their cheeks flushed, their scarves colorful, their generous bosoms covered with gold, and the image of the saint impressed on their hats, we ran, we pushed, we shoved, and we jumped onto the other car, which was already reserved and singled out by a piece of cardboard with Jacinto's initials. The train pulled out immediately. At that moment I thought about our Grilo, about the thirty-seven trunks! And leaning against the small door, I caught a glimpse of a mountain of baggage still piled next to a corner of the station beneath eucalyptus trees and men wearing caps with braided bills, who, standing in front of the trunks, were waving desperately.

Dropping back on the cushions, I muttered, "What service!"

Nestled in a corner, without opening his eyes, Jacinto sighed, "What a nuisance!"

For one whole hour we whisked through wheat fields and vineyards, and still the sun, hot and dusty, beat on the windows when we arrived at the Gondim station, where Jacinto's agent, the excellent Sousa, was supposed to be waiting for us with horses in order to go up the mountain to his ancestral Torges home. Behind the station's garden, also all abloom in roses and daisies, Jacinto recognized right away his carriages still covered with canvas.

But when we stepped down onto the small white platform, there was only solitude and silence all around us. Neither agent nor horses! Only the station chief! When I anxiously asked him "whether or not Senhor Sousa had shown up there, whether or not he knew Senhor Sousa," he affably removed his braided cap. He was a stout, portly young man with the coloring of a pippin apple, and he carried, tucked under his arm, a volume of verses. "He knew Senhor Sousa very well! He had played cards with Senhor Sousa three weeks ago! However, that afternoon unfortunately he had not seen Senhor Sousa!" The train had disappeared behind the tall cliffs that overhang the river there. A porter was rolling a cigarette and whistling, while an old woman dressed all in black was dozing, curled up on the ground next to the garden gate with her basket of eggs. And our Grilo? And our baggage? The station chief cheerfully shrugged his plump shoulders. All our possessions had been stranded for sure at that station with the white roses that had a sonorous name ending in *ola*. And there we were, lost on that agrestic mountain, without an agent, without horses, without Grilo, without trunks.

Why narrate in great detail that lamentable predicament? At a farmhouse for the estate's tenants that stood on a mountain slope near the station, we were given—to take us and guide us to Torges—a starving mare, a white donkey, and a boy and his hound. And from there we began to climb, wearily, the very same rural paths trod for sure by the Jacintos of the fifteenth century, coming and going from the mountain to the river. But once we made our way over a shaky wood bridge that crosses a brook punctuated by cliffs (a brook in which abound delightful trout), our woes were forgotten in the presence of the unexpected, incomparable beauty of that blessed mountain. The divine artist in the heavens had certainly composed that mountain on one of his mornings of most solemn and bucolic inspiration.

The grandeur was as all-encompassing as grace. To speak of the gentle green valleys, the nearly sacred forests, the fragrant orchards in blossom, the freshness of the murmuring waters, the small white hermitages on the hilltops, the moss-covered rocks, the air of a sweetness like paradise, all the majesty and splendor … that's not for me, a man of limited art. Nor do I believe it would be for Master Horace. Who can speak of the beauty of such simple and inexpressible things? Jacinto, ahead on the sluggish mare, muttered, "Ah! What beauty!" I, behind on the donkey with my legs wobbly, muttered, "Ah! What beauty!" Frolicking streams bubbled, splashing from rock to rock. Thin branches of flowering shrubs brushed our faces with familiarity and affection. For a long time a blackbird followed us, flying from poplar tree to chestnut tree, singing our praises. A truly amiable and welcoming mountain. Ah! What beauty!

Amidst marvelous *Ahs* we arrived at an avenue lined by beech trees that had a classic, noble appearance. Cracking his switch once again on the mare and the donkey, our guide boy, his hound at his side, shouted, "Here we are!" And, in effect, at the end of the beeches there appeared a country house gate that was greatly ennobled by a coat of arms on an old moss-pitted stone. Inside, dogs were barking furiously. And as soon as Jacinto, and I behind him on Sancho's donkey, neared the manorial entrance, a man ran toward us from the top of a flight of steps—a white-haired man, clean-shaven like a cleric, wearing neither vest nor jacket, his arms up in the air, clearly astonished and disconsolate. It was the caretaker, Zé Brás. And then, right there on the courtyard cobblestones, surrounded by yelping dogs, a tumultuous story ensued, which the poor man, rattled as he was, babbled, causing Jacinto's face to flush with lividity and rage. The caretaker hadn't expected His Excellency. No one had expected His Excellency. (He pronounced it *His Inselency*.)

The agent, Senhor Sousa, was at the border, and he had been there since May caring for his mother, who had been kicked by a mule. And for sure there had been a mix-up, lost letters. Because Senhor Sousa only expected His Excellency in September, for the grape harvest. And, unfortunately for His Excellency, no work had begun in the house—the roofs were still without tiles and the windows without glass.

I crossed my arms in justifiable consternation. But those crates—those crates shipped to Torges so prudently in April, replete with mattresses, treats, civilization? The caretaker, in the dark and not understanding, opened his small eyes even wider, eyes in which tears had already welled up. The crates? Nothing had arrived, nothing had appeared. And in his agitation Zé Brás looked around the arches of the courtyard, searched the pockets of his pants. The crates? No, he didn't have the crates!

It was then that Jacinto's coachman (who had brought the horses and carriages) approached, gravely. *He* was a civilized man, and he immediately blamed the government. Back when he worked for the Viscount of Saint Francis, two crates, one of aged wine from Madeira and another of a lady's underwear, had been lost like that, too, from the city to the mountain, on account of negligence on the part of the government. Therefore, having learned his lesson, and with no confidence now in the nation, he had not forsaken the brake carriage, the victoria, the coupé, and the bells, knowing that they were all that His Excellency had left. But on that rugged mountain there were no roads to accommodate them, and since they could only come up to the farm on big ox carts, he had kept them down there at the station tied up in canvas.

Jacinto had remained standing in front of me with his hands in his pockets. "Now what?"

There was no alternative except to bear up, have Uncle Zé Brás's soup for supper, and sleep on the straw mats that fate had ordained for us. We went up. The noble stairway led to a balcony completely covered by an overhang tile roof that extended all along the façade of the big old house, and it was adorned—between its massive granite pillars—with huge earth-filled tubs in which carnations flourished. I picked one of them. We went inside. And my poor Jacinto contemplated, at long last, the rooms of his manor house! They were enormous, the high walls stuccoed with whitewash begrimed by time and neglect—and empty, desolately bare, presenting scarcely a vestige of habitation and life, with mounds of baskets or hoes in the corners. On the ancient ceilings of black oak, whitish gaps showed: it was the already pale, late afternoon sky peeking through holes in the roof. Not a single windowpane remained. From time to time a rotten board creaked and sagged under the weight of our footsteps.

We stopped, finally, in the last one, the biggest one, where there were two bins for storing grain. And there we laid down, wistfully, what was left to us of the thirty-seven trunks: our somewhat white coats, a walking stick, and an issue of the *Afternoon Daily*. Through the paneless window, where you could distinguish the tops of trees and the blue mountains beyond the river, the air came in—plenteous, mountainous air circulating freely like on an open terrace, with the fragrances of wild pine trees. And from down below in the valley rose, bereft and sad, a shepherd girl's voice singing. Jacinto blurted out, "It's awful!" I muttered, "It's country!"

IV

ZÉ BRÁS, meanwhile, had vanished with his hands on his head in order to arrange supper for *Their Inselencies*. Poor Jacinto, crushed by the disaster, deprived of resistance in the face of that brusque disappearance of all civilization, had flopped down on the stone bench by a window, and from there he stared out at the mountains. As for me, those mountain airs and the singing of the shepherd girl had invigorated me, and I ended up going down to the kitchen, led by the coachman along flights of steps and blind turns where the darkness stemmed less from twilight than from dense spider webs.

The kitchen was a thick mass of black forms and hues the color of soot. On the earthen floor at the back a red hearth glowed, its flames licking substantial iron pots and disappearing in a cloud of smoke through the meager grid that filtered light. A chatty, excited group of women there plucked chickens, beat eggs, and cleaned rice with saintly fervor. From the middle of them, the good caretaker turned toward me, looking dazed yet swearing that *Their Inselencies'* supper would be ready in no time. And since I asked about beds, the worthy Brás muttered a timid, vague reply with regard to makeshift "pallets of straw on the floor."

"They'll do, Senhor Zé Brás," I hastened to console him.

"Then, thus may God be served!" sighed the excellent man who, at that moment, was dealing with the most bitter predicament of his mountain life.

Going back up with this consolatory news of supper and beds, I found my Jacinto still sitting on the stone bench by the window, drinking in all of the sweet twilight air that was slowly and silently blanketing the valley and the mountain. High above, a star glimmered—the adamantine Vesper, which is all that remains of the corporal splendor of Venus in this Christian sky! Jacinto had never closely regarded that star, nor had he ever been present at this majestic and gentle spectacle of things falling asleep. That darkening of mountains and groves, the clear clusters of houses receding in shadows, the dull peal of a bell coming from the slopes, the murmur of rivulets meandering through low grass … for him they were like initiations. I was opposite him, on the other stone bench. And I heard him sigh like a man who is finally resting.

So it was in the midst of this contemplation that Zé Brás came to us with the welcome announcement that the *light supper* was on the table. It was farther on, in another room, blacker and more bare. And there my overcivilized Jacinto flinched with genuine horror. On a pine table completely covered with a hand towel and set against a squalid wall, a half-melted tallow candle in a brass holder illuminated two dishes of yellow china flanked by wood spoons and iron forks. The tumblers, made of heavy, opaque glass, retained the purplish tint of the wine that had been poured into them in the plentiful years of plentiful vintages. The small earthenware bowl of olives would delight Diogenes for its Attic simplicity. Plunged into the wide cornbread was a big knife…. Poor Jacinto!

But he sat down there for a long time, resigned and pensive, before he wiped his black fork and his wood spoon with his handkerchief. Then, quiet and wary, he sampled a scant spoonful of the soup, which was chicken and smelled wonderful. Tasting it, he glanced up at me, his companion and friend, with wide-open eyes that shone with surprise. He swallowed a spoonful again, a fuller one, and more slowly. And he smiled, murmuring in astonishment, "It's good!" It really was good: it contained the liver and the gizzard, and the smell was out of this world. Three times did I avidly attack that soup, although Jacinto was the one who mopped up the tureen. But pushing aside both the cornbread and the candle, good old Zé Brás had already set on the table a glazed platter overflowing with rice and beans. Now, despite the fact that beans (which the Greeks called *ciboria*) are identified with superior eras of civilization and do so much to promote the wisdom that existed in Sicyon, in Galatia, a temple dedicated to Minerva Ciboriana, Jacinto had always detested beans. Nonetheless, he tried a timid forkful. Once again his eyes, wide open in amazement, sought mine. Another forkful, another moment of concentration. And here you have my very difficult friend exclaiming, "It's excellent!" Was it the pungent mountain air? Was it the delectable art of those women downstairs, stirring pots, singing *Vira, meu bem*? I don't know. But Jacinto's praise was growing in extent and conviction with each platter. And gazing at the blond chicken in front of him, roasted on a wood skewer, he ended up shouting, "It's divine!" However, nothing aroused his enthusiasm like the wine—wine poured from a coarse green jug held high, penetrating and alive and warm, that had in it more soul than many a poem and holy book! Eyeing in candlelight the crude tumbler that he filled to the brim with foam, I recalled the georgic day when Virgil—at Horace's home, beneath the arbor—sang of the fresh claret of Rhaetia. And Jacinto, with a color I had never seen in his Schopenhauerian pallor, whispered at once the sweet verse: *Rethica quo te carmina dicat.* Who will sing to you with dignity, wine of those mountains?

Thus did we enjoy a delicious supper under the auspices of Zé Brás. And afterward we returned to the only joys of the house, to the paneless windows, to contemplate in silence a sumptuous summer sky so star-spangled that the entirety of it resembled a dense cloud of glittering gold, suspended, motionless, high above the black mountains. As I observed to my Jacinto, in the city stars are never viewed on account of the artificial illumination that obfuscates them, and for that reason one never enters into a complete communion with nature. Men in capitals belong to their houses, or if they are driven by strong tendencies of sociability, to their environs. Everything isolates them or separates them from the rest of nature: the obstructive six-floor buildings; the smoke from chimneys; the slow, leaden rolling of omnibuses; the imprisoning intrigue of urban life. But what a difference on a mountaintop like Torges! There, all those beautiful stars gaze down on us from nearby, shining brilliantly like conscious eyes, some fixedly, with sublime indifference, others anxiously, with light that pulsates, a light that beckons, as if they were attempting to reveal their secrets or to understand ours. And it is impossible not to feel perfect solidarity between those immense worlds and our poor bodies. All are the handiwork of the same will. All live from the act of that immanent will. All, therefore, from the Uranuses to even the Jacintos, constitute diverse manifestations of a single being and through their transformations amount to the same oneness. There is no more consolatory idea than this one: that I, and you, and that mountain, and the sun, which is now hiding, are molecules of the same Everything, governed by the same Law, rolling toward the same end. The tormenting responsibilities of individualism vanish in an instant. What are we? Forms without force, which a Force impels. And there is a delightful breather, albeit fleeting, in this certainty, of which an individual is the mote of passive, irresponsible dust that is carried off by the great gust of wind, or the drop lost in the torrent! Jacinto concurred, immersed in darkness. Neither he nor I knew the names of those admirable stars. I, on account of the bachelor's massive and unimaginable ignorance with which I issued from the belly of Coimbra, my spiritual mother; Jacinto, because in his ponderous library he had *three hundred eighteen* treatises on astronomy! Besides, what did it matter to us that the one star out there was named Sirius and the other one Aldebaran? What did it matter to them that one of us was José and the other Jacinto? We were transitory forms of the same eternal being, and in us there was the same God. And if they understood it in like manner, there we were, we at the window of a big mountain house, they in their marvelous infinite, completing a sacrosanct act, a perfect act of Grace, which was to feel consciously our unity and attain for an instant, in conscience, our divinization.

We were vaguely philosophizing this way when Zé Brás, with an oil lamp in his hand, came to inform us that "*their Inselencies*' beds were made…." From ideality we went down to reality, and what did we see then, we brothers of the stars? In two dark, concave rooms, two pallets laid out on the floor, in a corner, with two chintz coverlets; at the head, a brass candle holder set on a bushel; and at the feet, as a washbowl, a glazed basin on a wood chair!

In silence, my overcivilized friend touched his pallet, and he felt the rigidity of granite. Then, running his lax fingers over his fallen face, he considered that with his trunks being lost he had neither slippers nor robe! And it was still Zé Brás who provided: he brought to poor Jacinto, for him to relieve his feet, some formidable wooden clogs; and to wrap his body, which had been sweetly educated in Sybaris, an enormous chemise that belonged to the housekeeper, a garment made of burlap more coarse than a penitent's serge, with stiff, uneven flounces like needlework on wood. To console him, I remembered that Plato, when he was composing *The Banquet*, and Xenophon, when he commanded the Ten Thousand, slept on worse camp beds. Austere pallets strengthen souls, and it is only if dressed in serge that one enters Paradise.

"Do you have something that I can read?" murmured my friend in a dry, absent-minded way. "I can't go to sleep without reading!"

I only had the issue of the *Afternoon Daily*, which I tore in half and fraternally shared with him. And the person who at that moment did not see Jacinto, the master of Torges, huddled at the edge of the pallet, next to the candle that was dripping onto the bushel, with his bare feet squeezed into thick wooden clogs, swimming in the housekeeper's chemise with all its flounces, perusing half of the *Afternoon Daily* and the advertisements of packet boats with bleary eyes ... that person cannot know what is an emphatic and real image of dismay.

I left him like that, and shortly afterward, stretched out on my similarly Spartan pallet, I rose—by means of an erudite, jovial dream—to the planet Venus, where I encountered, amid elm and cypress trees in an orchard, Plato and Zé Brás in lofty, intellectual camaraderie, drinking wine from Rhaetia in glasses from Torges. The three of us abruptly became engaged in a controversy about the nineteenth century. Far off, in a forest of rosebushes taller than oaks, the white marble monuments of a city stood out, and sacred chants reverberated. I do not recall what Xenophon maintained about civilization and the phonograph. And then all of a sudden everything was disrupted by dark clouds, in the midst of which I discerned Jacinto, fleeing on a donkey that he furiously urged onward—with his heels, with a switch, and with screams—in the direction of Jessamine.

V

EARLY AT DAYBREAK, so as not to awaken Jacinto, who, with his hands folded over his chest, slept peacefully on his granite bed, I left for Guiães.

And for three weeks in that village where they preserve the customs and ideas of the time of King Dom Dinis I learned nothing about my disconsolate friend, who most certainly had fled his holey roofs and immersed himself once again in civilization. At the end of my stay there, I journeyed back to Torges on a sweltering August morning and tramped anew that avenue of beech trees, where I entered the manorial gate amid the furious barking of the guard dogs. Zé Brás's wife appeared at the granary door, and her news, which she delivered immediately, was that Senhor Dom Jacinto (in Torges they accorded my friend the *Dom*) could be found down in the fields of Freixomil with Sousa.

"Then, Senhor Dom Jacinto is still here?"

His Inselency was still in Torges … and *His Inselency* was staying for the grape harvest! I had just noticed that the windows of the manor house now had panes in them, and that two buckets of whitewash sat in a corner of the patio. A stonemason's ladder leaned against the balcony, and two cats slept in an open crate still full of packing straw.

"And has Grilo turned up?"

"Grilo's in the orchard, in the shade."

"Good. And the baggage?"

"Senhor Dom Jacinto has his little leather bag now."

God be praised! My Jacinto was, finally, provided with civilization! I climbed the steps happily. In the noble room, where the floor had been restored and scoured, there was a table covered with oilcloth, pine shelves with white Barcelos earthenware, and cane chairs along the highly whitewashed walls that gave off the freshness of a new chapel. In another room next to that one, also of a sparkling whiteness, I discovered the unexpected comfort of three wicker chairs from Madeira with wide arms and calico cushions, as well as a pine table on which were untrimmed paper, an oil lamp, and duck quills stuck in a friar's inkwell—the necessaries for a calm, fruitful study of humanities. A small bookcase that hung on the wall by two nails contained four or five books that showed signs of use: *Don Quixote*, a Virgil, a *History of Rome*, and Froissart's *Chronicles*. Farther on was another room, which for certain was Dom Jacinto's, a chaste, bright student's room with a simple iron bed, an iron washbasin, and clothes hung on crude pegs. Everything proclaimed cleanliness and order. The closed windows guarded against the August sun that outside burned the stone sills. From the floor sprinkled with water, a welcome coolness rose, and in an old blue glass a bunch of carnations dispensed cheer and fragrance. With Torges slumbering in the splendor of a siesta, not a sound could be heard. And enveloped in that repose of a remote monastery, I ended up stretching out on a wicker chair by the table, where I listlessly opened the Virgil, muttering:

> *Fortunate Jacinthe! tu inter arva nota*
> *Et fontes sacros, frigus captabis opacum.*

I had just irreverently fallen asleep on the divine writer when a friendly shout awakened me. It was our Jacinto. I immediately compared him to a half-wilted plant etiolated in darkness that had been profusely watered and then revived in broad daylight. He didn't walk hunchbacked. Imposed on his pallor of an overcivilized man, the mountain air or the reconciliation with life had effected in him a strong, swarthy complexion that rendered him magnificently virile. His eyes, which in the city I had always thought resembled twilight, now emitted a midday brightness, resolute and expansive, that keenly penetrated the beauty of things. No longer did he run weak hands over his face: he slapped his thighs with them. What can I say? It was a reincarnation. And everything that he related to me, cheerfully walking the floor in his white shoes, was that he had felt—at the end of three days in Torges—as though relieved of concerns, and that he had ordered the purchase of a soft mattress, had collected five never read books, and there he was.

"For the entire summer?"

"Forevermore! And now, city man, come and lunch on some trout that I fished, and finally understand what heaven is."

The trout was, in fact, heavenly. And there also appeared a chilled green bean and cauliflower salad, as well as a white wine from Azães. But who will sing to you, adequately, of the food and drink of those mountains?

In the afternoon, the intense heat having ended, we hiked the paths that zigzag across the vast farm that stretches from valleys to mountains. Jacinto stopped from time to time, fondly contemplating tall stalks of corn or, with the palm of his now strong hand, patting the trunks of chestnut trees, as one would pat the back of a recuperating friend. Every trickle of water, every tuft of grass, every vine shoot concerned him like filial lives of which he was responsible. He recognized certain blackbirds that sang in certain poplars, and he exclaimed in a moving way, "What a delight clover flowers are!"

That evening, after a meal of roast suckling goat, to which Master Horace would have dedicated an ode (perhaps even a heroic poem), we discussed Destiny and Life. I mentioned, with discreet mischief, Schopenhauer and Ecclesiastes. But Jacinto shrugged his shoulders, his disdain patent. His confidence in those two gloomy expositors of life had vanished— and irremediably, unable ever to return, like a fog dispersed by the sun. Tremendous foolishness! To affirm that life is composed merely of an extended illusion is to construct a grandiose system predicated on a particular, narrow view of life, leaving outside of the system all of the rest of life, like a grand and permanent contradiction. It was as if he, Jacinto, pointing to a nettle plant, declared triumphantly, "Here is a nettle plant! The entire Torges farm, therefore, is a mass of nettle plants!" But it would suffice for a guest to raise his eyes and see grainfields, orchards, and vineyards! Besides, of those two illustrious pessimists, one, the German … what did he know of life—of that life of which he had postulated, with enlightened majesty, a painful, definitive theory? All that can be known by someone who, like this brilliant fraud, lived for fifty years in a gloomy provincial boardinghouse, barely raising his spectacles from books to converse, during meals, with the junior officers of the garrison! And the other one, the Israelite, the man of the *Songs*, the very pedantic king of Jerusalem, discovers that life is an illusion only at the age of seventy-five when power slips from his shaky hands, and his harem of three hundred concubines becomes ridiculously superfluous to his frigid skeleton! The one dogmatizes funereally about what he does not know and the other about what he cannot know. But let there be granted to that good Schopenhauer a life as complete and full as that of Caesar, and where will Schopenhauer be then? Let that sultan who built and taught so much in Jerusalem have his virility, daubed with literature, restored to him, and where will Ecclesiastes be then? Besides, what does it matter to speak well or ill of life? Fortunate or painful, fruitful or futile, life must be lived. Mad are those who, in order to pass through it, wrap themselves at the outset in burdensome veils of sadness and disillusion, so that on the road they travel all is blackness, not only on the truly dark stretches, but even on those where a welcoming sun shines. On Earth everything lives, and only people feel the pain and disillusion of life. And the more they are felt, the more extended and augmented is the work of that intelligence that makes them people, and that separates them from the rest of non-thinking, inert nature. It is at the height of civilization that they experience the height of tedium. Wisdom, consequently, lies in withdrawing even from that honest minimum of civilization, which consists of having a thatch roof, a furrow of land, and grain to sow in it. In short, so as to recover happiness, it is imperative that we return to Paradise with its vine leaves and stay there calmly, completely shorn of civilization, watching the lamb spring through thyme plants, and without searching for, not even with desire, the ill-fated tree of Knowledge! *Dixi*!

I listened, astonished, to this newest Jacinto. It was truly a resurrection in the magnificent manner of Lazarus. At the *surge et ambula* that the waters and forests of Torges had whispered to him, he was rising from the depths of the grave of Pessimism, shedding Poole's coats, *et ambulabat*, and beginning to be happy. When I withdrew to my room—at that decorous hour so suitable to the country and to optimism—I took my friend's now firm hand in mine, and, thinking that he had finally attained true reality because he possessed true freedom, I shouted my congratulations to him like the moralist of Tivoli, *Vive et regna, fortunate Jacinthe*!

Shortly afterward, I heard laughter through the door that separated us—a fresh, youthful, genuine, consoling peal of laughter. It was Jacinto, who was reading *Don Quixote*. Oh fortunate Jacinto! He preserved his acuity of mind and had recovered the divine gift of laughter!

Four years have gone by. Jacinto still lives in Torges. The walls of his manor house continue to be well whitewashed, but bare.

In winter he wraps himself in a coarse wool capote and lights a brazier. In order to summon Grilo or the serving girl, he claps his hands, as did Cato. Enjoying his delightful leisure, he has already read the *Iliad*. He does not shave. On paths out in the country, he stops and talks to the children. All the mountain dwellers revere him. I hear that he is going to marry a hardy, healthy, pretty girl from Guiães. For sure a tribe will grow there and be most pleasing to the Lord!

Since he recently sent word asking for books from his library (a *Life of Buddha*, a *History of Greece*, and the works of Saint Francis of Sales), I went, after these four years, to the deserted Jessamine. Each step of mine on the soft rugs from Caramania sounded forlorn, like on a floor of the dead and gone. All the brocade covers were wrinkled, frayed. Hanging on the walls, like eyes outside of their sockets, were the electric buttons of the bells and lights, and there was a jumble of strands of wire, loose and twisted, on which a spider with free rein had spun dense webs. In the library, all the vast knowledge of centuries lay in boundless silence, beneath boundless dust. On the spines of the tomes of philosophical systems, the white fuzz of mold had taken hold; and because moths had voraciously devoured the Universal Histories, a pervasive smell of putrid literature hung in the air. And I left there with my handkerchief on my nose, certain that not a single live truth remained in those twenty thousand volumes. I wanted to wash my hands, which were stained by contact with the detritus of human learning; however, the marvelous devices of the washroom and the bathroom had become rusted, corroded, stuck, and did not discharge one drop of water. And consequently, since it was raining that April afternoon, I had to go out onto the balcony to ask heaven to wash me.

On my way down, I entered Jacinto's workroom and tripped over a black pile of hardware, wheels, prints, bells, screws.... I half-opened the window and recognized the telephone, the théâtrophone, the phonograph, and other devices, all of them in pieces or various stages of disassembly, and having become dirty and undone beneath the dust of years. I pushed aside this waste of human ingenuity with my foot. The typewriter, completely uncovered, with black holes marking the uprooted keys, was like a toothless, doltish mouth. The telephone seemed squashed, tangled in its wire insides.

In the phonograph's horn—askew, chipped, forever mute— beetles teemed. And those brilliant inventions, so lamentable and so grotesque, lay there while I exited laughing at that overcivilized palace as if it were a hilarious joke.

The April rains had run their course: the remote roofs of the city were turning black over a sunset of crimson and gold. As I walked along the most refreshed streets, I was thinking that this magnificent nineteenth century of ours would, one day, resemble that abandoned Jessamine, and that other men, with a clearer certainty of what life and happiness are, would kick aside, as I did, the detritus of overcivilization and gaily laugh at the grand illusion that had ended, futile and blighted with rust.

For surely at that hour, Jacinto, on the balcony in Torges

without a phonograph and without a telephone, having entered simplicity anew, saw in the leisurely peace of early evening—when the first star glimmered—the drove of oxen gathering at the call of the drovers.

Glossary to "Civilization"
(in order of appearance)

TRÁS-OS-MONTES: province in the northeastern corner of Portugal.

ORESTES: in Greek mythology, the son of Clytemnestra and Agamemnon; a possible reference to his strong friendship—or relationship—with Pylades.

SEPTA-SINDU: Seven Rivers, presently in eastern Pakistan.

CARAMANIA [KARAMANIA]: a part of the Ottoman Empire (Turkey).

ADAM SMITH (1723–90): Scottish economist and philosopher, sometimes known by the sobriquet "The Father of Capitalism."

WHATMAN SHEETS OF PAPER: named after the English papermaker James Whatman the Elder (1702–59), who invented woven paper.

THÉÂTROPHONE: a telephonic distribution system in parts of late nineteenth-century Europe that allowed subscribers to listen to opera and theater performances over telephone lines.

ARRAS: a city in the northwestern corner of France known for its cloth and wool industry, and in particular for its production of fine tapestries.

HESIOD: a Greek poet thought to have lived around the same time as Homer. Nereus is described as "the wise and unerring old man of the sea," at the bottom of which he dwelled; he appears in Hesiod's *Theogony* (233–36).

DIOCLES: early Greek comic poet (c. 500 BC), author of the play *Bees*.

ANAXAGORAS: Greek philosopher (c. 510–c. 428 BC).

SYBARIS: an important city of Magna Graecia (southern Italy). Its inhabitants became famous among the Greeks for their hedonism, hence "sybarite" and "sybaritic" to describe the excessive pursuit of pleasure.

JUNO [HERA]: the Olympian queen of the gods and the goddess of women, marriage, the sky, and the stars; Lacinia, the epithet by which she was known in the region of Calabria (southern Italy).

BENVENUTO CELLINI (1500–1570): Italian goldsmith and sculptor.

FRANÇOIS-DÉSIRÉ FROMENT-MEURICE (1802–55): French goldsmith renowned as a chaser (*ciseleur*).

BROCELIANDE: a forest in Brittany, France's northwesternmost region.

ARMIDA: a Saracen sorceress conceived by the Italian poet Torquato Tasso. Sent to murder Rinaldo, a fierce Christian soldier, she falls in love with him while he sleeps. She then creates an enchanted garden where she keeps him a lovesick prisoner.

JAEGER: a clothing company founded by the British businessman Lewis Tomalin in 1884, using materials advocated by the German scientist Dr. Gustav Jaeger.

ELECTRIC PEN: invented by Thomas Edison in 1875, a high-speed, battery-driven copying device.

CARCEL LAMP: an efficient oil lamp invented by the French watchmaker Bernard Guillaume Carcel (1750–1818).

GUIÃES: a town in the administrative district of Vila Real, in the southwestern corner of Trás-os-Montes.

ON SANCHO'S DONKEY: an express reference to *Don Quijote de la Mancha*.

DIOGENES: Greek philosopher (c. 404 BC–c. 323 BC) who made a virtue of poverty.

CIBORIA: plural of the Latin *ciborium*; in this context, a seed vessel of the Egyptian bean.

VIRA, MEU BEM: a traditional song and dance in Portugal, most often associated with the northwestern Minho region, which borders the Atlantic Ocean to the west and Spain to the north.

RHAETIA: a province of the Roman Empire, in parts of present-day Switzerland, Germany, Austria, and Italy.

IMMANENT: existing or remaining within; inherent.

COIMBRA: the University of Coimbra, established in 1290; the oldest university in the Portuguese-speaking world.

SIRIUS: the brightest star in the night sky.

ALDEBARAN: a red giant star and the brightest in the zodiac constellation Taurus.

XENOPHON (431 BC–354 BC): ancient Greek philosopher, soldier, and mercenary who commanded the group of mercenaries known as the Ten Thousand. He is credited with having devised and practiced the tactics of a retreat in order to stave off and annihilate an enemy.

KING DOM DINIS [DENIS] (1261–1325): called the Farmer King for his improvements in agriculture and the Poet King for his contribution to the development of Portuguese as a literary language. It was during his reign that what became the University of Coimbra was founded.

BARCELOS: the city in the Braga district (Minho) where blue and white earthenware has been made and painted by hand for centuries. It is also well-known for its colorful *galo*, the cockerel viewed as a symbol of Portugal.

FRIAR'S INKWELL: a statuette of a small friar's head with a well to contain ink.

JEAN FROISSART (1337–1405): a French-speaking author from Valenciennes whose *Chronicles* are a prose history of the Hundred Years' War.

FORTUNATE JACINTHE! TU INTER ARVA NOTA / ET FONTES SACROS FRIGUS CAPTABIS OPACUM: from verses 53–54 of Virgil's Eclogue I, the *Bucolics*. Loosely translated: "Oh fortunate

Jacinthe! Here amid known grainfields/And sacred fountains, you shall harvest a shady freshness."

AZÃES: Azaes is the ninth Atlantean king listed by Plato in his dialogue *Critias*; the name is a possible source for the present-day Azores.

DIXI: I have spoken.

SURGE ET AMBULA: get up and walk.

POOLE'S COATS: Henry Poole and Co., bespoke tailors, founded in London in 1806.

ET AMBULABAT: and he was walking.

[The Wet Nurse]
A Topic for Verse

The story that I have long wished to tell so that some poet who's fond of topics that enrich and stimulate our thoughts might compose it in sonorous verse (which I myself have not done on account of having tarried in erecting before it a frontispiece of general considerations) transpired in India. India—the land of precious stones, festivals, and glorious skies—immediately suggests to an artist extensive artistic details.

But my story needs to be presented with all the simplicity of its moral, naked reality, with no landscapes, clothing, or architecture to materialize it.

Because it takes place in India, the poet who embellishes it with palm trees, elephants, and bayaderes risks certain disaster.[1] With neither time period, nor names, nor locales that can be verified on a map, abstract and as though having happened in the country of souls, this story of one soul, which is directed only to the soul, should come enveloped in a minimum of literature, the kind that the people, in their ingenuousness, transform into something alive and poignant, affirming with magnificent indifference to time periods, emotions, customs ... that once upon a time there was a king....

*

1. Bayaderes: professional female dancers of India.

95

ONCE UPON A TIME, then, there was a valiant young king—lord of a kingdom abundant in cities and grainfields—who had gone off to battle in distant lands, leaving behind his queen and his infant son, the former alone and sad, the latter still in his cradle and wrapped in swaddling clothes.

The full moon that had seen him depart, driven by his dream of conquest and fame, was beginning to wane when one of his knights came back with his combat arms broken. Black with dried blood and covered over with dust from the roads, he brought the bitter news of a lost battle and the death of the king, who had been run through by seven lances on the bank of a great river, amid the flower of his noble warriors.

The queen wept the king magnificently. She even wept desolately the husband, who was handsome and jovial. But above all she woefully wept the father, who thus left his infant son helpless in the midst of so many enemies of his fragile life and the kingdom that would be his, left him without an arm to defend him—an arm strong by virtue of might and strong by virtue of love.

The most fearful of those enemies was his uncle, the king's bastard brother, a crude, depraved man consumed by vulgar greed, desirous of the kingship only because of its treasures. For years he had lived with his horde of rebels in a castle that stood high on a mountain, and like a wolf on the lookout, he avidly watched for prey. Alas! The prey now was that babe, the nursling king, lord of so many provinces, asleep in his cradle with his golden rattle in the tight grip of his hand!

Alongside him, another boy child slept in another cradle. But he was a little slave, the son of the beautiful, robust young slave woman who nursed the prince. Both had been born on the same summer night. The very same breast was nurturing the two of them. When the queen would come, before going to bed, to kiss the little prince who had fine blond hair, she would also, because she loved him, too, kiss the little slave who had curly black hair. The eyes of both boys shone like precious stones. Only the cradle of one was a magnificent piece of work made from ivory and brocade, while the other cradle was much inferior and made of wicker. However, the loyal slave woman embraced both babes with equal affection, because if one was her son, the other would be her king.

She had been born in the royal residence, and the king and the queen became her passion and her religion. No tears had flowed more sorrowfully than hers for that king killed by the bank of a great river. However, she belonged to a race that believes that our life on Earth continues in Heaven. The king, her lord, would surely be reigning already over another kingdom beyond the clouds, one also abundant in grainfields and cities. His charger, his arms, and his pages had risen to the heights with him. As his vassals gradually died, they would quickly join him in that celestial kingdom to resume their vassalage in his service. And one day, in her turn, she would ascend in a ray of light to inhabit her lord's palace and once again weave the linen for his tunics, and once again light his cup of perfumed essences, and be in Heaven as she had been on Earth, happy in her servitude.

Nonetheless, she also trembled for her little prince! How many times, with him clinging to her breast, did she think about his fragility, his long infancy, the slow years that would pass before he grew at least to the height of a sword, and about that cruel uncle with his face darker than the night and his heart darker than his face, hungry for the throne, watching from his mountaintop amid the scimitars of his horde! Her poor, precious little prince! She would then clutch him with greater tenderness, although if her son gurgled alongside, it was to him that she extended her arms with even happier ardor. That one, in his indigence, had nothing to fear from life.

Misfortunes, onslaughts of bad luck would never leave him more deprived of glories and worldly goods than he already was, there in his cradle, lying under the piece of white linen that guarded against his nakedness. His existence was in fact more precious and worthy of being preserved than that of her prince, because none of the harsh concerns with which life darkens the souls of the mighty would so much as graze his free, simple slave's soul. And, as if she loved him more on account of that happy, humble state, she would cover his chubby little body with firm, devouring kisses, whereas she gave her prince's hands light, feathery kisses.

Meanwhile, great fear engulfed the palace where a woman now reigned among women. The bastard, the man of pillage who roamed mountaintops, had come down to the plain with his horde and was already leaving a wake of bloodshed and ruin through peaceful hamlets and villages. The gates of the city had been secured with stronger chains. Fires built on the watchtowers burned higher, but the defense lacked the strong hand, the discipline, of a man. A distaff does not rule like a spear. All of the faithful noble warriors had perished in the great battle. And the unfortunate queen could do naught but run repeatedly to the cradle of her little son and bewail over him her widow's weakness. Only the loyal wet nurse seemed certain of resistance, as if the arms with which she clutched her prince were walls of a citadel that no amount of daring could bridge.

Now, one night—a night of silence and darkness—when she had already disrobed and was about to drop off on her shabby bed positioned between her two little boys, she suspected rather than heard a dull sound of sword striking sword, from afar, at the entrance of the royal gardens. Hastily tossing a wrap about her and drawing her hair back, she listened, anxiety-ridden. Heavy, bestial footsteps tramped the sandy ground around the jasmine bushes. Then there was a moan, a body feebly falling onto flagstones like a bale of straw, and she violently yanked open the curtain. Down at the bottom end of the gallery she saw men, the flash of lanterns, glances of weapons.... In a heartbeat she understood everything—the palace taken by surprise, the cruel bastard coming to plunder, to kill the prince! Then swiftly, without hesitating for a second, without doubting for a second, she swooped up the prince from his ivory cradle and deposited him in the poor wicker one; and lifting her son from his menial cradle while planting desperate kisses on him, she laid him in the royal cradle, covering it with brocade.

Suddenly, a giant of a man with a fiery face and a black cloak over his coat of mail appeared at the door of the room, surrounded by others holding their lanterns high. He glanced all around, ran over to the ivory cradle with the bright brocade, snatched the child as one would a purse of gold, and, muffling the little one's cries in his cloak, dashed off furiously.

The prince slept in his new cradle. The wet nurse stood there, motionless in the silence and in the darkness.

But cries of alarm suddenly rang out in the palace. Long tongues of torch flames were visible through the windows, and the courtyards resounded with the clash of arms. And the queen, disheveled, almost naked, burst into the room with her maids, shouting for her son! When she saw that the ivory cradle was empty and the swaddles undone, she collapsed onto the floor and wailed, grief-stricken. Then quietly, very slowly, ghostly pale, the wet nurse uncovered the poor wicker cradle. There lay the prince, peacefully asleep, deep in a dream that made him smile and light up a face peeping through golden ringlets of hair. His mother fell over the cradle, with a sigh, as would a corpse.

And in that instant a new clamor shook the marble gallery. It was the captain of the guard, the queen's faithful adherents. However, in all the hubbub there was more sadness than triumph. The bastard was dead! Caught as he fled between the palace and the citadel and overwhelmed by the hardy legion of archers, he had succumbed, he and twenty of his horde. His arrow-riddled body lay in a pool of blood. But, alas! Ineffable grief! The prince's tender little body lay there, too, wrapped in a cloak, already cold yet still purple from the fierce hands that had strangled him! Thus were the men-at-arms tumultuously blurting out the cruel news when the queen, with tears in her eyes but radiating joy, lifted in her arms, to show them all, the prince who had awakened.

Cries of amazement and acclamation rose. Who had saved him? Who had…? There beside the empty cradle, silent and unmoving, was the one who had saved him! The sublimely loyal slave woman! It was she who, in order to save the life of her prince, had set in motion her son's death. Then, only then, did the happy mother, emerging from her ecstatic joy, passionately embrace the distressed mother and kiss her, and call her "beloved sister." And from amid that multitude squeezing into the gallery a new, ardent acclamation sprang up—appeal after appeal that the admirable slave woman who had saved the king be magnificently recompensed.

But how? What sacks of gold could pay for a son's life? Then an old man of noble pedigree suggested that she be taken to the royal treasure chamber and there choose from among those riches, which were the greatest to be found in India, all the ones that her heart desired.

The queen took the slave woman by the hand. And her marble face not yet having shed its rigidity, and walking like a dead woman in a dream, she was led in that state to the Treasure Chamber. Lords and ladies, maids, and men-at-arms followed, their respect so moving and so hushed that the tap-tapping of their sandals on the flagstones could scarcely be heard. The heavy doors of the Chamber turned slowly. And when a serf unbarred the windows, the already bright and pink light of dawn, streaming through the iron grilles, set ablaze a marvelous, glittering fire of gold and gemstones! Throughout the entire Chamber, from the stone floor to the somber vaults, there gleamed, scintillated, and sparkled gold escudos, inlaid arms, mounds of diamonds, heaps of coins, and long strings of pearls, all the riches of that kingdom accumulated by a hundred kings for twenty centuries. A slow, prolonged *Ah* rippled through the throng that had been struck with amazement. A charged silence then ensued. And in the middle of the Chamber, enveloped by such precious resplendence, the wet nurse was not moving. Only her bright, dry eyes … to glance up, high above the bars, at that sky now tinged with rose and gold. It was there, in that fresh early morning sky, that her little boy now dwelled. He was there, and the sun was already rising, and it was late, and surely he was crying and looking for her breast! Then the wet nurse smiled and extended her hand. Everyone followed breathlessly that slow movement of her open hand. What wondrous piece of jewelry, what strand of diamonds, what fistful of rubies was she going to choose?

She reached for and grasped a dagger from among the many arms piled on a bench next to her. It was an old king's dagger, with an emerald-encrusted hilt and crossguard, and worth a veritable fortune many times over.

Having grasped the dagger and gripped it tightly, she pointed it skyward, to the heavens where the first rays of the sun were rising. She then faced the queen and the multitude, crying out, "I saved my prince, and now … I am going to nurse my son!"

And she sank the dagger up to its hilt into her heart.

*

This is my story. Or rather this is the rough first draft of a marvelous legend of soul. So beautiful that it seemed to me that it could only be told in a fitting manner if sung to the music of a lyre. Thus do I offer it to poets. And the one who makes an attempt with it but does not create a work of art will, at the very least, see justice done by popularizing this poor Indian slave, so unknown and so sublime a woman.

The Treasure

THE THREE MEDRANHOS brothers, Rui, Guanes, and Rostabal, were at that time the hungriest and shabbiest noblemen in the entire kingdom of Asturias.

In the run-down Medranhos ancestral home, from which the mountain wind had swept away windows and tiles, they spent the afternoons of that winter hunched in their goatskin jerkins and stamping the cracked soles of their boots on the kitchen flagstones in front of the huge black fireplace, where it had been a long time since a flame flared or an iron pot boiled. When night fell, they would devour a crust of black bread rubbed with garlic. Then, without a candle for light while crossing the courtyard and tramping through the snow, they would head for the stable to sleep in order to take advantage of the warmth given off by three emaciated mares who, as famished as they were, nibbled at the wood of the manger. And misery had made these gentlemen as fierce as wolves.

Now, one quiet Sunday morning in spring, as all three of them were plodding through the Roquelanes woods to search for game tracks and gather mushrooms from around the oak trees while the three mares grazed on the fresh April grass, the Medranhos brothers stumbled upon an old iron chest behind a tangle of thorn bushes at the mouth of a cave. Its three keys were still in its three locks, as if it had been safeguarded in a secure tower. On the lid, barely decipherable through the rust, was a couplet in Arabic characters. And inside, nearly overflowing, it was full of gold doubloons!

In the terror and splendor of emotion, the three gentlemen turned more pale than candle wax. Then, rabidly sinking their hands into the gold, they burst out laughing, and so booming was the sound of their laughter that all around them the tender leaves of the elms trembled. Abruptly drawing back, though, they faced one another with fiery eyes and such ill-tempered distrust that Guanes and Rostabal felt for the hafts of the big knives at their belts. At that point portly, sandy-haired Rui, who was the most prudent one, raised his arms like an arbitrator and began by stating that the treasure, whether it came from God or from the Devil, belonged to the three of them, and would be strictly divided among the three of them by weighing the gold on scales. But how would they lug that coin-filled chest over the sierra back to Medranhos? And then, too, it wouldn't make sense to leave the woods with their find before total darkness. For that reason he proposed that their brother Guanes, as the fleetest of foot, swiftly set out for the nearby village of Retortilho with some of the gold in his pocket and there buy three leather saddlebags, three sacks of barley, three meat pies, and three bottles of wine. The meat and wine were for them, as they had not eaten since the day before; the barley was for the mares. And thus replenished, men and mounts, they would pack the gold into the saddlebags and go back up to Medranhos under the safety of the moonless night.

"Good thinking!" shouted Rostabal, a man taller than a pine tree, with a long shock of hair and a beard that fell from below his bloodshot eyes down to his belt buckle.

But Guanes would not move away from the chest. His face was set in a frown of distrust as he twisted and tugged at the dark skin of his cranelike neck. He finally blurted out, "Brothers! The chest has three keys.... I want to lock my lock and take my key!"

"By God, then I want to take mine, too!" Rostabal bellowed for his part.

Rui smiled. Certainly, certainly! So each owner of the gold got one of the keys to keep. And each one, crouched in front of the chest, silently and forcefully secured his lock. Relieved now, Guanes leaped at once onto a mare and rode off toward Retortilho along a path lined with elms, reciting to the branches his customary, sorrowful ditty:

> *Olé! Olé!*
> *Sale la cruz de la iglesia*
> *Vestida de negro luto....*

II

IN THE CLEARING opposite the thicket of thorn bushes that had concealed the treasure (and that the three had hacked open), a thread of water issuing from among the rocks fell on a huge, hollowed stone, where it pooled, clear and still, before continuing to flow toward a stretch of high grass. And next to it, in the shade of a beech tree, lay an old moss-covered pillar. It was there that Rui and Rostabal sat down, their tremendous swords set between their knees. The two mares were grazing on the good grass dotted with poppies and buttercups; a blackbird sang in the beech's branches as a drifting smell of violets sweetened the clear air; and Rostabal, glancing at the sun, yawned with hunger.

Rui, who had taken off his hat and was smoothing the old purple feathers on it, began to reflect—in his gentle, rational voice—that Guanes had not wanted to come down with them to the Roquelanes woods that morning. What rotten luck they had! Because if Guanes had stayed in Medranhos, only the two of them would have discovered the chest, and only the two of them would have to split the gold! What a great pity! All the more so because Guanes's share would soon be frittered and gambled away on wine, women, and song.

"Ah! Rostabal, Rostabal! If Guanes, passing by here alone, had found this gold, he would not have shared it with us, Rostabal!"

A sullen Rostabal grumbled, tugging angrily at his black beard. "No, by God! Guanes is greedy. Last year, if you remember, when he won a hundred ducats off that swordsman from Fresno, he refused to lend me even three for me to buy myself a new jerkin!"

"Do you see?" shouted Rui, glowing with excitement.

Both had stood up from beside the granite pillar, as if carried away by the same idea—an idea that fascinated them. And as they paced back and forth, the high grass whistled and whistled.

"And why?" Rui went on. "Why does he need all the gold that he's taking from us? Don't you hear him at night … the way he coughs? All around the straw where he sleeps the floor's black from the blood that he spits. He won't last out the winter snows, Rostabal! But by then he will have frittered away the gold doubloons that ought to be ours—so that we can put the house to rights, and you have horses, arms, attire fit for a nobleman, a body of warriors due the lord of a manor, as behooves you, being the eldest of the Medranhos."

"Then let him die, and die today!" thundered Rostabal.

"Really?" Rui had eagerly grasped his brother's arm, pointing to the elm-lined path along which Guanes had made tracks while singing. "Farther on, right at the end of the path there's a good place by a bramble patch. And it must be you, Rostabal, as you're the strongest and most skilled. A single thrust through the back. And it's divine justice that it be you, because oftentimes in taverns Guanes has shamelessly called you a 'pig' and a 'blockhead' since you can't read and don't know numbers."

"The scoundrel!"

"Come on!"

They went, and both lay in wait behind the bramble patch that provided a good view of the cutoff, which was narrow and strewn with stones like the bed of a stream. Rostabal, hiding in the ditch, already had his sword out. A light breeze ruffled the leaves of poplars on the hillside, and they heard the faint peal of the bells of Retortilho. Rui, scratching his beard, calculated the hour by the sun, which was already starting to dip below the mountains. A murder of cawing crows passed over them. And Rostabal, who had followed the flight, began to yawn again, so hungry was he thinking about the meat pies and wine that Guanes was bringing in the saddlebags.

Finally! An alert! It came from the path, that hoarse, sorrowful ditty sung to the branches:

> *Olé! Olé!*
> *Sale la cruz de la iglesia,*
> *Toda vestida de negro luto....*

Rui said in a low voice, "Right in his side. As soon as he passes by!"

The clippety-clop of the mare's trot sounded on the stones, and the red feather of a hat danced above the brambles.

Rostabal jumped out through an opening in the tangle of the bushes, brandishing his long sword, and the length of the blade swiftly penetrated his brother's side when, on account of the noise, Guanes abruptly shifted in the saddle. With a sudden start, he fell sideways, making a thud on the stones just as Rui was throwing himself at the mare's reins. Guanes had begun to gasp for breath, and Rostabal fell on him, again sinking his sword—held now by the blade, like a dagger—into his chest and throat.

"His key!" yelled Rui.

After Rostabal wrested the key from the dead Guanes's breast, both he and Rui fled along the path, Rostabal in the lead running hard, the feather of his hat broken and askew, still squeezing the naked sword against his arm, still flinching with horror from the taste of the blood that had spurted into his mouth. Behind him, Rui was pulling desperately on the mare's reins even as she was pounding her hooves into the pebble-strewn ground, baring her long yellow teeth, refusing to leave her master stretched out and abandoned along the hedgerows.

He had to jab the mare's scrawny hindquarters with the point of his sword to get her to move, and he finally ran her—his blade held high, as if in pursuit of a Moor—into the clearing where the sun no longer gilded the leaves. Rostabal had tossed his hat and sword on the grass and, with his sleeves rolled up and lying face down over the hollowed stone in the pool, was noisily washing his face and beard.

The mare quietly began to graze, still carrying the saddlebags that Guanes had bought in Retortilho. The biggest one bulged with the necks of two bottles of wine. Rui then slowly withdrew his hefty knife from his belt, and without making a sound on the dense grass, stole over to Rostabal, who was panting, his long hair dripping profusely. And calmly, as if he were nailing a stake into a bed of flowers, he buried the length of the blade into his brother's broad, bent back, straight through to his heart.

Rostabal, already prone, dropped over the pool with nary a moan, his face and long hair floating in the water. His old leather pouch had become wedged against his thigh, and in order to get at the key to the chest, Rui turned his body over, and a thicker blood oozed, steaming, as it spilled out by the edge of the pool.

III

NOW THE THREE KEYS to the chest were his, only his! And Rui, stretching his arms, breathed delightedly. As soon as it grew dark, he would pack the saddlebags with the gold and, leading the mares along the mountain trails, go up to Medranhos and bury his treasure in the cellar! And when only a few unidentified bones remained beneath the December snows there by the pool and farther on near the brambles, he would be the magnificent lord of Medranhos, and in the new chapel of the renovated manor house he would have several glittering masses said for his two dead brothers. Dead how? As Medranhos men should die—fighting the Turks!

He opened the three locks and grabbed a handful of doubloons, which he let slip and clink on the stones. What a sound, what pure gold, what superior worth! And it was *his* gold! He then went to check on the capacity of the saddlebags and, finding the two bottles of wine and one fat capon, instantly experienced intense hunger. Since the day before he had only eaten a morsel of dried fish. And he hadn't feasted on capon in such a long time!

With what delight Rui sat down on the grass, his legs open in a vee, between them the golden bird—which smelled delicious—and the amber-colored wine! Ah! Guanes had indeed been a good steward: he hadn't even forgotten the olives! But why had he bought, for three dinner companions, only two bottles of wine? Rui tore off a capon wing and proceeded to devour it with ravenous bites. Evening was coming on, sweet and wistful, as sparse pink clouds threaded the sky. Overhead, farther down the path, a murder of crows was cawing; the sated mares were drowsing, their muzzles nearly to the ground; and the spring was singing while washing the dead man.

Rui held the bottle of wine up to the light. With that warm

red color it must have cost at least three maravedis. And putting the bottle to his lips, he drank in slow swallows that made his hairy neck bob with pleasure. Oh, blessed wine that so quickly warms the blood! He tossed the empty bottle and opened the other one. However, since he was prudent, he did not drink any of it, because the trek to the sierra with the treasure called for good judgment and resolve. Propped by an elbow while resting on the grass, his thoughts turned to a Medranhos manor house with a new tiled roof, flames dancing in the hearth on snowy nights, and his brocaded bed, in which he would always have women.

All of a sudden, seized by anxiety, he hurried to load the saddlebags, as already shadows were deepening among the trees. He walked one of the mares over to the chest, raised the lid, took a handful of gold…. But he wavered, dropping the doubloons, which clinked together on the ground as he clutched his chest with both of his afflicted hands. What is it, Dom Rui? Good God! It was a fire, a blazing fire that had been lit inside him and was rising in his throat! He had already ripped open his jerkin, had already wobbled; and gasping now, with his tongue hanging out, he wiped away big beads of horrendous, freezing sweat. Oh, Virgin Mother! Once again the fire, more devastating and spreading, tormented him. He cried out, "Help! Someone! Guanes! Rostabal!"

His distorted arms beat the air desperately. And the flame inside him leaped, and he felt his bones cracking like the beams of a house on fire.

Stumbling over Rostabal, he staggered to the spring to extinguish that blaze, and with one knee on his brother's body, and clawing at the stone and howling in anguish, he lunged for a trickle of water to drip over his eyes and hair. He tottered back and fell on the grass, which he uprooted by the handful, biting into it and his fingers to taste the coolness. He still managed to get to his feet, slobbering drool onto his beard. All of a sudden, his eyes becoming dreadfully protuberant, he bellowed as if he finally understood the treachery in all of its horror: "It's poison!"

Oh, Dom Rui, you prudent one, yes, it was poison! Because Guanes, as soon as he had arrived at Retortilho, had run, singing—even before buying the saddlebags—to an alley behind the cathedral to buy poison from an old Jewish druggist, and that poison, mixed with wine, would make him, and only him, the owner of the treasure.

Night fell. Two crows, from among the murder that was cawing beyond the brambles, had already alighted on Guanes's body. The singing spring continued to wash the other dead man. Half buried in the dark grass, Rui's entire face had turned dark. A little star twinkled in the sky. The treasure is still there, in the Roquelanes woods.

Glossary to "The Treasure"
(in order of appearance)

RUI: Although the story takes place in Spain, Eça uses the Portuguese spelling of this first name, which in Spanish would be *Ruy*.

KINGDOM OF ASTURIAS: a [former] kingdom (718–924) and province in northwestern Spain.

OLÉ! OLÉ! / SALE LA CRUZ DE LA IGLESIA / VESTIDA DE LUTO ...: Here Eça does use Spanish: "Olé! Olé! / The cross is leaving the church ... / Draped in the black of mourning...."

AS IF IN PURSUIT OF A MOOR: a reference to the wars with the Moors to drive them out of Spain (the Reconquista, from the Middles Ages to 1492). Saint James the Great, the Moorslayer—Santiago de Compostela, Matamoros—is often depicted on a white horse wielding a sword to do battle with them.

FIGHTING THE TURKS: a possible reference to the Battle of
Lepanto (October 7, 1571), the naval engagement in which
Christian forces, spearheaded by Philip II of Spain, defeated
the Ottoman Turks.

MARAVEDI: a former gold coin issued by the Moors in Spain.

The Dead Man

I

IN THE YEAR 1474, which was so abundant in divine mercies throughout all of Christendom with King Henry IV reigning in Castile, a young gentleman of pure lineage and genteel bearing named Dom Rui de Cardenas came to live in the city of Segovia, where he had inherited a residence and a garden.

That house, which had been bequeathed to him by his uncle, an archdeacon and master of canon law, stood in silent shadow beside the Church of Our Lady of the Pillar; and facing it, beyond the churchyard where the three spouts of an ancient fountain trickled, was the dark, grated palace of Dom Alonso de Lara, a nobleman of great wealth and somber demeanor who, already advanced in years and with his hair completely gray, had married a young lady who was much talked-about in Castile on account of her white skin, hair the color of bright sunshine, and graceful neck like that of a capped heron.

It had been determined right at his birth that Dom Rui would have for his godmother Our Lady of the Pillar, to whom he always remained a devoted and faithful servant, despite his makeup as a cheerful, courageous gentleman who loved arms, hunting, courtly soirees, and even an occasional boisterous night at a tavern with dice and mugs of wine. But since his arrival in Segovia he had become accustomed, out of love and this holy proximity, to visiting his divine Godmother every morning at the hour of prime and asking for her blessing and

113

favor with three Hail Marys. Even at dusk, after a rigorous gallop through open hill country with his hounds or his falcon, he would still return for the start of vespers and devoutly murmur a Salve Regina. And every Sunday he would buy—from a Moorish flower girl in the churchyard—a bouquet of jonquils or carnations or plain roses, which he would then spread before the altar of Our Lady with tenderness and gallant care.

Dona Leonor also came every Sunday to this venerated Church of Our Lady of the Pillar. This much-talked-about and beautiful wife of Senhor de Lara was always accompanied by a surly lady's maid with eyes rounder and harder than an owl's, and by two strong-looking lackeys who, walking on either side of her, guarded their mistress like two towers. So jealous was Senhor Dom Alonso that only having been given strict orders by his confessor, and for fear of offending Our Lady, his neighbor, did he permit these fleeting Sunday visits, all the while anxiously spying on his wife's every step and brooding over her delay from between the bars of a grated window. Senhora Dona Leonor spent every slow day of the slow week shut up in that black granite mansion, not enjoying recreation or relief, even in the heat of summer, except for a section of a dreary garden surrounded by walls so high that only the crowns of some sad cypress trees could be seen rising above them here and there. But that brief visit to Our Lady of the Pillar sufficed for Dom Rui to fall madly in love with her on the May morning that he spotted her kneeling before the altar, limned in a sunbeam, her head graced by an aureole of golden hair, her long eyelashes cast down over the Book of Hours, and her rosary wrapped around her slender fingers; indeed, all of her was slender and soft and white, the whiteness of a lily abloom in shade, whiter in the midst of the black laces and black satins that hugged her graceful figure and fell to the chapel's flagstones, which were old tombstones. When, after a moment of hesitation and delightful astonishment, he knelt down, it was less for the Virgin of the Pillar, his divine Godmother, than for that mortal apparition whose name and life he did not know, only that for her he would give his life and name, if she surrendered herself for such an uncertain offering. Mumbling with unseemly haste the three Hail Marys with which he greeted Our Lady of the Pillar each morning, Dom Rui grabbed his hat, walked down the resonant nave with nimble feet, and stopped at the doorway, waiting for her by the starving beggars who were delousing themselves in the sun. But after a short while, during which Dom Rui felt his heart beating with uncommon anxiety and fear, Senhora Dona Leonor passed by and paused, wetting her fingers in the marble holy water stoup, not raising her veil-covered eyes to peek at him, either timidly or absent-mindedly. With her wide-eyed maid glued to her person, and walking between the two lackeys who looked like twin towers, she leisurely crossed the churchyard flagstone by flagstone, no doubt relishing, like a prisoner, the open air and clear sunlight that flooded it. And it filled Dom Rui with consternation to see her slip into the gloomy arcade with the great pillars on which the palace stood, disappearing through a side door overlaid with iron fittings. That, then, was the much-talked-about Dona Leonor—the very lovely and noble Senhora de Lara.

There followed seven long, drawn-out days that Dom Rui spent sitting on a stone bench by his window, watching that black door overlaid with iron fittings as if it were the one to Paradise, and that through it an angel would come out to announce Heavenly Bliss to him. Finally, the long-desired Sunday arrived, and while the bells were pealing at the hour of prime, he crossed through the churchyard with a bunch of yellow carnations in hand for his divine Godmother just as Dona Leonor was exiting from between the pillars of the dark arcade, her countenance white, pensive, and resigned, like a moon breaking through clouds. He nearly dropped the carnations as a result of the pleasurable agitation in which his chest rose and fell like a storm-driven sea, his soul having fled from him in turmoil as he devoured her with his gaze. And Dona Leonor acted in kind as she riveted her eyes on Dom Rui, although hers were calm eyes, serene eyes that betrayed neither curiosity nor even consciousness of encountering others so inflamed and darkened by desire. The young gentleman did not enter the church on account of a pious fear of not paying to his divine Godmother the attention that surely would have been robbed from her by all that was merely human, and yet that "all" was already mistress of his heart, already deified in it.

He waited eagerly at the door, by the beggars, the carnations wilting in the heat of his trembling hands as he thought of how much time she spent saying her rosary. And while Dona Leonor was walking down the nave, he already felt in his soul the sweet rustle of the silks that she dragged along the flagstones. The pale Senhora de Lara passed by, and the same calm, distracted, and mindless glance that she had swept over the beggars and the churchyard she now let sweep over him, either because she did not understand why that young man had suddenly turned so pallid, or because she did not yet distinguish him from indifferent objects and shapes.

Heaving a deep sigh, Dom Rui left the doorway and returned to his room, where he devoutly placed before the image of the Virgin the flowers he had not spread before her altar in the church. His whole life then turned into one long lament upon seeing the cold, inhuman demeanor of that woman, unique as she was among all other women for having captured his heart and made it serious, a heart that heretofore had been capricious and shallow. Spurred by hope, even though suspecting that disillusionment awaited him, he began to patrol her high garden walls or, disguised in a cloak, to back a shoulder against the corner of one and while away slow hours contemplating the bars of the palace's prison-like grilles, but no chinks opened in the walls, no rays of promising light shone through the bars. The entire edifice was like a tomb in which lay an insensitive woman, and behind those cold stones there was, moreover, a cold heart. So as to unburden himself on nights that he kept vigil, he composed, with pious-minded care, plaintive ballads that brought him no relief. At the church, he would kneel before the altar of the Lady of the Pillar—on the very same flagstones where he had seen Dona Leonor kneel—and remain there, no words of prayer occurring to him, adrift in bittersweet meditation, hoping that his heart would be calmed and consoled under the influence of the Lady who consoles and calms everything. But he would always get to his feet more unhappy, yet scarcely feeling the sensation of how cold and hard the stones were where he had been kneeling. The whole world seemed to him to consist of naught but hardness and coldness.

He did meet Dona Leonor on other Sunday mornings, but her eyes always remained dispassionate and as though oblivious, or when they happened to cross with his, that instant was lifeless, with hers so devoid of all emotion that Dom Rui would have preferred seeing them displeased or flashing with indignation, or arrogantly averted with arrogant disdain. Certainly Dona Leonor knew him by now, albeit in the same way that she also knew the Moorish flower girl who crouched by her basket alongside the fountain, or the poor who deloused themselves in the sun in front of Our Lady's doorway. So now Dom Rui could not think that she was inhuman and cold. Like a star that turns and twinkles in the heavens, she was merely majestically remote, not knowing that down below, in a world she does not comprehend, eyes she does not suspect gaze at her, adore her, and surrender to her the governance of their happiness and fortune.

Dom Rui thought, *She does not want it to be, I cannot make it so. It was a pipe dream that has ended, and may Our Lady keep both of us in her embrace!*

And because he was a very discreet gentleman, once he acknowledged her steadfast indifference, he did not continue to pursue her, did not so much as glance up at the bars on her grated windows, did not even go inside the Church of Our Lady when, from the doorway, he chanced to see her kneeling, and looking so very graceful, her golden head slanted over the Book of Hours.

II

THE OLD MAID with eyes more wide-open and harder than an owl's had not wasted time in telling Senhor de Lara that a bold young man of refined appearance—the inhabitant of the archdeacon's former residence—was constantly walking the churchyard and taking up a spot at the front of the church in order to capture Dona Leonor's heart with the looks he darted at her. Only too well and too bitterly did the jealous nobleman know of those doings, because while spying like a hawk from his palace window on the graceful Dona Leonor as she walked to church, he had observed that gallant young man fidgeting and waiting for her, never taking his eyes off her. And he had pulled furiously at his beard. From the time, then, that the old maid went to Senhor de Lara, the latter's most intense occupation was hating Dom Rui, that canon's impudent nephew who dared to elevate his sordid desire to the level of the lofty Senhora de Lara. So now he had the young man watched around the clock by a servant, and he soon came to know his every move and the friends with whom he hunted or consorted, and even who tailored his jackets, and even who polished his sword—each hour of his life. And still more anxiously did he keep an eye on Dona Leonor: all of her movements; her most fleeting moods, silences, and conversations with maids; her distractions while embroidering; the way she would daydream sitting under the trees in the garden; her mien and her color upon coming back from church.... But so unalterably serene in the calm of her heart did Senhora Dona Leonor prove to be, that not even the most imaginative kind of jealousy wanting to find fault would have been able to discover stains on that pure white snow. Dom Alonso then redoubled his harsh rancor toward the canon's nephew for having aspired to that purity, and that hair the color of bright sunshine, and that neck like a capped heron's, which were only his, for the exquisite pleasure of his life. And when he paced the gloomy, resonant corridors of his vaulted mansion, wearing his shepherd's coat edged with fur, the point of his gray beard jutting out before him, his curly mop of hair bristling at the back, and his fists clenched, it was always to brood over the same bitterness.

"He tempted her virtue, he sullied my honor.... He's guilty on two accounts and deserves to die two deaths!"

But his fury nearly transformed into terror when he learned that Dom Rui no longer waited for Senhora Dona Leonor in the churchyard, nor lovingly patrolled the palace walls, nor went inside the church when she prayed there on Sundays. Even worse was that so absolutely had Dom Rui become distanced from her that one morning Dom Alonso spotted him close to the arcade where that young gentleman could clearly hear the squeak of a door being opened—the door through which Senhora de Lara was going to exit—and he had stood still, his back turned while laughing with a portly acquaintance who was reading a parchment to him. No doubt such well-affected indifference only served (thought Dom Alonso) to hide some accursed design. What was that devious schemer plotting? Everything in the ill-tempered nobleman then became exacerbated: jealousy, rancor, vigilance, notwithstanding his ugly, gray old age. In Dona Leonor's calm manner he suspected cunning and pretense, and so he immediately forbade her visits to Our Lady of the Pillar.

On the mornings that she would have customarily attended church, Dom Alonso now hurried there to say the rosary and to express Dona Leonor's regrets—*que no puede venir* (he would murmur while bowing before the altar) *por lo que sabéis, Virgen purísima*!

And so he carefully inspected and reinforced every one of the black bolts of the gates to his manor house, and at night he unleashed two watchdogs into the shadows of the walled garden.

By the headboard of the vast bed—next to the night table, on which sat a lamp, a reliquary, and a glass of warm clove- and cinnamon-spiced wine—there always glittered a naked sword. But even with so many precautionary measures, he slept poorly and would wake up with a start from among the stacked pillows, grasping Senhora Dona Leonor with his brutal, greedy hands and bruising her neck, to whisper ever so softly in a fit of longing, "Say that you love only me!" Then, at the onset of dawn he would go off, like a hawk alighting on its roost, to spy on Dom Rui's windows. Dom Alonso never caught sight of his antagonist now, neither by the door of the church at Mass times nor returning from the country on horseback at the ringing of the Hail Marys bell.

And it was on account of realizing that Dom Rui had vanished from all the sites he used to frequent that the jealous husband suspected even more strongly that the young gentleman had found a place in Dona Leonor's heart.

Finally, after a night of tramping back and forth on the floor tiles of the corridor, inwardly brooding over his suspicion and hatred, he shouted for his majordomo and ordered that trunks and mounts be prepared. Early in the morning he would leave with Senhora Dona Leonor for his country estate in Cabril, two leagues from Segovia! The departure did not start at dawn, like the flight of a miser who is going to hide his treasure a long way off; rather, it was effected pretentiously and leisurely. The litter was brought in front of the arcade where it waited a number of hours with the curtains open while a stableboy walked the nobleman's white mare mule—bedizened Moorish style—all around the churchyard, and a team of male mules hooked to hitching rings stood beside the garden, beneath the sun, pestered by flies, and loaded down with trunks, the din from their bells pervading the alleyway. Thus did Dom Rui learn of Senhor de Lara's journey, and thus did the entire city learn of it.

Going to Cabril occasioned great contentment for Dona Leonor. She loved its lush orchards and gardens onto which opened—fully and without bars—the windows of her bright rooms, and there at least she had lots of fresh air, plenty of sunshine, flower boxes to water, an aviary, and such long paths bordered by laurel and yew that they were almost like gateways to freedom. And then, too, she hoped that being in the country would alleviate the worries that of late had caused her lord and husband to be so taciturn and his features to wrinkle with rage. But this hope bore no fruit, because after one week Dom Alonso's features were still clouded, for there were no fresh groves, no running, murmuring waters, no rose gardens in bloom perfuming the air—nothing that could allay such deep and bitter turmoil. As he had done in Segovia, he paced the resonant, vaulted gallery nonstop, huddled in his shepherd's coat. With the point of his beard jutting out before him and his thick mop of hair bristling at the back, he silently curled his lips into a sneer, as if he were contemplating evil acts, the acrid foretaste of which he seemed to be already enjoying. And all of his interest in life centered on a servant who continually galloped back and forth between Cabril and Segovia, and sometimes he even waited for him on the outskirts of the village by the Cruzeiro, staying there to hear the man hurriedly give him the news once he dismounted out of breath.

One night when Dona Leonor was in her room, praying the chaplet with the maids by the light of a large wax candle, Senhor de Lara came in very slowly, carrying in his hands a parchment roll and a quill dipped in his bone inkwell. With a brusque gesture he dismissed the maids, who feared him as they would a wolf. And pushing a bench beside the table and turning toward Dona Leonor with a face on which he had impressed tranquility and pleasantness, he started to speak as if he had come to her only about some simple, ordinary concern.

"Senhora," he said, "I want you to write a letter here that is of great importance to me."

So accustomed was she to submission that with neither comment nor curiosity, only going over to the bedpost to hang her rosary, with studied application for her hand to be neat and clear she penned the first short line that Senhor de Lara dictated, which was: *My lord....* But when he dictated the following line, longer and voiced bitterly, Dona Leonor threw down the quill as if it had scalded her, and, backing away from the table, she cried out in distress, "Senhor, why is it so important to you that I write such things—such false things?"

In an outburst of fury, Senhor de Lara yanked from his belt a dagger that he flourished next to her face, bellowing, "Either you write what I am ordering you to write, which is of great importance to me, or by God, I'll stab you in the heart!"

Whiter than the wax of the candle that provided their light and her skin tingling on account of that luminous blade, supreme trepidation prompted Dona Leonor to resign herself to all that he demanded of her and she murmured, "In the name of the Virgin Mary, do not hurt me! And do not become mad with rage either, Senhor, for I live to obey you and serve you. Order me and I shall do your bidding."

Then, with his taut fingers gripping the edges of the table where the dagger lay, and overwhelming the fragile, unhappy woman with a forceful, unyielding stare, Senhor de Lara dictated in a hoarse, violent rant, all composure lost. The finished letter, written by an unsteady, tremulous hand, read as follows: *My lord: Very badly have you understood, or very badly do you repay, the love that I have for you and could never openly declare to you in Segovia. Now I am here in Cabril, longing to see you, and if your desire coincides with mine, you may easily make it come true, because my husband happens to be away on another property, and this one here in Cabril is accessible and easily approached. Come tonight, enter by the garden gate, next to the narrow footpath, and then pass by the pond to reach the terrace. There you will see a ladder propped against a window of the house, which is my window, where you shall be sweetly received by the one who anxiously awaits you.*

"Now, Senhora, sign your name at the bottom, because this is what matters most!"

Dona Leonor slowly scratched her name, as red-faced as if she were being disrobed in front of a crowd.

"And now," ordered her husband more softly through his clenched teeth, "address it to Dom Rui de Cardenas!"

She dared to glance up at him, surprised by that unknown name.

"Do it!" commanded the somber man with a shout. "To Dom Rui de Cardenas!"

And she addressed her dishonest letter to Dom Rui de Cardenas.

Dom Alonso stuck the parchment inside his belt, next to the dagger he had resheathed, and left in silence, his beard jutting out, and his footsteps sounding muffled on the floor tiles of the corridor. Dona Leonor, her tired hands sunk in her lap, continued to sit on the bench, overcome with infinite foreboding, her gaze lost in the darkness of the silent night. Less dark did death seem to her than that dark adventure in which she felt herself embroiled! Who was that Dom Rui de Cardenas, about whom she had never heard a word, who had never figured in her life, which was so placid and so little occupied by memories and men? And yet he surely knew her, had most likely followed her with his eyes, and therefore would think it a natural and logical consequence to receive from her a missive of so much passion and promise.

So a man—no doubt young and wellborn, perhaps genteel—brought by her husband's hand, would brusquely gain entrée into her destiny! So intimately had that man now invaded Dona Leonor's life, without her fathoming what was afoot, that the gate of her garden was to be opened at night, and a ladder was to be stood against her window at night for him to climb up to her room! And it was her husband who would very secretly fling open the gate, and very secretly bring the ladder. What for?

Then, in a heartbeat, Dona Leonor understood the truth, the shameful truth, which wrung from her an anguished, ill-stifled cry. It was a trap! Senhor de Lara would entice that Dom Rui with a magnificent promise in order to overpower him and no doubt murder him, inasmuch as he would be defenseless and alone. And she, her love and her body, were the promises the unfortunate young man was going to see glittering before his seduced eyes. Thus did her husband use her beauty, her bed, as the golden web into which that brash prey was meant to fall! What greater offense could there be? And the imprudence of it all, too! Well might that Dom Rui be suspicious, not agree to such a candidly amorous invitation, and then, laughing and triumphant, show throughout all of Segovia that letter in which the wife of Alonso de Lara offered him her bed and her body! But no! The poor devil would hasten to Cabril, to die—to die miserably in the black silence of night, with neither priest nor sacraments, his soul mired in the sin of love! And surely to die, for never would Senhor de Lara permit the man who had received such a letter to live. Thus was that young man going to die out of love for her, and out of a love that would swiftly bring him death, while it had never brought him any joy! Doubtless on account of his love for her, because hatred like that of Senhor de Lara—which must have fed on disloyalty and villainy—could only have been born of jealousy that overshadowed every obligation that befits a gentleman and a Christian. Without doubt he had spied glances, moves, and intentions of this Senhor Dom Rui, a Dom Rui made incautious for being so much in love.

But how? When? She vaguely remembered a young man who one Sunday had crossed by her in the churchyard and waited for her at the door of the church with a bunch of carnations in his hands. Would he be the one? He was of noble appearance, very pale, with big, black, warm eyes. She had continued on … indifferent to him. The carnations that he clutched in his hands were red and yellow. To whom was he taking them? Oh! If only she could warn him right away, before dawn!

How, if there was no servant or maid in Cabril whom she trusted? But to let a brutal sword treacherously pierce a heart that was coming so full of love for her, beating for her, staking all its hopes on her!

Oh! Dom Rui would arrive on the heels of an ardent, devil-may-care gallop from Segovia to Cabril aglow with the promise of the enchanting open gate and the ladder propped against the window in the silence and protection of night! Would Senhor de Lara really order a ladder to be propped against her window? By all means, so that he might more easily kill the poor, and sweet, and innocent young man when he climbed up, unsteady on the flimsy rungs, his hands hindered, his sword beyond reach in its scabbard. And so at night the window facing her bed would be open, and a ladder would be stood against it, waiting for a man! Huddled in the shadows of the room, her husband would ambush and surely kill that man.

But suppose Senhor de Lara decided to bide his time outside the estate walls so as to brutally assault that Dom Rui de Cardenas on some path, and either being less proficient or less powerful in a clash of arms, he fell having been run through, without the other man being aware of whom he had killed? And she, there in her room, unknowing, with all the doors unlocked and the ladder raised, and that man appearing at the window in the soft shadows of the tepid night, and the husband who should be at her side to defend her, lay dead deep in a lane.... Virgin Mother, what would she do? Oh! She would intrepidly repulse the bold young man. But his astonishment and anger at having been duped would provoke him to blurt out, "You are the reason I'm here! You asked me to come here, Senhora!" And he would have with him, close to his heart, her letter, signed by her and written by her. How could she tell him about the ambush and the hoax? It would take so long in that silence and solitude of the night, while he kept his moist black eyes fixed on her, imploring her and boring into her. Poor, unfortunate Dona Leonor if Senhor de Lara were to die and leave her alone, defenseless, in that huge, wide-open house! But how much more unfortunate too if that young man whom she had summoned—and who loved her, and who because of that love would be dazzled and come on the run—was to encounter death at the site of his hopes, which was the site of his sin, and, having died in the clutches of sin, were to fall headlong into eternal despair. Twenty-five years old ... if he was the same one she remembered—pale, and so elegant in his purple velvet jerkin as he stood at the door of the church in Segovia with a bunch of carnations in his hand.

Two tears welled up in Dona Leonor's eyes. Kneeling down then, and raising her soul to the heavens, where the moon was beginning to rise, she murmured with infinite heartache and faith:

"Oh! Holy Virgin of the Pillar, Mother mine, watch over both of us, watch over all of us!"

III

DOM RUI was entering the cool courtyard of his house at the hottest hour of the day when a country boy jumped up from a stone bench in the shade and withdrew a letter from his pouch, which he handed over, saying deferentially, "Senhor, please read fast, for I must return to Cabril, to the person who sent me."

Dom Rui unrolled the parchment and, astounded by the contents, hugged it to his breast, as if to bury it in his heart.

The boy insisted anxiously, "Hurry, please, Senhor! Hurry! You needn't reply. A sign that you have received the message will do."

A very pale Dom Rui took off one of his silk-embroidered gloves and handed it to the boy, who then rolled it up and tucked it into his pouch. And he was already skipping away on the tips of his sandals when Dom Rui called out and stopped him with a wave.

"Tell me. What road do you take back to Cabril?"

"The shortest one, which is only for the fearless, because it takes you by Hangedmen's Hill."

"All right."

Dom Rui bounded up the stone steps, and in his room, without even taking off his hat, he stood by the jalousie and re-read that divine parchment in which Dona Leonor summoned him to her room at night, to possess her body and soul. And this offer did not surprise him ... after such a constant, impassive indifference. Rather, he immediately perceived in it a very astute love that, by virtue of being so strong, is kept hidden in light of obstacles and dangers in order to prepare that hour of contentment silently, thus making it a better and more delectable hour for having been prepared patiently. She had always loved him, then, from the blessed morning when their eyes met at the door of Our Lady of the Pillar. And while he was pacing up and down those garden walls, cursing a coldness that seemed colder to him than those cold walls, she had already given him her soul, and, imbued with constancy, with loving wisdom, repressing the slightest sigh and quelling suspicions, she was actually preparing for the radiant night when she would give him her body.

So much determination, such keen ingenuity in questions of love, caused her to be still more beautiful in his eyes!

With what impatience he glanced at the sun, which was in no hurry late that afternoon to dip behind the hills! Then, up in his room, with the shutters closed in order to concentrate better on his happiness, in a flurry of activity he lovingly made ready for his triumphal journey: fine clothes, fine lace, a black velvet jerkin, and perfumed essences. And twice he went down to the stable to ascertain whether his horse was well shod and well fed. To test the blade of the sword that he would gird to his waist, he flexed it a number of times on the ground. But his greatest concern was the road to Cabril, despite knowing it and the village that abutted the Franciscan monastery, as well as the old Roman bridge with its cross of Calvary and the narrow path that led to Senhor de Lara's estate. He had even passed by there that winter to go hunting with two friends from Astorga, and when he had caught sight of the Laras's tower on that outing, he had thought, *There's my ungrateful lady's tower*! How mistaken he had been! The nights were moonlit now, and he would quietly leave Segovia by the Saint Mauros Gate. A short gallop would put him at Hangedmen's Hill, a site he also knew. It was one of sadness and dread with its four stone pillars on which criminals were hanged, and on which their bodies remained to swing in the wind and be parched by the sun, until the ropes rotted and their bones—white and pecked clean of flesh by crows—fell to the ground. The Lake of the Ladies was behind the hill, and the last time he had ridden there was on the feast day of the Apostle Saint Matthew, when the magistrate and the confraternities of charity and peace went in procession to give sacred burial to the bones that had fallen onto black earth, only to be torn apart by birds. From there the road ran smooth and straight to Cabril.

As evening fell, thus did Dom Rui ponder his adventurous journey. Then, when it got completely dark with bats having begun to fly around the church towers, when in the corners of the churchyard candles had been lit in the niches of the De-parted, the brave young man experienced a strange kind of fear—fear of that happiness soon to be his, and that struck him as supernatural. Was it true, then, that this woman of divine beauty, famous in Castile and more inaccessible than a star, would presently be his, all his, in the silence and security of a bedroom, even before the devotional candles burning in front of the retables of the Departed had died out? And what had he done to merit such a great boon? He had walked the flagstones of a churchyard, he had waited at the door of a church, trying with his eyes to meet two other eyes that, indifferent and heed-less, were never upturned. Then, without pain, he had aban-doned his hopes.... But all of a sudden those distracted eyes seek him out, and those folded arms open up to him, and with her body and with her soul that woman cries out to him, "Oh, you foolish man! You misunderstood me! Come! The woman who discouraged you now belongs to you!" Had there ever been a like good fortune? So lofty, so rare was it, that surely be-hind it—if human law does not err—misfortune must already be lurking! In truth, it was already lurking, for could there be any greater misfortune than to know that after such rapturous fortune he would be leaving those divine arms at the crack of dawn, having to return to Segovia, whereas his Leonor—the sublime good of his life and so unexpectedly possessed for but an instant—would immediately revert to another master!

What did it matter! Let days of sorrow and jealousy come! That night was gloriously his, the whole world a vain appearance and the only reality that dim room in Cabril, where she would be waiting for him, her hair in loose tresses! With covetous anticipation he skipped down the steps and hopped onto his horse. Then, out of prudence, he crossed the churchyard very slowly, with his hat leaving his face in full view as if he were taking an ordinary ride to seek the coolness of the night outside the walls. No encounter held him up until he approached Saint Mauros Gate. There, a beggar, crouched in the darkness of an archway where he was monotonously playing his hurdy-gurdy, petitioned the Blessed Virgin and all the saints in a pitiful lament to keep that genteel rider in their sweet and holy care. Dom Rui had paused to toss him alms when he remembered that he had not gone to church that evening for Vespers, to pray and ask his divine Godmother's blessing. He dismounted in a leap, for next to that old archway a lamp flickered, illuminating a niche with a recessed altarpiece. On it was an image of the Virgin, her heart pierced by seven swords. Dom Rui knelt, set his hat on the flagstones, and, his hands raised, very fervently prayed a Salve Regina. A yellow gleam enveloped the face of Our Lady, who—not feeling the seven sorrows from the seven swords or perhaps feeling that they only gave her ineffable joy—smiled with rich, red lips. While Dom Rui was praying, the bell of the close-by monastery of Saint Dominic began to toll the death knell. In the black shadows of the archway, the hurdy-gurdy stopped, and the beggar murmured, "A friar is dying!" Dom Rui said a Hail Mary for the moribund religious. The Virgin of the Seven Swords still smiled sweetly: the death was not, consequently, a bad omen!

Beyond Saint Mauros Gate, past some potters' shanties, the byway continued, narrow and black between tall century plants. Behind the hills, at the end of the dark plain, there rose the first languid, yellow glimmer of a still hidden full moon. And Dom Rui slowly rode on, afraid of arriving too early, before the maids and servant boys finished their evening chores and said the rosary. Why had Dona Leonor not stipulated a time in a letter that was so clear and so well-thought-out in other respects? Then his imagination ran away with him … he was breaking into the garden at Cabril … he was flying up the promised ladder.… And all the while he rode hard, pushing his mount on an eager gallop that caused stones from the lumpy surface to shoot every which way. Afterward he reined in his panting horse. It was early, it was early! And he resumed his deliberate, painstaking pace, feeling his heart beat against his breast like a captive bird flapping its wings against the bars of its cage.

In this frame of mind he arrived at the Cruzeiro, where the road split into two byways closer together than the prongs of a pitchfork, both of them cutting through a pine forest. Having taken off his hat before the image of the crucified Christ, Dom Rui suffered a moment of anguish because he did not recall which of the two led to Hangedmen's Hill. He had already begun to head along the denser one when a light, dancing in the dark, rose from among the silent pine trees. It was an old woman, dressed in rags and tatters, with long, disheveled hair, stooped over a walking stick and carrying a candle.

"Where does this lead?" shouted Dom Rui.

The old woman dangled her candle higher up to look at that rider. "To Xarama."

And the light and the old woman vanished instantly, blending into the shadows as if they had arisen solely to warn the rider that he was going the wrong way. Abruptly turning around the cross of Calvary, he set out at a gallop along the other, wider byway until sighting, beneath the bright night sky, the black pillars and crossbeams of Hangedmen's Hill. He stopped, then, to stand straight up in the stirrups. The four pillars rose on a high, arid knoll with neither grass nor heath; enormous and black against a pale moon, they were joined by a low, collapsed wall and looked like the four corners of a dilapidated house. On top of the pillars rested the four massive wood crossbeams from which hung four hanged men, black and stiff in the still, silent air. All around everything was dead, like them.

Fat birds of prey slept, perched on the cross pieces; and in the distance the dead water of the Lake of the Ladies shone faintly while the big, full moon dominated the sky.

Dom Rui murmured the Our Father that every Christian owes to those guilty souls. Then he urged his horse forward and was continuing on when in the immense silence and immense solitude a voice rang out—a slow, suppliant voice calling him.

"Senhor, stop. Come here!"

Dom Rui tugged at the reins. Standing up again in the stirrups, he riveted his startled eyes all around that sinister wilderness, where he saw only the rugged hill, the quiet, luminous water, and the four dead men. He thought it had been a nighttime illusion or deviltry on the part of some errant demon. And calmly, no longer uneasy or in a hurry, he rode on as if he happened to be on a street in Segovia. But behind him he heard the voice a second time, calling him now with greater urgency and anxiety, almost in distress, "Senhor, wait. Don't keep going. Turn around and come back here!"

Once more Dom Rui stopped, and, shifted around now on his saddle, he boldly stared straight at the four bodies hanging from the crossbeams. The voice had sounded from their direction, and being a human voice, it could only have come from a human form! Therefore, it must have been one of those hanged men who called out to him in such an urgent, anxious manner.

Might there possibly remain in one or two of them, by the wondrous mercy of God, some breath and life? Or might it be, by virtue of a yet greater wonder, that one of those half-putrefied corpses was detaining him so as to deliver warnings to him from Beyond the Grave? But whether that voice issued from a live breast or a dead breast, great cowardice it would be to bolt, panic-stricken, without minding it and listening to it.

And so he pressed his hesitant horse up to the hill and stopped, one hand at his side. After gazing at the four corpses, one by one, he shouted, "Which of you hanged men dared to call out to Dom Rui de Cardenas?"

Then the one with his back turned to the full moon, coils of rope high on his neck, responded very placidly and naturally, like a man at a window in conversation with somebody in the street, "Senhor, it was me."

Dom Rui rode closer to him. He could not make out the man's face because his head was drooped, his features hidden by long, disheveled black hair. In the darkness he discerned only that his hands were loose and untied and that his bare feet were also loose and already desiccated and the color of bitumen.

"What do you want from me?"

Sighing, the hanged man said in a low voice, "Senhor, do me the great mercy of cutting this rope by which I am hanging."

Dom Rui drew his sword and with one practiced blow slashed the half-rotten rope. With a sinister sound of jarred bones the body fell to the ground, where it lay for a moment, stretched out. But it straightened immediately on unsteady, still inert feet and raised a dead, sunken face, the skin taut and yellower than the moonlight that shone on it, to Dom Rui. His eyes had no movement, no light, and his lips were opened into a hard, stony semblance of a sneer. From between his snow-white teeth emerged the tip of a very black tongue.

Dom Rui betrayed neither terror nor aversion and calmly sheathed his sword. "Are you dead or alive?" he asked.

The man slowly shrugged his shoulders. "I do not know, Senhor. Who does know what life is? Who does know what death is?" With his long, fleshless fingers the hanged man undid the knot of the rope still binding his neck and declared with the utmost serenity and firmness, "I must go to Cabril with you, Senhor. To the place where you are going."

Dom Rui shuddered, so taken aback that he jerked the reins, which caused his trustworthy horse to rear, as if it too had been taken aback.

"Go with me to Cabril?"

The hanged man bent over, and through a long tear in his woolen jersey his bones, sharper than the teeth of a saw, stood out all along his spinal column. "Senhor," he implored him, "do not deny me this opportunity, for I am to receive great recompense if I render you great service!"

All of a sudden it occurred to Dom Rui that the request might well be a formidable trick on the part of the Devil. And fixing his lustrous eyes on the dead face raised up to him, a face anxiously waiting for his consent, Dom Rui made a very slow, very long Sign of the Cross.

The hanged man went down on bended knee with scared reverence. "Why do you test me with that Sign of the Cross, Senhor? It is by it that we gain remission of sins, and only by it do I hope for mercy."

Dom Rui then considered that if the man had not been sent by the Devil, he could well have been sent by God! And swiftly and devoutly, he consented and accepted his frightful companion.

"Come with me to Cabril, then, if God so ordains! But I ask you nothing and nothing will you ask me."

Kneeing his horse, he descended the hill to the road bathed in moonlight and resumed his journey. The hanged man followed at his side so fleet of foot that even when Dom Rui rode at a gallop, he stayed close to the stirrups, as if swept onward by a silent wind. Now and then, in order to breathe more freely, he pulled at the knot of the rope wound around his neck. And when they passed by hedgerows redolent of the fragrance of wildflowers, the man would say softly, "How good it is to run!"

Dom Rui continued on in an astonished, turbulent state of mind. He fully comprehended now that the hanged man at his side was a corpse reanimated by God for a strange and undisclosed service. But why did God give him such a frightening companion? To protect him? To prevent Dona Leonor, beloved by Heaven for her piety, from falling into mortal sin? And for such a divine mission of such hallowed mercy the Lord had so few angels in heaven that he had to have recourse to a hanged man? Ah! How happily he would have turned his horse toward Segovia were it not for his gallant loyalty as a gentleman, his pride in never backing down, and his submission to the orders of God, which he felt weighing on him.

From an elevation on the road they suddenly caught sight of Cabril, the towers of the Franciscan monastery a bright white in the moonlight, and the hamlet asleep in the midst of gardens. Very quietly, without a single dog barking behind gates or from above walls, they made their way down to the old Roman bridge. In front of the cross of Calvary, the hanged man fell to his knees on the stone steps, raised the pale bones of his hands, and prayed a long time, amid long sighs. When they came to a lane, he drank deeply and gratefully from a fountain that ran and sang beneath the canopy of a willow's foliage. Since the lane was very narrow, he walked ahead of Dom Rui, stooped, and with his arms squeezed tight against his chest, not uttering a word.

The moon stood high in the sky. Dom Rui regarded that full, lustrous disk bitterly: so much indiscreet light was it spilling on his secret while emerging from between the hills to illuminate the entire landscape! Oh, how a night that should have been so divine was being ruined! A hanged man had escaped the gallows to follow him and know everything. But thus had God ordained matters. What sadness was his to gain access to that sweet door, sweetly promised, with such an interloper at his side and beneath that clear, bright sky!

All of a sudden the hanged man stopped, raising an arm from which hung a sleeve in tatters; he had come upon the end of the lane that ran into a wider and more beaten pathway. Before them rose the long white wall of the environs of Senhor de Lara's country house with its lookout and ivy-covered terraces.

"Senhor," the hanged man said in a hushed voice, respectfully holding on to one of Dom Rui's stirrups, "in a matter of steps past the lookout we'll reach the gate through which you are to enter the garden. It would be wise to hitch the horse to a tree here, if you believe it sure and faithful, because as regards the affair we have undertaken, even the sound of our footsteps could be our undoing!"

Dom Rui silently dismounted and, knowing the horse was sure and faithful, hitched it to the trunk of a dried-up poplar. And so submissive had he become to that companion imposed on him by God that, with no other drawback to heed, he followed him close by the moonlit wall.

The hanged man now advanced slowly and cautiously, on tiptoe, while keeping watch on the top of that wall, scrutinizing the dark pockets of the bushes, and pausing now and then to listen to nocturnal sounds audible only to him, because never had Dom Rui known a night so deeply and silently asleep.

And that kind of fear in one who should have been indifferent to human perils was filling the courageous Dom Rui with such wariness that he drew his dagger from the sheath, rolled his cape around an arm, and proceeded ever vigilant, his eyes flashing, as if he were on the brink of an ambush or a fight. In this manner they arrived at a low gate, which the hanged man opened with deft hands to prevent the hinges from creaking. There they started along a path, lined by leafy yews, which led them to a pond that was full of floating water lilies and surrounded by rustic stone benches strewn with the petals of flowering shrubs.

"That way!" whispered the hanged man, pointing with a skinny arm.

Beyond the pond, dense old trees obscured and arched over an avenue. They took it, like shadows in the shade, the hanged man in the lead, Dom Rui following very nimbly without grazing a single branch, scarcely setting foot on the sandy soil. A susurrous thread of water flowed through the greensward, and the rose climbers on the tree trunks gave off a sweet fragrance. Dom Rui's heart began to beat anew with the hope of love.

"Shh!" hushed the hanged man.

And Dom Rui almost stumbled into that sinister companion, who had stopped, his arms open like the crosspieces of a gate. In front of them, four stone steps led up to a terrace suffused with bright light. They clambered up the steps in a crouch, and at the end of a garden with no trees, laid out in well-tended flower beds bordered by box shrubs, they saw one side of the house awash in a lunar glow. In the middle, between the closed windows, there was a stone balcony with crocks of basil positioned to keep the panes wide open. The room on the inside had no illumination and was like a hollow of darkness in the midst of the brightness of the façade, which was bathed by the moonlight.

And propped against the balcony stood a ladder with rope rungs.

The hanged man then forcefully pushed Dom Rui away from the steps, back into the darkness of the avenue. And there, in an urgent, commanding voice, he exclaimed, "Senhor! Now you have to give me your hat and your cape. You will stay here in the darkness of these trees. I am going to climb that ladder and peek into that room. And if it is as you desire, I will come back here—and then may you go happily with God."

Dom Rui recoiled at the prospect of such a creature climbing up to such a window! And stamping his foot, he muffled a cry, "No, by God!"

But the hanged man's hand, pale in the darkness, brusquely wrested the hat from his head and pulled the cape off his arm. Already covering and disguising himself, he spoke softly now, his tone an anxious plea, "Do not deny me this opportunity, Senhor, for if I do you great service, I shall be granted great mercy!"

And he climbed the steps and reached the broad, illuminated terrace.

Dom Rui, stupefied, then climbed them, too, to look on. And oh, what a marvel! It was him, it was Dom Rui himself—all of him, in figure and likeness of manner—who was advancing between the flower beds and low box shrubs, so graceful and so agile, his hand at his side, his face upturned to the window with a smile, the long scarlet plume of his hat swaying in triumph. The man continued to advance in the splendid moonlight. The love room awaited him there, open and black. And Dom Rui watched, trembling with amazement and rage, his eyes flashing. The man had reached the ladder: he loosened his cape and put his foot on the rope rung! "Oh, he's going up, the blackguard!" roared Dom Rui. The hanged man climbed steadily. Already the tall figure, who was him, Dom Rui, was halfway up the ladder, all black against the white wall. He stopped! No! He had not stopped! He kept climbing to the top, and now he rested a cautious knee on the edge of the balcony. Overcome with desperation, Dom Rui could only stare—with his eyes, with his soul, with his entire being. And lo and behold, all of a sudden a shadowy black shape emerged from the black room, and a furious voice thundered, "You villain, you villain!" And the blade of a dagger flashed in a shaft of moonlight, and fell, and rose again, and glinted, and struck, and still glittered, and still penetrated.... Like a dropped bundle, the hanged man fell heavily onto the soft earth. Windows and shutters were swiftly and noisily shut. And there remained only the silence, the soft serenity, the full moon high up and round in the bright summer sky.

Dom Rui had realized the treachery in a trice, had drawn his sword, and had begun to move back to the darkness of the avenue, when—oh, what a miracle!—the hanged man came running across the terrace. Approaching Dom Rui posthaste, he grabbed him by the sleeve, and said in a loud voice, "To the horse, Senhor, and let us be off, for the encounter was not with love, but death!"

With no time to waste, the two dashed down the avenue and skirted around the pond sheltered by flowering shrubs; veering onto the narrow pathway bordered by yews, they passed through the gate and, out of breath, stopped for a moment on the road where the more rounded, more brilliant moon was shining like the brightest of days.

Then, only then, did Dom Rui discover that the hanged man still had the dagger plunged into his chest, all the way to the haft, the clean, glossy point showing through his back! But the terrified man was pushing him, hurrying him "to the horse, Senhor, and let us be off, for treachery still hovers over us!"

Shuddering and yearning to put an end to an adventure so full of miraculous and horrible occurrences, Dom Rui grasped the reins and set out at a gallop. And with great urgency the hanged man immediately jumped up onto the rump of the faithful horse. The good young gentleman shivered from head to toe upon feeling his back brushed by that corpse, which had been dangling from the gallows and had subsequently been pierced by a dagger. With what desperation did he then ride hard along that endless road! Notwithstanding the frantic gallop, the hanged man—as rigid on the rump as a bronze statue on a pedestal—never faltered. And the whole time Dom Rui felt a gelid cold freezing his shoulders, as if he were carrying a sack full of ice on them. As they passed by the Cruzeiro he murmured, "Help me, Lord!" Beyond the Cruzeiro he suddenly shook with the chimerical fear that such a funereal companion might end up accompanying him forever, and that it might be his destiny to gallop through the world in an eternal night, carrying a corpse on his horse's rump. He could not contain himself, and he shouted toward his back, into the biting wind that lashed them as they raced on, "Where do you want me to take you?"

Holding so close that the haft of his dagger caused Dom Rui pain, the hanged man whispered, "Senhor, it's best that you leave me on the Hill!"

Sweet and infinite relief did the good young gentleman experience, inasmuch as the Hill was so near that in the faint light he could already make out the pillars and the black beams. Before long, the horse stopped, trembling, speckled with lather.

Then, without making a sound, the hanged man slid down from the horse and, like a good servant, held the stirrup for Dom Rui. And with his sunken face and his black tongue protruding further from between his white teeth, he made a quiet, respectful appeal: "Senhor, please now do me the great mercy of hanging me again from my beam."

Dom Rui shuddered, horrified. "Good God! Hang you? You want me to—?"

The man sighed, opening his long arms. "Senhor, it is by the will of God, and by the will of the Lady who is most dear to God!"

Resigned, then, and submissive to the orders of the Almighty, Dom Rui finally dismounted to follow the stooped man, who, lost in thought, had begun to walk up to the Hill, the glittering, tapered point of the dagger protruding from his back. Both of them stopped beneath the empty beam. The other corpses hung from the other beams there on Hangedmen's Hill, and the silence was sadder and deeper than other silences on Earth. The lake water had turned black, and the moon was descending and growing faint.

Dom Rui regarded the beam on which dangled the short piece of rope that remained after he had slashed the corpse's knotted one with his sword.

"How do you expect me to hang you?" he asked. "I can't reach that short piece with my hand, nor could I raise you by myself."

"Senhor," the man responded, "there should be a long coil of rope at a corner. You tie one end of it to this knot here on my neck and fling the other one over the beam, and then, strong as you are, you'll have to pull me up and hang me again."

With their backs bent, the two slowly walked the Hill, searching for the coil. It was the hanged man who found it and unwound it. Dom Rui took off his gloves, and, instructed by the hanged man become hangman (so well did he learn from him), Dom Rui tied one end of the rope to the severed piece still around the man's neck and pulled the other one tight, which he whipped through the air and over the beam, the rope having been paid out to hang to the ground. And the strong Dom Rui, planting his feet and tautening his arms, tugged until he drew the man up and had him hanging, back in the air, just like any of the other hanged men there.

"Are you all right this way?"

The dead man's voice came out slowly, faintly. "Senhor, I am as I ought to be."

Then, to hold him fast, Dom Rui looped the thick rope around the stone pillar a number of times. Taking off his hat afterward and wiping sweat from his brow with the back of his hand, he contemplated his sinister and miraculous companion. He was already as rigid as before, his sunken face veiled by long, disheveled hair, his feet stiff, his body abraded and decayed like an old carcass. The dagger stayed plunged into his chest. Above him on the beam, two crows slept quietly.

"Do you want something else now?" asked Dom Rui, beginning to put his gloves back on.

Weakly, from high up, the hanged man spoke in a low voice, "Senhor, I ask most humbly that upon your return to Segovia you faithfully recount everything to Our Lady of the Pillar, your Godmother, and say that from her I hope there will be great mercy for my soul, owing to this service which, at her behest, my body has performed on your behalf!"

Dom Rui de Cardenas then understood all that had occurred, and devoutly kneeling on the ground of pain and death, he said a long prayer for that good hanged man.

Afterward he galloped back to Segovia. Dawn was breaking, and in the pure air clear bells were pealing for matins when he passed through Saint Mauros Gate. Still scruffy from his terrible journey, he entered the Church of Our Lady of the Pillar and, prostrating himself before her altar, related to his divine Godmother the evil temptation that had lured him to Cabril, the help he had received from Heaven, and with hot tears of repentance and gratitude, swore to her that never again would he pursue desire where there was sin, nor admit into his heart any mundane and evil thoughts.

IV

AT THAT HOUR IN CABRIL, Dom Alonso de Lara, his eyes bulging with astonishment and dread, was examining every path, corner, and shaded nook of his garden.

After listening at daybreak by the door of the room in which he had shut Dona Leonor that night, he had stealthily gone down to the garden and not found close to the ladder beneath the balcony—as he had delightedly expected would be the case—Dom Rui de Cardenas's body, for he was certain that when the odious man fell, he still had a residue of life in him, and so must have dragged himself away, bleeding and gasping for breath in an attempt to reach his horse and abscond from Cabril. However, with the sturdy dagger that he had plunged into his chest three times, and left in his chest, the villain could not have dragged himself very far, and must be lying in some corner, cold and stiff. He then searched again, every path, every patch of shade, every cluster of bushes. And—marvelous circumstance!—he discovered no body, no footprints, no scratched earth, not even a trace of blood on the ground! And yet with a certain and ravenous hand he had stabbed him in the chest three times and had indeed left the dagger in his chest!

And the man he had killed was surely Rui de Cardenas. He had recognized him immediately from the deep darkness of the room where he was spying, had seen him in the bright moonlight coming across the terrace—confident, light of foot, his hand at his side, his face raised with a smile, and the plume of his hat swaying in triumph! How could such an odd thing occur ... a mortal body surviving three stabs in the heart? And the greatest oddity was that not even on the ground below the balcony, where there ran all along the wall a row of gillyflowers and white lilies, had that strong body left a trace after falling from such a height, heavily, inertly, like a hefty bale of wares!

Nor did he glimpse a single crushed flower—dotted with light dewdrops, all of them remained upright, luxuriant, as if they had just bloomed. Motionless with fear, almost panic-stricken, Dom Alonso de Lara stood there, contemplating the balcony, measuring the height of the ladder, gazing with glassy eyes at the fresh gillyflowers with no bent stems or leaves. And then, in a precipitate dash, he ran madly around the terrace, along the avenue, and down the path bordered by yews, with the hope of still discovering a footprint, a broken branch, a bloodstain on the fine sand.

Nothing! Presenting a picture of uncommon order and neatness, the entire garden looked as if no leaves had been stripped by the wind or wilted by the sun.

Then, consumed by uncertainty and mystery as nightfall approached, he took a horse and, unaccompanied by neither servant nor stableboy, left for Segovia. Stooped and moving furtively like a fugitive, he entered his palace by the orchard gate, and his first concern was to hurry to the vaulted gallery, unlock the shutters, and avidly spy on Dom Rui de Cardenas's house. All the jalousies of the archdeacon's old residence were dark, open, taking in the fresh night air, and sitting on a stone bench by the door a stableboy was lazily tuning his bandore.

A pale Dom Alonso de Lara went down to his room thinking that certainly no disaster had occurred in a house where all the windows were open to cool down the interior, and where servant boys amuse themselves at the street entrance. Then he clapped his hands, furiously calling for his dinner. And as soon as he sat down at the head of the table on his high chair of tooled leather, he sent for his steward, to whom he promptly offered—with unusual familiarity—a glass of aged wine. While the man stood there, drinking respectfully, Dom Alonso, smoothing his beard and forcing his somber face into a smile, asked about the news and gossip in Segovia. During his stay in

Cabril, had no incident generated alarm or murmured gossip throughout the city? The steward wiped his lips and replied that nothing untoward had given rise to talk, unless it was the fact that Senhor Dom Gutierres's daughter, so young and such a wealthy heiress, had taken the veil in the Convent of the Discalced Carmelites. Dom Alonso insisted, staring voraciously at the steward. Had no great quarrel arisen? Had no much-talked-about young gentleman been found wounded on the road to Cabril? The steward shrugged his shoulders. He had not heard a thing in the city about quarrels or wounded gentlemen. With a gesture of annoyance, Dom Alonso dismissed his steward.

After rushing through a meager dinner, he returned at once to the gallery to spy on Dom Rui's windows. They were closed now, but in the last one, on the corner, a light flickered. Dom Alonso kept watch all night long, tirelessly brooding over the same astonishing fact: How had that man been able to escape with a dagger plunged into his heart? How had he been able to …? At daybreak he wrapped himself in a cape, put on a wide-brimmed hat, and went down to the churchyard under cover, disguised, and—on the lookout—started pacing back and forth near Dom Rui's house. The bells pealed for matins. Merchants with their jackets not completely buttoned were coming out to raise the shutters of their shops and hang their signs. Gardeners already goading donkeys laden with panniers cried their fresh vegetables, and discalced friars with sacks on their shoulders begged for alms and blessed young girls.

Pious women wrapped in cloaks and carrying bulky black rosaries avidly threaded their way into the church. Then the town crier, standing in a corner of the churchyard, blew a horn, and in a booming voice began to read a proclamation.

Senhor de Lara had stopped next to the fountain, preoccupied, as if engrossed in the musical trickle of the three spouts of the fountain. All of a sudden he wondered whether that proclamation had to do with the disappearance of Dom Rui. He ran to the corner, but the man had already rolled up his vellum and was majestically withdrawing, tap-tapping the flagstones with his white walking stick. And upon turning around to watch the house again, whom do his astonished eyes behold but Dom Rui—the Dom Rui whom he had killed—coming toward the Church of Our Lady with an airy step and elegant mien, his smiling face raised up in the fresh morning air, wearing a jerkin that was light-colored like the plumes on his hat, one hand at his side, the other one distractedly fingering a staff tasseled with golden cords of silk!

Dom Alonso then dragged himself home, looking aged. At the top of the stone stairway he ran into his old chaplain, who had come to greet him and who, entering the antechamber with him after reverentially asking for news of Senhora Dona Leonor, proceeded to relate to him a most astounding occurrence, which occasioned grave mumbling and terror throughout the city. Late the previous evening, when the magistrate went to visit Hangedmen's Hill, for the Feast of the Holy Apostles was drawing near, he discovered to his great astonishment and scandal that one of the hanged men had a dagger plunged into his chest! Was it the joke of some sinister scoundrel? Vengeance that not even death would satisfy? And a still greater marvel was that the body had been taken down from the gallows and dragged through a garden or a flower bed (since young leaves had been found adhering to its old rags) and then hanged again with new rope! This was the turbulence of the times, that not even the dead escaped outrages!

Dom Alonso listened with his hands trembling and his hair standing on end. Instantly seized by anxiety and agitation, and shouting and bumping into doors, he wanted to leave without delay to verify with his own eyes that ghastly profanation. On two quickly readied mules, they rode posthaste to Hangedmen's

Hill—he and the stunned chaplain, for Dom Alonso dragged him along. A crowd of people from Segovia had already congregated on the Hill, gawking in wonder at that astonishing sight: the dead man put to death by a dagger! They all backed away as the noble Senhor de Lara rushed up the incline to the gallows and stopped to stare, his expression frantic, wild as he took in the hanged man and the dagger in his chest. It was his dagger. He was the one who had killed the dead man!

Panic-stricken, Dom Alonso dashed off at a gallop to Cabril, where he shut himself up with his secret. He soon began to turn sallow and waste away, always shunning Senhora Dona Leonor, hiding in the shadowy paths of the garden, and babbling words into the wind, until early in the morning of the feast day of Saint John when a maid, who was returning from the fountain with her pitcher, found him dead beneath the stone balcony, stretched out on the ground, his fingers dug into the bed of gillyflowers where he seemed to have been scrabbling at the earth for a long time, searching for....

V

SO AS TO ESCAPE such harrowing memories, Senhora Dona Leonor, heiress of all the assets of the House of Lara, withdrew to her palace in Segovia. But since she now knew that Senhor Dom Rui de Cardenas had miraculously escaped the ambush in Cabril, she peeked every morning through the half-closed jalousies with eyes that did not tire, but did grow moist, to watch him as he crossed the churchyard to enter the house of God. Fearful, though, of the haste and impatience of her heart, she herself did not want to visit Our Lady of the Pillar while her period of mourning lasted. Then, one Sunday morning, discarding her black crepes when she could wear purple silks, Dona Leonor descended the steps of her palace with a new, divine emotion, and looking pale as she stepped onto the flagstones, she walked the churchyard and passed through the doors of Our Lady of the Pillar. Dom Rui de Cardenas was already on his knees before the altar, where he had placed his votive bouquet of yellow and white carnations. Upon hearing the rustle of her fine silks, he glanced up, his eyes aglow with a hope so pure and so fraught with celestial grace, it was as if an angel had summoned him. Dona Leonor knelt with her breast heaving, so pale and so happy that the wax of the great candles was not paler, nor the swallows happier as they freely flapped their wings about the ogives of the old church.

Before that altar, and kneeling on those flagstones, Dom Rui and Dona Leonor were married by Dom Martinho, bishop of Segovia, in the autumn of the year of Grace 1475, when the powerful Catholic monarchs, Isabella and Ferdinand, through whom God worked great deeds on land and on sea, already reigned over Aragon and Castile.

Glossary to "The Dead Man"
(in order of appearance)

THE CHURCH OF OUR LADY OF THE PILLAR: location in Segovia is invention on the part of Eça de Queirós. The Basilica of Our Lady of the Pillar (Nuestra Señora del Pilar) is in the city of Saragossa [Zaragoza], in northeastern Spain.

SALVE REGINA [LATIN: HAIL, QUEEN]: a Roman Catholic hymn or prayer sung or said after compline (the last of the seven canonical hours).

BOOK OF HOURS: a book of prayers said at various hours of the day.

QUE NO PUEDE (…) PURÍSIMA: Eça does not explain his switch to Spanish here, but presumably it is because the story takes place in Spain: *she cannot come (…) for the reason that you know, Virgin most pure!*

CRUZEIRO: a large stone cross, usually erected on a stepped, stone platform, seen in churchyards, cemeteries, public squares, and occasionally on roads.

CHAPLET: a string of beads, one-third the length of a rosary, for counting iterations in a sequence of prayers.

ASTORGA: a city in northwestern Spain with walls built by the Romans in the thirteenth century; it is a starting point for the Camino de Santiago.

HURDY-GURDY: a lute-shaped stringed instrument that produces sound by cranking a rosined wheel that rubs against the strings.

IMAGE OF THE VIRGIN … SEVEN SWORDS: Catholic tradition has it, going back to the fourteenth century, that Mary's heart was pierced seven times with seven swords of sorrow, which gave rise to the veneration of the Mater Dolorosa, Our Lady of Sorrows. They are: (1) Simeon's prophecy, Luke 2:34–35; (2) The flight into Egypt, Matthew 2:13; (3) The three days loss in the temple; (4) Meeting Jesus with his cross; (5) The crucifixion; (6) Taking Jesus down from the cross; and (7) The burial of Jesus. This Virgin appears in Marian iconography the world over.

BANDORE: a plucked instrument of six or seven pairs of strings with the pear-shaped soundbox of the old citterns.

Perfection

I

ULYSSES, THE MOST SUBTLE OF MEN, sat on a rock on the island of Ogygia, his beard buried in hands that no longer showed traces of the callused, blackened roughness brought about by weapons and oars. He found himself in a dark and weighty sadness as he gazed at the navy-blue sea that gently and harmoniously washed onto the snow-white sand. A tunic embroidered with scarlet flowers covered his powerful but now fat body in soft folds. Emeralds from Egypt glittered on the thongs of the sandals that he wore; his feet were softened and perfumed with fragrances. And his staff was a marvelous coral branch crowned with a cluster of pearls, like the ones used by sea gods.

With its alabaster cliffs, its aromatic woods of cedar and thuja, its eternal harvests gilding the valleys, and the freshness of rosebushes dotting the snug hills, the divine island gleamed, somnolent in the laziness of midday, completely encircled by a resplendent sea. Not a single breeze of the curious Zephyrs of the Archipelago sundered the serenity of the luminous air, sweeter than the sweetest wine, and saturated with the delicate perfume of meadows of violets. In the silence pregnant with pleasant warmth, the murmurs of brooks and fountains made for a lulling harmony, as did the cooing of doves flying from cypresses to plane trees and the slow rolling and breaking of gentle waves on the smooth sand. And in this ineffable peace and immortal beauty the subtle Ulysses, his eyes riveted on the luminous waters, groaned bitterly, stirring the complaint of his heart.

Seven years, seven prolonged years, had passed since Jupiter's fulgent ray had rent his ship with its high red prow, and he, clinging to mast and keel, had pitched in the roaring fury of the dark billowy sea for nine days and nine nights, until he had gained calmer waters and washed ashore on the sands of that island where Calypso, the radiant goddess, had given him shelter and loved him! And during those long years, how had his life—his great, strong life—dragged on after his departure for the fatal walls of Troy, abandoning amid copious tears his clear-eyed Penelope and his infant son, Telemachus, swaddled in the nursemaid's lap? Had he not been endlessly beset by dangers and wars, and intrigues and tempests, and errant courses? Ah, fortunate were the dead kings at the gates of Troy with praiseworthy wounds on their chests! Happy their comrades who were swallowed by the bitter wave! Happy would he have been if Trojan lances had pierced him that afternoon of the great wind and dust, when, near Phaia with a resounding sword, he had defended the dead body of Achilles from outrages! But no! He had lived! And now, every morning as he joylessly left Calypso's bed, the nymphs who served the goddess bathed him in the purest of waters and perfumed him with voluptuous essences, and they clothed him in an always new tunic, sometimes embroidered with fine silks, sometimes embellished with pale gold! Meanwhile, on a resplendent table set at the entrance of a cave in the shade of branches near the drowsy murmur of a limpid stream, wicker baskets and chased platters overflowed with cakes, fruits, tender meats still steaming, and fishes glistening like silver tendrils. The goddess's venerable maidservant chilled sweet wines in bronze kraters rimmed with roses. And sitting on a bench, he would reach his hands to grasp the perfect delicacies, while alongside him on an ivory throne, Calypso emitted through her snowy tunic the brightness and fragrance of her immortal and sublimely serene body and, with a reserved smile, not partake of the food of humans, but pick at her ambrosia as she sparingly sipped the transparent red nectar. Then, grasping the staff of Prince-of-Peoples that Calypso had presented to him, he would go off and roam, indifferently, the familiar paths of the island, which were so smooth and well-tended that his gleaming sandals never became sullied with dust, and so permeated with the goddess's immortality were those same paths that neither a dry leaf nor a wilting flower on its stem could be found on them. Then he would sit down on a rock, contemplating the sea that also bathed Ithaca, a sea so wild there, yet so calm at Ogygia, and he would think, and moan … until shadows fell over the waters and paths, and he withdrew to the cave to sleep unwillingly with the goddess who loved him! And during these long, long years, what fate had befallen his Ithaca, the rough island of shady forests? Were his loved ones still alive? Did his palace with its beautiful red and purple porticos still stand on the imposing hill that overlooked the Reitros inlet and the pine forests of Neus? After such slow and fruitless years, with no news and all hope extinguished like a lamp, had his Penelope taken off her transient widow's tunic and embraced the arms of another strong husband, who now wielded Ulysses's spears and harvested his vineyards? And his sweet son, Telemachus? Would he reign in Ithaca, seated with the white scepter on the high marble of the Agora? Idle and passing through courtyards to no purpose, would he look down on the harsh empire of a stepfather? Would he wander through strange cities, begging to earn his bread? Ah! If Ulysses's existence, thus forever severed from the wife and son so dear to his heart, were at least given over to illustrious deeds! Ten years before, he did not know Ithaca's fate, nor that of the precious beings he had left there, alone and vulnerable; but a heroic undertaking had stirred him, and every morning his fame grew, like a tree on a promontory that fills the sky, a tree that all men contemplate. At that time it was the plain of Troy and the white tents of the Greeks along the sonorous sea! He pondered unceasingly the stratagems of war; with impressive eloquence he held forth at the Assembly of Kings; he firmly hitched rearing horses to a chariot's yoke; and with his javelin held high and screaming, he ran apace at the Trojans in their high helmets as they stormed out of the Skaias Gates in full cry! Oh, and when he, Prince-of-Peoples—humped beneath a beggar's rags, his arms disfigured with false sores, limping and moaning—had penetrated the walls of proud Troy at the Phaia side by night with incomparable artifice and bravery to steal Pallas Athena, the city's tutelary! And when, inside the darkness and confines of the belly of the wooden horse, he calmed the impatience of all those motionless, iron-clad warriors who were suffocating; and when with his hand he covered the mouth of Anticlus who was raging furiously upon hearing Trojan insults and ridicule outside on the plain, he murmured to all of them, "Quiet, quiet! Night is drawing near, and Troy is ours." And after those prodigious journeys! The dreadful Polyphemus, mocked with an astuteness that will forever be the marvel of succeeding generations! The sublime ruses to escape Scylla and Charybdis! While tied to a mast, with silent, glaring eyes sharper than darts, repulsing the Sirens even as they were singing and whirling around him! The descent to hell, never granted to a mortal! And now a man of such glowing feats lay on a soft island eternally captive, without love, because of the love of a goddess! How could he escape, surrounded by an indomitable sea, with no ship and no comrades to man the long oars? The fortunate had clearly forgotten one who had fought so much on their behalf and had always devoutly rendered the oblations due them, even through the clamor and smoke of subjugated citadels, even when his prow ran aground on rustic lands! And to the hero, who had received Achilles's armor from the king of Greece, fell the bitter fate of getting fat in the idleness of an island more languid than a basket of roses, and of reaching for abundant delicacies with softened hands, and, when the waters and paths became covered with shadows, of sleeping, bereft of desire, with a goddess who desired him endlessly.

Thus did the magnanimous Ulysses groan by the shore of the shining sea when ... behold! All of a sudden a trail of uncommon brilliance—more glitteringly white than that of a falling star—blotted out the splendor of the sky, from the highest point to the fragrant stands of thujas and cedars that shaded a serene gulf east of the island. The hero's heart pounded. Such a refulgent trail, in the refulgence of the day: Only a god could have followed it across broad Uranus. Had a god, then, descended on the island?

II

A GOD HAD DESCENDED, a great god. It was the messenger of the gods, the light, eloquent Mercury. Wearing those sandals on which sprouted two white wings, his wine-colored hair covered by a helmet whose two additional wings also flap, and holding high the caduceus in his hand, he had cleaved the ether, had skimmed the smoothness of the calm sea, and had trod the island sand, where his footprints ended up glinting like impressions of new gold. Despite ranging over all of Earth with countless messages from the gods, the luminous messenger was not familiar with that island of Ogygia, and with a smile he admired the beauty of the meadows of sweet violets where nymphs ran and gamboled, and the harmonious sparkle of brooks that coursed amid tall, languid lilies. Propped by jasper supports, a vineyard laden with bunches of ripe grapes led—like a fresh portico sprinkled with sunlight—to the entrance of the grotto, all of polished rocks, where there hung jasmine and honeysuckle flowers enveloped in the faint buzz of bees. And then he caught sight of Calypso, the happy goddess, sitting on a throne and spinning beautiful crimson wool on a gold distaff with a gold spindle. A band of emeralds pinned her very wavy and glowing blonde hair. Under a diaphanous tunic, the immortal youthfulness of her body glistened, like snow when dawn tinges it with roses on the eternal hills populated by gods. And as she twisted the spindle, she sang a trilled, refined song, akin to a tremulous crystal thread vibrating from Earth to Heaven. Mercury thought: *Lovely island, and lovely nymph*!

From the clear plume of cedar and thuja there rose, directly skyward, a fine smoke that perfumed the entire island. Sitting in a circle on mats laid out on the agate-covered ground, the nymphs—servants of the goddess—wound skeins of wool, embroidered airy flowers on silk, and wove delicate woofs on silver looms. They all blushed in the presence of the god. And without stopping her golden spindle, Calypso had recognized the messenger at once, since all immortals know one another's names, deeds, and sovereign faces, even when they inhabit remote retreats separated by ether and sea.

Mercury had halted, smiling in his divine nudity and exhaling the perfume of Olympus.

Then, with composed serenity, the goddess raised to him the all-embracing splendor of her green eyes. "Oh Mercury! Why have you come down here to my humble island? You, venerable and loved, whom I've never seen set foot on Earth? Say what you expect from me. My open heart is already telling me to accommodate you if your wish falls within my purview and fate. But come, rest, that I may serve you like a sweet sister at the table of hospitality."

She pushed the distaff away from her waist and brushed

aside the loose locks of her radiant hair; and with her nacre-
ous hands she set on the table, which the nymphs had brought
close to the aromatic fire, the plate overflowing with ambrosia
as well as the crystal goblets glittering with nectar.

Mercury murmured, "Sweet is your hospitality, oh goddess!" He hung the caduceus from the fresh branch of a buttonwood tree and with his shining fingers reached for the platter of gold as he smilingly praised the excellence of that island
nectar. And with a contented soul, his head leaning against the
smooth trunk of the buttonwood now enveloped in brightness,
he began, "You asked, oh goddess, why a god has descended to
your abode! And certainly no immortal would travel without
reason from Olympus to Ogygia, this deserted immensity of
the salty sea where no cities of men can be found, nor temples
surrounded by forests, not even a small shrine from which the
aroma of incense could rise, or the smell of votive candles, or
the pleasant murmur of prayers. But it was our Father Jupiter,
the tempestuous one, who sent me on this errand. You took in,
and retain by dint of the immeasurable force of your sweetness,
the most subtle and unhappy of all the princes who fought high
Troy for ten years, and afterward embarked on deep-sea ships
to return to the land of their birth. Many of them managed to
resume life in their rich homes, possessed of fame, spoils, and
wonderful stories to tell. However, hostile winds and an even
more inexorable fate drove to this your island, awash in filthy
foam, the eloquent and astute Ulysses. Now, the destiny of this
hero is not to remain here in the immortal idleness of your bed,
far from those who weep for him, and who lack his strength
and divine cunning. That's why Jupiter, the regulator of order, ordains that you release the magnanimous Ulysses from
your lustrous arms, and return him—with the presents rightly
owed—to his beloved Ithaca, to his Penelope, who weaves and
unweaves her crafty web of deceit surrounded by arrogant suit-

ors, voracious consumers of her fat oxen, great imbibers of her new wine!"

The divine Calypso bit her lip lightly, and the shadow of her dense, hyacinth-colored eyelashes fell over her luminous face. Then, with a harmonious sigh, in which undulated her entire radiant bosom, she exclaimed, "Ah, great gods, fortunate gods! How harshly jealous you are of the goddesses who, without hiding in the depths of forests or the dark folds of mountains, love strong and eloquent men! This one, whom you gods begrudge me, washed ashore on the sands of my island, naked, hurt, starving, lashed to a broken keel, persecuted by all the fits of rage, all the gusts of wind, and all the furious thunderbolts at Olympus's disposal. I took him in, I washed him, I fed him, I loved him, and I tended him so that he would be eternally protected from torments, pain, and old age. And now, after eight years during which my sweet life has been twined around this attachment like a grapevine around an elm, thunderous Jupiter has determined that I should sever myself from the companion I had chosen for my immortality! You really are cruel, you gods who constantly increase the turbulent race of demigods by sleeping with mortal women! And how do you expect me to send Ulysses to Ithaca if I possess neither ships, nor rowers, nor a knowledgeable pilot to guide him through the islands? But who can resist Jupiter, the one who gathers clouds? So be it! And let obeyed Olympus laugh! I will teach the intrepid Ulysses to build a safe raft with which to again plow the green back of the sea."

Mercury the messenger immediately rose from the bench put together with gold nails, grasped his caduceus, and, drinking a last cup of the island's excellent nectar, praised the goddess's obedience.

"You are wise to do so, oh Calypso! Thus do you avoid the thunderous Father's wrath. Who will resist him? His omniscience directs his omnipotence. And he sustains, like a scepter, a tree that has Order for a flower. His decisions, clement or cruel, always result in harmony. That's why his arm becomes terrifying to rebellious breasts. Because of your swift submission, you shall be an esteemed daughter, and you shall enjoy an immortality replete with calm, free from intrigues and free from surprises."

The impatient wings of his sandals were already fluttering, and his body swayed with sublime grace over the lea and the flowers that carpeted the entrance to the grotto.

"Besides," he added, "your island, oh goddess, stands on the course of the daring ships that cleave the waves. Soon, perhaps, another robust hero, having offended the immortals, will turn up on your sweet beach, clutching a keel. Light a torch at night, high up on the rocks!"

And, laughing, the divine messenger serenely soared, leaving an elegant trail of effulgence in the ether, which the nymphs, having forgotten their tasks, followed with fresh, parted lips and raised breasts in their desire for that beautiful immortal.

Pensive then, Calypso tossed a saffron-colored veil over her wavy hair and set out through meadows for the seashore, walking in such haste that her tunic twisted about her round, rosy legs as would a patina of foam. So lightly did she step on the sand that the magnanimous Ulysses did not hear her approaching, lost as he was in the contemplation of the lustrous waters, his black beard in his hands, the heaviness of his heart alleviated with moans. The goddess smiled with fleeting, sovereign bitterness. Then, resting fingers as roseate as those of Eos, goddess of the dawn, on the hero's shoulders, she spoke to him.

"Lament no longer, unhappy Ulysses! Do not consume yourself gazing at the sea! The gods, superior to me by virtue of intelligence and willpower, have determined that you are to leave, and to confront the inconstancy of the winds, and to tread again the earth of your native land."

Suddenly, like a condor rending its prey, the divine Ulysses jumped down from the mossy rock, astonishment writ on his face. "Oh goddess, are you saying...!"

With her beautiful arms enveloped in the saffron-colored veil fallen at her sides, she continued calmly as a wave—sweeter and more harmonious in amorous respect for her divine presence—washed ashore.

"You know full well," she said, "that I have no high-prow ships, nor robust rowers, nor a pilot knowledgeable about the stars to guide you. But you can surely wield the bronze ax that belonged to my father to fell trees that I shall mark for you, and thus will you construct a raft to make your voyage. Then I shall provision it with wineskins, perfect victuals, and propel it with a friendly breath out into the untamed sea."

The cautious Ulysses drew back slowly, fixing on the goddess a hard stare darkened by mistrust. And raising his trembling hand, he spoke with the anxiety of his heart.

"Oh goddess, you cloak a terrible thought, since in this way you invite me to confront, on a raft, difficult waves where deep-sea ships navigate poorly. No, dangerous goddess, no! I fought in the great war and I know the infinite malice harbored in the bosoms of the immortals! If I resisted the irresistible Sirens, escaped due to sublime stratagems through Scylla and Charybdis, and triumphed over Polyphemus by means of a ruse that made my name eternally renowned among men, it certainly was not, oh goddess, so that now on the island of Ogygia I should fall—like a little bird scarcely covered with down, and in its first flight from the nest—into a simple trap facilitated by your honeyed words! No, goddess, no! I will only embark on your extraordinary raft if you swear, by the terrible oath of the gods, that you are not preparing my irreparable downfall with those quiet eyes!"

Thus did Ulysses, the prudent hero, cry out at water's edge

with his chest heaving. Then the merciful goddess laughed a bright, musical laughter. And, approaching the hero, she ran her celestial fingers through his thick, blacker-than-pitch hair.

"Oh marvelous Ulysses," she said, "you are, truthfully, the most perfidious and cunning of men, since you cannot even conceive of the existence of a spirit with neither artifice nor falsity! My illustrious father did not beget me with a heart of iron! Despite being immortal myself, I understand mortal misfortunes. I only recommended to you what I, a goddess, would undertake to do if Fate obliged me to depart Ogygia across an uncertain sea!"

The divine Ulysses slowly and somberly withdrew his head from the rosy caress of Calypso's fingers. "But swear.... Oh goddess, swear so that a savory trust will wash over my breast like a wave of milk!"

She raised her fair arm to the blue where the gods dwell. "By Gaius and by the Heavens, and by the subterranean waters of the river Styx, which is the greatest invocation that immortals can call upon, I swear, oh man, that I am not preparing your ruin or even greater tribulations."

The valiant Ulysses breathed deeply. And then, rolling up the sleeves of his tunic and rubbing his robust hands together, he asked, "Where is the ax of your magnificent father? Show me the trees, oh goddess! Daylight is waning, and the work will take a long time!"

"Not so fast, you eager man of human woes! The greater gods in their wisdom have already determined your fate. Return with me to the sweet grotto to regain your strength. When red Eos appears, tomorrow, I shall take you to the forest."

III

IT WAS INDEED THE HOUR when mortal men and immortal gods alike approach well-laid tables, where awaiting them are abundance, rest, absence of concerns, and amiable conversations that gladden their souls. In no time Ulysses sat on the ivory bench on which lingered the aroma of Mercury's body, and before him the nymphs—servants of the goddess— set cakes, fruits, tender smoky meats, and fish as gleaming as silver filigree. Perched on her throne of pure gold, the goddess received from her venerable waiting woman the dish of ambrosia and the cup of nectar. Both the mortal and the immortal reached their hands toward the perfect foods of Earth and Heaven. And as soon as they had given an abundant offering to hunger and thirst, the illustrious Calypso, leaning her face on rosy fingers and thoughtfully observing the hero, spoke these winged words.

"Oh so very subtle Ulysses, you wish to return to your mortal dwelling and to your native land. Ah! If you knew, as do I, how many harsh evils you must undergo before you catch sight of the rocks of Ithaca, you would stay in my arms—pampered, bathed, well-nourished, clothed in fine linens, never losing your valued strength, nor the sharpness of your mind, nor the warmth of your eloquence, since I would communicate to you my immortality! But you wish to return to your mortal wife, who lives on that rough island where the woods are dark, sinister. And yet I am not inferior to her, neither in beauty, nor in intelligence, because mortal women shine before immortal goddesses as do smoky lamps before pure stars."

The eloquent Ulysses stroked his scruffy beard. Then, raising his arm, as was his wont at the Assembly of Kings in the shade of the high sterns before the walls of Troy, he said, "Oh venerable goddess, do not be offended! I know perfectly well that Penelope is very inferior to your beauty, wisdom, and majesty. You will be eternally lovely and youthful so long as gods exist, while she, in a matter of years, will experience the melancholy of wrinkles, white hairs, pains of old age, and the unsteady steps taken with a shaky walking stick. Her mortal spirit roams through darkness and doubt; you, beneath that luminous brow, possess luminous certainties. But, oh goddess, precisely because of what she has that's incomplete, fragile, unrefined, and mortal, I love her and long for her company as a kindred spirit. Consider how painful it is for me that at this table, every day, I eat my fill of lamb from the pasture lands and fruits from the orchards, while you at my side, by virtue of the ineffable superiority of your nature, raise divine ambrosia to your lips with sovereign deliberation! Never in eight years, oh goddess, has your face glowed with a moment of joy; nor has a tear escaped from your green eyes; nor have you stamped your foot with angry impatience; nor, groaning from pain, have you ever stretched out on a soft bed. And thus do you render useless all the virtues of my heart, for your divinity does not permit me to congratulate you, to console you, to calm you, or even to massage your aching body with the essences of beneficial herbs. Consider besides that your godly intelligence possesses all wisdom and always ascertains the truth; and, in the whole time that I have slept with you, never have I enjoyed the pleasure of correcting you, of contradicting you, and of feeling the force, the power, of my comprehension in light of a weakness of yours! Oh goddess, you are that terrifying being who's always right! Consider besides that, as a goddess, you know all of the past and all of the future of men. I have never been able—drinking fresh wine of a night— to savor the incomparable delight of relating to you my illustrious deeds and my sublime travels! Oh goddess, you have no faults, and when I slip on a rolled-out carpet or snap a strap of my sandal, I cannot yell at you like mortal men yell at their mortal wives, 'It was your fault, woman!' and thereby raise a nasty ruckus in front of the fireplace! Consequently, I shall suffer, in a spirit of patience, all the many ills that the gods will heap upon me on the gloomy sea so as to return to Penelope, a human

Penelope whom I can command, and console, and reprimand, and accuse, and contradict, and teach, and humiliate, and dazzle, and as a result love with a love that constantly feeds on these fluctuating modes, like a flame that feeds on contrary winds!"

Thus did the eloquent Ulysses unbosom himself, his gold cup empty; and serenely did the goddess listen to him, with a quiet smile, her hands motionless in her lap, her fingers curled around the end of her veil.

Meanwhile, Phoebus Apollo was making a westward descent, and already a golden, rubied vapor rose from the hindquarters of his four sweating horses and spread over the sea. Soon the island's paths became covered with shadows, and on the precious fleeces of the bed deep inside the grotto, Ulysses with no desire and the goddess with desire, enjoyed sweet love and afterward sweet sleep.

Early the next morning, as Eos was just beginning to open the gates of Uranus, the divine Calypso, who had dressed in a tunic whiter than the snow of Mount Pindus and pinned in her hair a transparent blue veil as light as ether, exited the grotto. The magnanimous Ulysses was already sitting at the entrance beneath foliage, with a cup of clear wine in front of him, and she brought him her illustrious father's powerful double-bit bronze ax, the handle of which had been hewed from an olive tree on the slopes of Olympus.

Quickly wiping his stiff beard with the back of his hand, the hero grabbed the venerable ax.

"Oh goddess, it's been so many years since I've touched a weapon or a tool, I, a man who lays waste to citadels and is a builder of ships!"

The goddess smiled and, her smooth face aglow, spoke these stirring words: "Oh Ulysses, conqueror of men, if you were to stay on this island, I would order marvelous weapons for you from Vulcan and his forges on Etna."

"What worth have weapons without battles or men to admire them? Besides, oh goddess, much have I already battled, and my glory across generations is proudly secure. I only aspire to a peaceful rest, to watch over my livestock, to frame laws for my peoples. Be benevolent, oh goddess, and show me the strong trees that it behooves me to cut down!"

She walked, silently, along a shortcut abloom with tall, radiant lilies that led to a point on the eastern side of the island thick with woods, and the intrepid Ulysses, the shiny ax on his shoulder, followed behind her. Doves flew off the branches of cedars, or up from the hollows of rocks where they drank, to flutter about the goddess in an amorous flurry. As she passed by, a more delicate scent rose from the opened flowers, like from censers, and the grass grazed by the hem of her tunic turned a fresher, deeper, lusher green. And Ulysses, indifferent to the goddess's illusions and impatient with the divine serenity of her harmonious spirit, thought about his raft, anxious to reach the forest.

At long last he sighted it, dense and dark, full of oaks and age-old teaks, as well as pines that rustled in the high ether. From its fringe, the wood fell to a sandy beach where no shell, no broken coral polyp, no pale flower of a marine thistle marred its perfect enchantment. And the sea glittered with the brilliance of a sapphire in the still of the clear, pink-hued morning. Going from the oaks to the teaks, the goddess marked for the attentive Ulysses the dry trunks—strengthened by innumerable sunny days—that would float more swiftly and steadily on the treacherous waters. Then, caressing the hero's shoulder as if it were another robust tree also consigned to the cruel waters, she withdrew to the grotto, where she sat at her gold distaff and spun all day, and sang all day.

With excited, unbridled joy Ulysses drove the ax into a mighty oak, and it shook. And soon the entire island echoed with his superhuman labor. Seagulls, asleep in the eternal silence of those cliffs, flew away en masse, startled and squawking. The fluid divinities of the lazy streams, shuddering and quaking, fled toward the canebrakes and alder roots. On that short day the valiant Ulysses felled twenty trees: oaks, pines, teaks, and poplars; and he pruned, squared, and aligned all of them on the beach. His neck and broad chest were steamy with sweat when he slowly trudged back to the grotto to satisfy his bearish hunger and drink ice-cold beer. And never had he seemed more beautiful to the immortal goddess who, with the onset of night, readily and tirelessly embraced on her bed of precious pelts the strength of those arms that had felled twenty trees.

Thus did the hero labor for three days. And, swept up in this magnificent activity that shook the island, the goddess helped Ulysses, bringing in her delicate hands lengths of rope and bronze nails from the grotto to the beach. The nymphs, having set aside their easy tasks at her command, were weaving a strong cloth for a sail to be lovingly driven by favorable winds. And the venerable waiting woman was already filling leather costrels with strong wines and generously preparing the numerous foodstuffs for the dubious crossing. In the meantime, the raft was taking shape with the hewn planks securely lashed and a framework raised in the middle to accommodate the pine mast, trued rounder and smoother than an ivory wand. Each afternoon the goddess, seated on a rock in the shade of the forest, would contemplate the admirable builder hammering furiously and heartily singing a rower's song. And, nimble-footed on shining tiptoes, the nymphs—slipping away from their tasks—would come to peek through the trees with bright, avid eyes at that solitary force who was magnificently raising a ship on that solitary sand.

IV

FINALLY, on the morning of the fourth day, Ulysses finished squaring the rudder, the base of which he reinforced with alder wood supports to better withstand the crash of waves. Then he gathered a plentiful ballast comprised of the island's soil and its polished stones. Without pause, in a merry longing, he tied the sail cut by the nymphs to the tall yard. On heavy rollers, and maneuvering the lever, he eased the immense raft onto the foam wash of the breakers in a sublime effort, with muscles so strained and veins so swollen that he himself seemed made of trunks and cords. One end of the raft heaved, rising rhythmically with the harmonious waves, and the hero, raising arms shiny with sweat, praised the immortal gods.

Then, since the work had been completed and the afternoon sparkled, a propitious one for a departure, the generous Calypso, winding her way through violets and anemones, brought Ulysses back to the fresh grotto. With her divine hands she bathed him in a nacre shell, and perfumed him with supernatural essences, and dressed him in a beautiful tunic of embroidered wool, and draped over his shoulders a cloak impervious to sea mists, and laid out the table for him to satisfy his ravenous hunger with the heartiest and finest foods on Earth. The hero accepted her loving care with patient magnanimity. Her gestures serene, the goddess smiled dolefully.

Then she took Ulysses's hairy hand in hers, feeling pleasurably the calluses brought about by the ax, and, following the seashore, led him to the beach where waves gently lapped the planks of his sturdy raft. Both the mortal and the immortal rested on the mossy rock. Never had the island shone with such serene beauty, in the midst of such a blue sea, under such a soft sky. Neither the fresh water of Mount Pindus drunk on a torrid march nor the golden wine produced by the hills on the island of Chios were sweeter to savor than that air imbued with aromas generated by the gods for a goddess to breathe. The everlasting freshness of the trees penetrated the heart, almost asking for a caress from fingers. All the sounds of streams coursing over grassland, waves washing onto the beach, and birds singing in the leafy shade rose softly and subtly, intermingled like the sacred harmonies of a distant temple. The splendor and charm of the flowers retained the awe-struck rays of the sun. So plentiful were the fruits of the orchards and the harvest-ready grain fields, that the island seemed to be collapsing, sinking into the sea under the weight of its abundance.

Then the goddess, at the hero's side, sighed easily and, a gentle smile on her lips, murmured, "Oh magnanimous Ulysses, you are truly leaving! Desire impels you to see mortal Penelope again, and your sweet Telemachus, whom you left in the nursemaid's lap when Europe ran against Asia, and who now already holds a feared lance in his hand. A flower, even a sad one, will always sprout in time from an old love with deep roots. But do tell! If on Ithaca no wife awaited you weaving and unweaving cloth, or no anxious son who gazes at the sea with tireless eyes, would you, oh prudent man, leave this sweetness, this peace, this abundance and immortal beauty?"

Beside the goddess, the hero extended his powerful arm as was his custom in the Assembly of Kings, before the walls of Troy, where he planted the persuasive truth in the souls of his listeners. "Oh goddess, do not be shocked! But even if there did not exist a son, a wife, or a kingdom to impel me, I would still joyfully confront the seas and the wrath of the gods! Because in truth, oh so very illustrious goddess, my sated heart can no longer bear this peace, this sweetness, and this immortal beauty. Consider, oh goddess, that in eight years never have I seen the leaves of these trees turn yellow and fall; never have I seen this bright sky become overcast with dark clouds; never have I had the satisfaction of holding my hands near a sweet fire, dressed warmly while a big storm raged about the mountains. All those flowers that glitter on elegant stems are the very same, oh goddess, that I admired and drank in the first morning that you showed me these perpetual meadows. And there are lilies that I hate, with a bitter hate, because of their insurmountably eternal albescence! These seagulls repeat their white, harmonious flights so incessantly, so inexorably, that I hide my face from them, as others hide theirs from Harpies! And how often do I seek refuge in the depths of the grotto so as not to hear the always languid murmur of the always pellucid streams! Consider, oh goddess, that on your island I have never come across a swamp, or a decayed trunk, or the carcass of a dead animal covered with buzzing flies. Oh goddess, for eight years, eight terrible years, I have been deprived of seeing work, effort, struggle, and suffering. Oh goddess, do not be shocked! I have been desperate to behold a body bent over a burden; two sweaty oxen pulling a plow; men insulting one another on the way across a bridge; the supplicant arms of a crying mother; a cripple leaning on his crutch and begging at the gate of a village. Oh goddess, in eight years I have not spotted a grave. I have had enough of this sublime serenity! My entire soul burns with a desire to see something become deformed, get dirty, be broken into pieces, made corrupt. Oh immortal goddess, I dreadfully miss seeing death!"

Motionless, with her perfectly still hands in her lap clutching the ends of her yellow veil, the goddess had listened to her captive hero's furious complaint with a serenely divine smile. In the meantime, the nymphs—servants of the goddess—were coming down the hill carrying on their heads, with the support of their arms, the jugs of wine and leather sacks that the venerable waiting woman was sending to provision the raft. Silently, the hero positioned a plank for them to proceed from the sand and go on board. And while the nymphs nimbly walked it, their golden anklets tinkling on sleek feet, the attentive Ulysses counted the sacks and wineskins, enjoying in his noble heart that generous plenty. But as soon as those excellent bales of provisions were tied to pegs, all the nymphs slowly sat down on the sand around the goddess to watch the farewell, the embarkation, and the hero's seamanship on the water.

Rage, then, flashed in Ulysses's wide eyes. And, furiously crossing his valiant arms in front of Calypso, he spoke these words: "Oh goddess, do you truly believe that nothing is missing for me to unfurl the sail and set out? Where are the rich presents that you owe me? Eight years, eight years, I was the magnificent guest on your island, in your grotto, in your bed. The immortal gods have always ordained that, at the friendly moment of departure, considerable presents are to be offered to guests! Where are they, oh goddess? Those abundant riches that you owe by custom on Earth and by law in Heaven?"

The goddess smiled with sublime patience. And with winged words that wafted in the breeze, she replied, "Oh Ulysses, you are clearly the most self-interested of men! And also the most distrustful, since you suppose that a goddess would deny presents owed to one she has loved. Calm down, my subtle hero. The rich presents, extensive and splendid, are on the way."

And, sure enough, other nimble nymphs were coming down the low hill, their veils fluttering, their arms laden with lustrous riches that shone in the sun! The magnanimous Ulysses extended his hands, his eyes devouring what they beheld. And while the nymphs passed over the squeaky plank, the astute hero counted, and in his noble spirit he appraised the ivory chest, bolts of embroidered cloth, ewers of chased bronze, and gem-encrusted shields.

So rich and beautiful was the gold vase that the last nymph was carrying on her shoulder that Ulysses stopped her, snatched it, hefted it, examined it, and shouted with a proud and strident laugh, "This truly is choice gold!"

After the precious riches were stored and fastened under the wide bench, the impatient hero grabbed the ax, slashed the rope securing the raft to the trunk of an oak, and jumped onto the broadside engulfed in foam. But then he remembered that he had not even kissed the generous and illustrious Calypso. Quickly flinging off his cloak, Ulysses cleared the foam, ran along the sand, and planted a serene kiss on the goddess's aureoled brow.

She took hold of his strong shoulder. "How many evils await you, oh unfortunate Ulysses! Better that you should remain throughout all immortality on my perfect island, in my perfect arms."

Ulysses flinched with a magnificent cry. "Oh goddess, the irreparable and supreme evil consists in your very perfection!"

And he fled through the wave, eagerly climbed aboard the raft, loosed the sail, and, seaward bound, headed for labors, torments, and miseries—for the delight of imperfect things!

Glossary to "Perfection"
(In order of appearance)

ULYSSES: the Latin variant of Odysseus. Ulysses/Odysseus and the Trojan War present a familiar cast of characters, many of whom appear in "Perfection," as do the hero's stratagem of the Trojan horse and his twenty-year odyssey to return home to Ithaca.

OGYGIA: the island where Calypso kept the hero for seven years.

THUJAS: coniferous trees that grow from ten to two hundred feet.

ARCHIPELAGO: the Aegean Sea.

CALYPSO: a nymph in Greek mythology who lived on the island of Ogygia.

THE AGORA: a marketplace or public square.

SKAIAN GATES: the gates from which Priam watched the Trojan War.

ANTICLUS: a Greek warrior who hid inside the Trojan horse and wanted to respond to the voice of his wife (imitated by Helen) but was prevented by Odysseus, who thereby saved his companions.

POLYPHEMUS: the one-eyed giant who lived on the island of Cyclops and was blinded by Odysseus.

SCYLLA AND CHARYBDIS: mythical sea monsters and maritime hazards to passing sailors.

SIRENS: depicted as female figures with the legs and wings of birds, they were dangerous creatures who lured sailors with their enchanting music and singing voices to shipwreck on their island.

ACHILLES'S ARMOR: the armor that Achilles lent to Patroclus and was subsequently taken by Hector as a spoil of war.

RIVER STYX: a mythological river that forms the boundary between Earth and the Underworld.

PHOEBUS APOLLO: Greek god of the sun, prophecy, and archery.

COSTREL: a pear-shaped flask with ears to attach it to one's waist.

MOUNT PINDUS: mountain range in northern Greece and southern Albania.

VULCAN: the ancient Roman god of fire and metalworking.

CHIOS: island in the Aegean Sea, known for its export of high-quality wine during the time of the ancient Greeks.

HARPIES: in Greek myth, female monsters—half-human, half-bird—known for their hideous appearance and smell.

José Matias

A BEAUTIFUL AFTERNOON, my friend! I'm waiting for the funeral of José Matias … José Matias de Albuquerque, nephew of the Viscount of Garmilde. Surely you knew him—a slender young man as blond as an ear of corn with a paladin's curly mustache above the indecisive mouth of a contemplative sort, a skilled horseman, and possessed of a refined, sober elegance. He had an inquisitive mind, too, so engrossed in general ideas and so discerning that he understood my *Defense of Hegelian Philosophy*! This image of José Matias dates from 1865, because the last time that I ran into him, on an inhospitable January afternoon, he was huddled in a doorway on Rua de São Bento, reeking of brandy and shivering in a honey-colored jacket that was threadbare at the elbows.

But on one occasion, my friend, when José Matias stopped in Coimbra, on his way from Porto, you had supper with him at the Paço do Conde. Craveiro, who at the time was writing *The Ironies and Agonies of Satan* in order to provoke further the break between the Purist and Satanic schools of thought, even recited that sonnet of his, which is imbued with such mournful idealism: "In the cage of my breast, my heart.…" And I can still picture José Matias, wearing that wide cravat of black satin tucked inside his white linen vest, not taking his eyes off the flames of the serpentine candelabras and smiling wanly at that heart roaring in its cage. It was an April night with a full moon. Afterward, as a group and with guitars, we took a walk across the bridge and strolled through that poplar grove. Januário sang romantic verses of our time in a heartfelt manner:

> At sunset yesterday evening,
> Silently did you contemplate
> The torrential cascade that
> Was boiling at your feet....

And José Matias, his hands on the parapet of the bridge, was gazing skyward, his soul and eyes entranced by the moon! Why do you not accompany this interesting young man to the Cemetery of Pleasures? I have a coach, one for public hire, as befits a professor of philosophy. What? Because of your light-colored trousers? Oh, my dear friend! Of all the materializations of sympathy none is more grossly material than black cashmere. And the man we are going to bury was of a great spiritual disposition!

The casket is being brought out of the church. Only three carriages accompany it. But you know that in reality José Matias died six years ago, in all his unsullied magnificence. The one we're taking away now, half-decomposed inside boards adorned with yellow bunting, is the corpse of a drunkard with neither history nor name who was killed by the February cold in the recess of a doorway.

The individual with the gold-rimmed glasses, in the coupé? I don't know him, my friend. Perhaps he's a rich relative, like the ones who show up at funerals, properly broadcasting their relationship in the black of mourning, when the deceased can no longer importune them or compromise them. The obese man with the ugly sallow face seated in the victoria is Alves Capão, who owns *The Joke*, a newspaper in which there is, unfortunately, a dearth of philosophy. What connection did he have with Matias? I don't know. Maybe they got drunk together in the same dives; maybe he contributed pieces of late to *The*

Joke; maybe beneath all that lard and that literature—the one as vile as the other—a compassionate heart is housed. Here's our coach. Should I lower the window? Would you like a cigarette? I've brought matches. Well. This José Matias was a perplexing sort for someone like me who loves logical evolution in life and expects corn to sprout consistently from seed. In Coimbra we always viewed him as a scandalously banal figure. Maybe his maddeningly fastidious appearance contributed to this judgment. Never did a conspicuous tear show on his academic gown! Never did an errant mote of dust show on his shoes! Never did you see a rebellious hair on his head or mustache escaping from the rigid alignment that used to drive us to distraction! Moreover, in our passionate generation he was the only intellectual who did not rage against the miseries of Poland, who read *Les Contemplations* without turning pale or shedding tears, who remained unmoved by the wound that left Garibaldi lame! And yet, in that José Matias there was no coldness or harshness or selfishness or lack of affability! On the contrary! A pleasant companion he was, always cordial and cheerful in a kindly way. All of his steadfast calm seemed to stem from an immense, sentimental superficiality; and in those days it struck us as rather reasonable and appropriate that we should nickname that young man who was so soft, so blond, and so slight, "Squirrel-Heart Matias." By the time he graduated from the University of Coimbra his father had died, as had soon afterward the refined, lovely lady who was his mother; and since José had inherited fifty *contos*, he left for Lisbon to gladden the loneliness of an uncle who adored him, a general, the Viscount of Garmilde. Surely you remember him, my friend: that perfect picture of the classic general with his highly waxed mustache, his pink trousers fully stretched to hook onto the loops of his gleaming boots, and a quirt tucked under his arm, the tip of the lash trembly and eager to flay the world! A grotesque warrior and a delightfully good man. At the time, Garmilde lived in the parish of Arroios, in an old house façaded with tile, adjacent to a garden where he lovingly grew beds of superb dahlias. That garden rose very gently to the ivy-blanketed wall that separated it from another garden: the beautiful, spacious rose garden of Councilman Matos Miranda, whose house with its airy terrace stood between two small yellow towers on top of the hill, and was known as the Casa da Parreira, after its vine trellises. I expect, my friend, that you know of the beautiful Elisa Miranda, the Elisa da Parreira (at least from celebrity, as one knows of Helen of Troy or Inês de Castro). She was the sublime romantic beauty of Lisbon toward the end of the Regeneration period. But in reality, Lisbon only caught a glimpse of her through the windows of her grand calash, or on an occasional night of illumination in the Passeio Público amid the dust and the multitude, or at the two balls held by the Carmo Assembly, of which Matos Miranda was a venerated member. Whether on account of the home-loving preference of a woman of the provinces, or on account of belonging to the serious Lisbon bourgeoisie of the times (which still adhered to the severely restrictive old customs), or on account of the paternal imposition placed on her by a sixty-year-old diabetic husband, the goddess rarely emerged from Arroios to let herself be seen in public by mortals. But the individual who did see her—with habitual ease and almost unavoidably—as soon as he settled in Lisbon was José Matias. And that was because the general's imposing residence stood at the foot of the hill, next to the garden and the Casa da Parreira, and the divine Elisa could not appear at a window, cross the terrace, or pick a rose from among the paths of boxwoods without being deliciously visible, especially given that not a single tree spread a curtain of dense foliage over the two sun-filled gardens. Surely, my friend, you have hummed, as we all have, those trite yet immortal lines:

It was autumn when your image so bright
And so striking in the moonlight….

As in those verses, so it was with poor José Matias when, upon returning from the beach at Ericeira in the fall, one October night he caught sight of Elisa Miranda on the moonlit terrace! You have never beheld that incomparable kind of loveliness so poetically brought to life by Lamartine. Tall, slender, lithe, worthy of the biblical comparison of the palm tree swaying in the breeze. An abundance of lustrous black hair in wavy locks. A complexion of the freshest camellias. Liquid black eyes, dispirited and melancholy, hooded by long lashes. Ah, my friend, even I, laboring as I was at the time to annotate Hegel, even I adored that woman for three impassioned days and wrote a sonnet dedicated to her after running into her one rainy afternoon as she waited for a carriage at the Seixas Gate! I don't know if José Matias dedicated sonnets to her. But all of us, his friends, instantly understood the powerful, profound, absolute love that on a moonlit October night had taken root in that heart, which in Coimbra we judged to be the heart of a squirrel!

Obviously, you realize that such a quiet, reserved man did not make a public spectacle of his sighs. However, as far back as the age of Aristotle it was said that love and smoke cannot be hidden, and from our self-effacing José Matias love began to escape at once, like tendrils of smoke through invisible fissures in a closed house caught up in a raging fire. Well do I remember visiting him one afternoon in Arroios after my return from the Alentejo. It was a Sunday in July. He was going to have dinner with a great aunt, a Dona Mafalda Noronha, who lived in Benfica on the Quinta dos Cedros, where Matos Miranda and the divine Elisa also habitually had dinner on Sundays. I even believe it was only there that she and José Matias would have met, especially with the means afforded by shady retreats and paths conducive to reflection. The windows of José Matias's room opened onto his garden as well as that of the Mirandas, and when I entered he was still slowly getting dressed. Never, my friend, have I marveled at a human countenance framed by an aureole of such unquestionable, serene happiness! When he embraced me, he was smiling radiantly with a smile that sprang from the depths of his radiant soul; he was still smiling, delightedly, while I related to him all the vexations I had suffered in the Alentejo. And then he smiled ecstatically, and mentioned the heat, absent-mindedly rolling a cigarette; and he kept on smiling, enraptured, as he selected a white silk cravat from a dresser drawer with religious scruple. And all the while, out of a habit that now was as ingrained in him as blinking, his tenderly smiling eyes kept returning irresistibly to the closed windows. And, trailing as I did that blissful love beam, I immediately spotted on the terrace of Casa da Parreira the divine Elisa wearing a light-colored dress and a white hat, pacing lazily while slipping on her gloves and stealing glances at my friend's windows, which an oblique sunray dazzled with golden flashes. Meanwhile, José Matias talked on, or rather mumbled about sundry pleasant matters, his perennial smile always in place. All his attention was fixed on the mirror in front of him, on the coral and pearl stickpin for fastening his cravat to his white vest, which he was buttoning and adjusting with the devotion of a newly ordained priest who, in the pure exaltation of preparing to say his first Mass, dons the stole and amice to approach the altar. Never had I seen a man sprinkle eau de cologne on a handkerchief with such abandon! And after putting on his frock coat and affixing a superb rose to the lapel with ineffable emotion, making no attempt to suppress a delightful sigh, he went and solemnly threw the windows wide open! *Introibo ad altare Dei*! I remained discreetly ensconced on the sofa. And, believe me, my dear friend, I envied that man at the window, motionless as he was, rigid in his sublime adoration, with his eyes and his soul and his entire being riveted on the terrace, on the woman in white slipping on her light-colored gloves, as indifferent to the world as if it were merely an aggregate of flagstones that she stepped on and covered with her feet.

And this bliss, my friend, lasted for ten years—ever splendid, pure, and distant, a love of the spirit! Don't laugh. They surely met at Dona Mafalda's home; they surely wrote to each other, and profusely, flinging their letters over the wall that separated the two gardens; but never, over the ivy at that wall, did they seek the rare delight of a stolen conversation or the still more perfect delight of a silent interlude while hidden in shadows. And never did they share a kiss. No doubt about that! A fleeting, ravenous squeeze of hands under Dona Mafalda's trees was the passionately extreme extent that their will forced upon their desire. I imagine you don't understand how two such fragile souls could have carried on in this terrible, morbid renunciation for ten years. Granted, they were denied an hour of safety or a small gate in the wall that might have allowed them to go astray. Also, the divine Elisa really did live as if confined in a convent, the bolts and grates of which were in place on account of the rigidly reclusive habits of the gloomy, diabetic Matos Miranda. But in the chasteness of this love there figured considerable moral nobility and lofty finesse of feeling. Love spiritualizes man and materializes woman. That spiritualization was easy for José Matias, who (without our suspecting it) had been born extravagantly spiritualistic; however, the human Elisa also experienced a delicate pleasure in that ideal adoration of his, which was akin to that of a monk who, with his tremulous fingers wrapped around a rosary, does not even dare to brush against the tunic of the sublime Virgin. He, of course, relished a superhuman enchantment in that transcendentally dematerialized love. And for ten years, like old Hugo's

Ruy Blas, he wandered, eager and fascinated, through his own radiant dream—a dream in which Elisa actually dwelled inside his soul, in a fusion so absolute that she became consubstantial with his very being! Can you believe, my friend, that he gave up his cigars—even while riding horseback alone in the outskirts of Lisbon—as soon as he learned one afternoon at Dona Mafalda's estate that smoke bothered Elisa?

And this real presence of the divine creature in his being, in his self, occasioned in José Matias strange new states of mind that stemmed from that very hallucination. Since the Viscount of Garmilde dined early, at the customary hour of old Portugal, José Matias followed suit after seeing his opera, and at that same delightful and nostalgic Central Café, where the sole seemed fried in heaven and the Colares wine bottled in heaven. And mind you, he never had dinner without a tableful of brightly burning candles and flowers. Why? Because Elisa also ate there, invisibly. All of which gave rise to those silences bathed in a religiously attentive smile. Why? Because he was always listening to her! I still remember him ridding his room of three classical engravings of audacious fauns with subdued nymphs. The ideal of Elisa hovered there in that atmosphere, and so he purified the walls and ordered them hung with cream-colored silks. Love induces luxury, especially love of such elegant idealism, and José Matias was lavish, prodigal with luxury that she enjoyed. He could not decently go around with Elisa's image in a coach for hire, nor permit such an august image to brush against the wicker chairs of the orchestra seats at the São Carlos opera house. As a result, he too took to riding in carriages of simple, sober good taste, and he subscribed to a box at the opera, where he installed—for her use—a papal-like armchair in white satin, embroidered with gold stars.

Moreover, when he discovered Elisa's generosity, he too, and at once, became similarly and sumptuously generous, and no one who lived in Lisbon at that time gave out one-hundred-*mil reis* bills more freely and cheerfully. Therefore, in no time at all he squandered sixty *contos* out of love for that woman to whom he had never even given a flower!

And all this while, what about Matos Miranda? I'm telling you, my friend, the good Miranda tainted neither the perfection nor the serenity of this happiness. Could José Matias's spirituality have been so absolute that he was only interested in Elisa's soul, that he was indifferent to the submissions made by her body, that inferior and mortal receptacle? I don't know. Truth be told, that worthy diabetic with his grayish sideburns and ponderous gold-rimmed eyeglasses, who was so grave and always wrapped in a dark woolen muffler, did not suggest disturbing ideas about a passionate husband whose ardor fatally and involuntarily awakens an equally inflamed response. Nonetheless, I, a philosopher, never understood that almost affectionate consideration on the part of José Matias for the man who, even disinterestedly, could by right and by custom watch Elisa unfastening her white underskirt! Might there have been some recognition or acknowledgment that Miranda had discovered that divine woman on a remote street in Setúbal (where José Matias never would have set eyes on her), had kept her in comfort, well fed, finely dressed, and driven about in the most comfortable calashes? Or had José Matias been given that customary assurance—"I'm not yours, nor his either"—that consoles a man for his sacrifices so much because it flatters his ego so much? I don't know. But certainly this magnanimous disdain of his for Miranda's physical presence in the temple inhabited by his goddess gave José Matias's happiness a perfect unity—the unity of a crystal that glitters on all sides, all of them equally pure, with neither scratch nor blemish. And this happiness, my friend, lasted ten years.... What scandalous luxury for a mortal!

But one day all of Earth trembled for José Matias in an earthquake of incomparable horror. In January or February of 1871, Miranda, already weakened by diabetes, died of pneumonia. Along these very streets, in a sluggish, hired coach, I joined his stately funeral procession, crowded as it was with dignitaries and ministers because Miranda belonged to various institutions. Afterward, taking advantage of the hire, I visited José Matias in Arroios, not out of any perverse curiosity, nor to extend indecent congratulations, but so that he would feel the moderating force of philosophy in that stressful situation. However, I found him with an older, closer friend, that brilliant Nicolau da Barca, whom I also followed to this cemetery, where now lie under their gravestones all those comrades with whom I once upon a time built castles in the air. Nicolau, summoned by a telegram from Matias, had arrived at dawn from Velosa, his estate in Santarém. When I entered the room, a servant was busy packing two enormous trunks. José Matias was leaving that night for Porto; he had even dressed already in his travel attire of black suit with yellow leather shoes. After shaking my hand while Nicolau mixed a grog, he continued pacing the floor, in silence, as if confused, with an expression that was neither emotion nor decorously disguised joy, nor surprise at his abruptly altered destiny. No! If the good Darwin does not mislead us in his book *The Expression of Emotions*, that afternoon José Matias only felt and only exhibited embarrassment! At Casa da Parreira on the other side of the gardens, all the windows remained closed in the sadness of the gray afternoon. And, nonetheless, I caught José Matias unawares, shooting a quick glance at the terrace, and what showed through that glance was disquiet, anxiety on the verge of terror! How shall I express it? It was the kind of glance that you let slip at an insecurely locked cage in which a lioness moves about restlessly! When José Matias went into his bedroom for a moment, I said sotto voce to Nicolau, over the grog, "Matias is doing the right thing by going off to Porto." Nicolau shrugged his shoulders. "Yes, I thought it was being sensitive, and I supported his decision. But only for a few months of prolonged mourning." At seven o'clock we accompanied our friend to Santa Apolónia train station. During our return, inside our coupé, with a heavy rain pounding the top, we philosophized. I smiled contentedly. "One year of mourning, and then a bundle of children and a bundle of happiness. It's a finished poem!" Nicolau promptly added, "And finished in delightful, succulent prose. The divine Elisa retains all of her divinity and Miranda's fortune, some ten or twelve *contos* of income. For the first time in our lives you and I will see virtue rewarded!"

*

MY DEAR FRIEND! The ritual months of mourning passed, followed by others, and José Matias did not budge from Porto. I found him that August settled in the Francfort Hotel, where he coped with the melancholy of the torrid days by smoking (because he had gone back to his cigars), reading novels by Jules Verne, and drinking ice-cold beer until early evening when it cooled off, at which time he dressed, applied a touch of cologne, and pinned a flower to his lapel to go and have dinner in Foz.

And although the blessed end of mourning and desperate waiting drew near, I didn't notice any genteelly suppressed excitement in José Matias, any rebellion against the slow march of time, which occasionally drags on like a sluggish, doddering old man. On the contrary! The smile of radiant certainty that in those years had illuminated him with a nimbus of supreme contentment had given way to cumbersome seriousness, all shadows and depressions, the demeanor of a man floundering in irresolvable doubt, an ever present, unrelenting, painful doubt. You want to know what I think? I think every moment of his life that José Matias was awake that summer in the Francfort Hotel—even while gulping down a cold beer, even while putting on his gloves to get in the calash that would take him to Foz—he would ask his anguished conscience, "What am I to do? What am I to do?" And then one morning at breakfast he really surprised me upon opening the newspaper and exclaiming, with a touch of color in his face, "What? It's already August 29? Good Lord! It's already the end of August!"

I returned to Lisbon, my friend. Winter passed, very dry and very blue. I worked on my *Origins of Utilitarianism*. One Sunday when carnations were already being sold in tobacco shops, I caught a glimpse of the divine Elisa with purple feathers in her hat inside a coupé on the Rossio. And that same week I noticed in my *Illustrated Daily* a brief, almost timid announcement of the marriage of Senhora Dona Elisa Miranda. To whom, my friend? To the well-known landowner, Senhor Francisco Torres Nogueira!

At that point my friend clenched his fist and pounded his thigh in amazement. I also clenched both of my fists, but to raise them to Heaven, where acts on Earth are judged, and to cry out furiously, rage against the falsity, against the fickle and perfidious inconstancy, against all the deceitful turpitude of women, and of that Elisa in particular, the most infamous woman of them all! For with her period of mourning scarcely having ended, she betrayed in haste, precipitately, that noble, pure, intellectual Matias and his submissive, sublime love of ten years!

And after pointing my fists toward Heaven, I then clutched them to my head and shouted, "But why? Why?" Out of love? She had loved this young man on an exalted plane for years, and with a love that had neither been disillusioned nor sated, because it remained suspended, incorporeal, dissatisfied. Out of ambition? Torres Nogueira was, like José Matias, an affable man who idled away his time; he possessed mortgaged vineyards that yielded the same fifty or sixty *contos* that José Matias had recently inherited from his uncle Garmilde in excellent, unencumbered lands. So why? Obviously because Torres Nogueira's dense black mustache held greater physical appeal for her than José Matias's wistful blond down! Ah, with what reason did Saint John Chrysostom teach that woman is a dunghill of iniquity at the gates of hell!

Anyway, my friend, one afternoon while I was carrying on like that, whom did I run into on Rua do Alecrim but our Nicolau da Barca, who bounded out of his carriage and ushered me into a doorway, excitedly squeezing my arm and practically choking on his words. "Have you heard yet? It was José Matias who turned her down! She wrote to him, she journeyed to Porto, she cried. He wouldn't even agree to see her! He didn't want to get married, does not want to get married!" I was shocked. "And what about her?" "Hurt, aggressively pursued by Torres, tired of widowhood, her beauty still blossoming at the age of thirty … what the devil! The poor thing got married!" I raised my arms up to the arch over the doorway. "But what of José Matias's sublime love?" Nicolau, his close friend and confidant, swore with categorical certainty, "It's the same as always! Infinite, absolute. But he does not want to get married!" We eyed each other a moment and then went our separate ways, shrugging our shoulders with that resigned amazement that behooves prudent souls who find themselves face to face with the Unknowable. Nevertheless, as a philosopher, and consequently an impudent spirit, that night I examined José Matias's behavior with the scalpel of a psychology that I had expressly sharpened, and by dawn I was exhausted and concluded—as one always concludes in philosophy—that I was confronting a first cause argument, therefore impenetrable, and one on which the point of my scalpel would be broken, with no advantage to him, to me, or to the world!

After the divine Elisa got married, she continued living in the Parreira with her Torres Nogueira in the comfort and quiet that she had previously enjoyed with her Matos Miranda. In midsummer, José Matias quit Porto to leave for Arroios and his uncle Garmilde's spacious house, where he took up residence once again in his old rooms with the balconies that gave onto the garden blooming with now neglected dahlias. August came, silent and hot, as always in Lisbon. On Sundays, José Matias had dinner with Dona Mafalda da Noronha, in Benfica, alone, because Torres Nogueira did not know that venerable lady from the Quinta dos Cedros. Wearing light-colored dresses, the divine Elisa took afternoon strolls among the rosebushes of her garden, so the only change in that sweet nook of Arroios seemed to be that Matos Miranda lay in his beautiful marble vault and Torres Nogueira in Elisa's excellent bed.

There was, however, one immense and painful change— and it was José Matias's! Can you imagine, my friend, how that wretch of a man spent his sterile days? With his eyes, and his memory, and his soul, and his entire being riveted on the terrace, the windows, and the gardens of the Parreira! But it was no longer from his wide-open windows in wide-open ecstasy with the smile of confident bliss; it was from behind closed curtains, through a minuscule slit, hidden while furtively catching glimpses of the white pleats of her dresses, his face totally devastated by anguish and defeat. And do you understand why this poor heart of his suffered to such an extent? Was it the likelihood that Elisa, spurned by his unresponsive arms, had run immediately, without struggle, without scruples, to other more accessible, willing arms? No, my friend! Not that! And bear in mind now the complicated subtlety of this passion. José Matias remained devoutly persuaded that Elisa loved him in the depths of her soul, in that sacred spiritual profundity where the impositions of conventions are of no consequence, nor are the decisions of pure reason, nor the impulses of pride, nor the stirrings of the flesh, and, what's more, that she loved him and only him, and with a love that had not waned, had not changed, that flourished in all its luxuriance, even without being nurtured and tended like the ancient Mystical Rose! What tortured him, my friend, what occasioned extensive wrinkles in his face in a few short months was that a man, a male, a beast with his wiry black mustache, should have possessed that woman who was his, and that said beast—in the most holy and socially decorous way, and tenderly sanctioned by church and state—could unstintingly defile the divine lips that he himself had never dared to brush out of superstitious reverence and what had nearly amounted to terror of her divinity! How can I explain it to you? The feelings of this extraordinary Matias were like those of a monk, prostrate before an image of the Blessed Virgin, when all of a sudden a sacrilegious beast of a man climbs up on the altar and obscenely lifts the Virgin's tunic! You smile. And how about Matos Miranda? Ah, my friend! That one was diabetic, and somber, and obese, and he was already in the Parreira with his obesity and diabetes when José Matias became acquainted with Elisa and gave her his life and heart forevermore. But this other one, this Torres Nogueira, he had brutally broken through Matias's purest of pure loves with his black mustache, his brawny arms, and the vigorous pluck of a one-time catcher of bulls and made off with that woman to whom he had, perhaps, shown what a real man is!

But, the devil to pay! José Matias had refused that woman when she had offered herself to him in the freshness and greatness of a feeling that no disdain had yet withered or diminished. What do you expect? It's the frightfully tortuous spiritual essence of this Matias! At the end of a few months he *had forgotten*, positively *had forgotten* that insulting rejection, as if it had been a slight disagreement over some social or material concerns of a number of months ago in the North, in Porto, the reality and slight bitterness of which had been dissipated by distance and time! And now here in Lisbon, with Elisa's windows facing his windows and the roses of the two contiguous gardens perfuming the shadows, his present heartache, his real heartache, was that he had loved a woman sublimely, and that he had placed her on a pedestal among the stars in order to achieve a more pure adoration, and that a dark-complexioned brute with a black mustache had snatched that woman from among the stars and flung her to bed!

And do you know what exacerbated this torment even more furiously? It was that poor Elisa *showed* her old love for him! What do you make of that? Diabolical, isn't it? At the very least, if she did not feel the same old love intact in its essence, as strong and unique as formerly, she retained an irresistible curiosity about Matias and repeated the gestures, the tokens of that love. Perhaps it was merely the fatality of neighboring gardens! I don't know. But as soon as September came, when Torres Nogueira left for his vineyards in Carcavelos to manage the grape harvest, she began anew—from the edge of the terrace overlooking the roses and dahlias in bloom—that sweet conveyance of sweet glances that for ten years had entranced the heart of José Matias.

I don't believe that they wrote billets-doux to each other over the garden wall as they had under the paternal regime of Matos Miranda. The new master, the robust man with the bushy mustache, imposed restraint and prudence on the divine Elisa, even from afar at his Carcavelos vineyards. And, calmed by that strong young husband of hers, she now felt less need for a discreet encounter in the tepid shadows of night, even if her moral elegance and José Matias's rigid idealism would have warranted taking advantage of a ladder propped against the garden wall. Besides, Elisa was fundamentally honest, and more than for her soul, she preserved a sacred respect for her body, on account of regarding it as beautifully and carefully created by God. And who knows? Perhaps the adorable woman belonged to the same fair race as that Italian marquise Júlia de Malfieri, who kept two lovers at her sweet service: a poet for her romantic refinements and a coachman for her crude needs.

At all events, my friend, let us not psychologize further about this living woman in order to follow behind the dead man who died for her! The fact of the matter is that Elisa and her friend unconsciously relapsed into the old ideal union across their two flowering gardens. And in October, since Torres Nogueira continued harvesting his grapes in Carcavelos, José Matias opened his windows again in order to contemplate, ecstatically and at leisure, the Parreira terrace.

Anyone would think that, having recaptured the ideal nature of his former love, such an extreme spiritualist might have also recovered the former perfect happiness of it. He reigned in Elisa's soul, so what did it matter that another had possession of her mortal body? But no! The poor man floundered in angst, and in order to rid himself of the distress of these torments, he—always so serene, always so gentle of disposition—turned into a restless, agitated soul. Ah, my friend, what a turbulent, chaotic life! Desperately, like a storm churning the sea, he stunned and scandalized Lisbon for a whole year! Some of his legendary extravagances date from that time. Do you know about the supper? A supper thrown for thirty or forty of the vilest, filthiest women picked up in the black alleys of the Bairro Alto and the Mouraria, whom he ordered to climb onto donkeys while he, grave and woebegone, rode at their head on a great white horse, an immense whip in hand, as he led them to the heights of Graça to greet the rising sun!

But all this hullabaloo did not dissipate his heartache, and it was then, that winter, that he began to gamble and drink.

All day long he would shut himself up in his house (for sure behind the windows now that Torres Nogueira had returned from his vineyards), with his eyes and his soul riveted on that fateful terrace; afterward, at night, he would go out in an old coach—always the same one, Gago's—to try his hand at roulette at the Bravo, then move on to the Cavalheiro Club, where he would gamble frenetically until having a late supper in the nook of some restaurant by the light of a multitude of brightly burning candles, with wine from Colares, champagne, and cognac flowing in reckless torrents.

And this life, encouraged by the Furies, lasted for years, seven long years! All the lands that his uncle had left him were lost almost in their entirety to gambling and drinking, and the only things that he still possessed were the big house in Arroios and the funds he had come by as a result of mortgaging it. But then, all of a sudden, he disappeared from all the gambling and drinking dens, and we learned that Torres Nogueira was dying of dropsy!

Around that time, and because of some business with Nicolau da Barca, who had telegraphed me anxiously from his estate in Santarém (an involved affair concerning a bill of exchange), I went to check up on José Martias in Arroios at ten o'clock one warm April night. The servant admitted me, and while leading me along the poorly illuminated hallway now emptied of the ornate chests and engravings from India collected by old Garmilde, he confessed that his master had yet to finish his dinner. I still remember with a shudder the desolate impression that the poor devil made on me! He was in the room that opened onto the two gardens. In front of the window covered by damask curtains stood a resplendent table with two multi-armed candelabrums, a basket of white roses, and some of Garmilde's princely silverware; and to one side, stretched out on an easy chair—his white vest unbuttoned, his sallow face drooped over his chest, and an empty glass in his flaccid hand—José Matias seemed to lie asleep or dead.

When I touched him on the shoulder, he raised his head with a start, his hair all disheveled. "What time is it?" he asked. In order to wake him up fully, I said—in a loud voice and in a jolly mood—that it was late, ten o'clock, at which point he hastily filled his glass with white wine from the nearest bottle and drank slowly, his hand trembling the whole time. Smoothing hair off his dank forehead, he asked, "So what's up?" With glazed eyes he listened in a fog, dreamlike, to the message sent to him by Nicolau. Finally, with a sigh, he spun a bottle of champagne that was icing in a bucket, and filled another glass, murmuring, "I'm hot! And thirsty!" But he didn't drink; he lugged his heavy body from the wicker armchair and staggered over to the window, yanked back the drawn curtains, and flung the window wide open. He stood there, perfectly still, as if in awe of the silence and dark calm of the star-spangled night. I took a good look, my friend! Opened to the gentle breeze, two brightly illuminated windows glowed in Casa da Parreira. And that clarity enveloped a white figure in the long folds of a white dressing gown—a figure standing at the edge of the terrace as if lost in thought. It was Elisa, my friend! Behind her, at the back of the room, lay her husband, no doubt gasping for breath in the throes of dropsy. Motionless, in repose, she was sending a sweet glance, perhaps a smile, to her sweet friend. The miserable man, fascinated and breathless, drank in the delight of that beneficial vision; and in between them, the sweet-smelling flowers suffused the two gardens in the softness of the night. All of a sudden, Elisa quickly withdrew, summoned perhaps by a moan or some grievance on the part of poor Torres. And the windows were closed at once, all the light and life vanishing from Casa da Parreira.

Then José Matias, in a heartbreaking sob overflowing with

torment, lurched, and so anxiously did he grab at the curtain that he tore it and tumbled helplessly into the arms I extended to him, and in which I cumbersomely dragged him like a dead man or a drunk to a chair. But much to my astonishment, the extraordinary man came to his senses for a moment; opening his eyes, he smiled a slow, limp smile and murmured almost serenely, "It's the heat! It's this terrible heat! Wouldn't you like to have tea?"

I declined and took my leave, while he—stretched out on the armchair, indifferent to my hasty departure—was lighting a huge cigar with trembling hands.

*

GOOD LORD! We're already at Rua Santa Isabel! How anxious these scoundrels are to commit poor José Matias to dust and the ultimate worm. Well, my friend, after that curious night Torres Nogueira died. During the new period of mourning, the divine Elisa withdrew to Corte Moreira, an estate near Beja that belonged to her sister-in-law, who was also a widow. And José Matias vanished completely, just dropped out of sight, so that no news about him reached me, not even hearsay; and the prospect of hearing news of any sort about Matias disappeared with the departure of his close friend—our brilliant Nicolau da Barca—for the island of Madeira. Although Nicolau's condition was hopeless, he soldiered on with the last lobe of his lung in order to carry out the classic duty, the almost social duty, of the consumptive.

All that year I was also fully absorbed in my *Essay on Affective Phenomena*. Then, one day at the beginning of summer, I was walking down Rua de São Bento while glancing up to locate number 214, where the library of Azemel's holdings was being catalogued, and whom did I spot on the balcony of a new house on the corner? The divine Elisa, slipping pieces of lettuce inside the cage of a canary! And beautiful, my friend, the epitome of feminine pulchritude—mature, and delectable and desirable, despite having celebrated her forty-second birthday in Beja! But that woman belonged to the great race of Helen, who forty years after the siege of Troy still dazzled mortal men and immortal gods. And curiously, later that afternoon, I learned the latest chapter in the life of this admirable Helen from Seco, the João Seco of the library, who was cataloguing Azemel's holdings.

The divine Elisa now had a lover. And he was only a lover because she could not, with her usual honesty, have him for a legitimate and third husband. As chance would have it, this fortunate man whom she adored was married to a Spanish woman in Beja, and at the end of one year of their marriage and a number of liaisons, she had decamped for Seville to devoutly observe Holy Week, and there she had slept in the arms of a wealthy cattle breeder. Her husband, a peaceful supervisor of Public Works, had remained in Beja where from time to time he also taught some kind of drawing on the side. It turned out that one of his charges was the daughter of the *senhora* of Corte Moreira, and while he guided the little girl's stump, Elisa met him there at the house. She soon fell in love with him with such urgent passion that she hurriedly wrested him from Public Works and dragged him off to Lisbon, a city, unlike Beja, more favorably inclined to scandalous pleasure, and one in which such pleasure can be hidden. João Seco is from Beja, where he spent Christmas, and he knew both the supervisor and the ladies of Corte Moreira very well. He instantly understood that it was a love affair when, from the windows of number 214 where he was doing his cataloguing, he not only recognized Elisa on the balcony of the corner house, but also subsequently spotted the supervisor, who looked very much at ease coming through the doorway. He was well-dressed, sporting elegant gloves and boots, and he carried himself with the air of a man infinitely more happy in those private works than in public ones.

And from that very same window of number 214, I also became acquainted, so to speak, with the supervisor. He was a handsome, solidly built man with a light complexion and a dark beard, in excellent circumstances of quantity (and perhaps even of quality) to fill a widowed heart, and therefore an "empty" heart, as the Bible has it. My interest in the catalogue and consequently in frequenting that number 214 stemmed from the ironic coincidence of inheritance: Azemel's estate possessed an incomparable collection of eighteenth-century philosophers. A few weeks went by, and one night (João Seco worked at night), I set the books down, left, and walked a short stretch before stopping alongside an open doorway to light a cigar. And by the flickering flame of the match, whom did I catch a glimpse of, under the cover of shadows, but José Matias! But what a José Matias, my friend! In order to distinguish him better, I struck another match. The poor man had let his beard grow into a strange, unkempt, and grubby sight, soft as yellowed fluff; and since he had let his hair grow, too, dry wisps of it peeked out from beneath an old derby. But in all respects he seemed diminished, shrunken inside a rumpled, patchwork jacket and black trousers with big pockets that allowed him to bury his hands in the infinitely sad and traditional manner of idle paupers. Taken aback by astonishment and pity, I barely managed to stammer, "Can it be? Is it you? What's going on?" With his cautious gentility, although somewhat brusquely in order to rid himself of me, he spoke in a voice made hoarse by brandy, saying, "I'm waiting for someone here." I didn't press him and continued on my way. However, I hadn't gone but a short distance when I stopped, wanting to verify what had come to me in a heartbeat—that the doorway stood directly across from the new building and Elisa's balconies!

So, my friend, José Matias lived for three years scrunched up and ensconced in that doorway.

*

IT WAS ONE OF THOSE COURTYARDS in old Lisbon: no doorkeeper, always wide open, and always dirty, like caves along the street from which no one ever chases away the miserable souls who were hiding there from destitution and adversity. On one side there was a tavern. Infallibly at nightfall, José Matias would walk down Rua de São Bento while hugging the walls, and like a shadow himself, blend into the shadow of the doorway. At that hour light shone in Elisa's windows, dimmed in winter by a fine mist and in summer still open to fresh air in the quiet and calm of the evening. Every half hour he would unobtrusively head over to the tavern. A glass of wine, a glass of brandy, and then he would meekly retrace his steps into the blackness of the doorway, into his ecstasy. When the lights in Elisa's windows went out, he would still drag himself through the long night, even through the dark nights of winter while hunched, numb with cold, and stamping his worn-out soles on the pavement or sitting on the steps of the stairs at the back, his bleary, subservient eyes on the black façade of that house where he knew she was sleeping with that other man!

At first, in order to smoke a quick cigarette, he would climb up to the deserted landing to conceal the flamed tip that would betray his hiding place. But with the passage of some time, he smoked incessantly, close by the doorjamb, puffing anxiously on the cigarettes to make them glow and cast light on himself! And do you understand why, my friend? Because by then Elisa had discovered that her poor José Matias stood inside that doorway, rooted there, submissively adoring her windows with the same depth of soul as formerly!

And would you believe that every night afterward she

would linger to gaze at the doorway, either from behind the windows or leaning on the balcony (with the supervisor inside, stretched out on the sofa, already in his slippers reading the *Evening Daily*)? And that she would keep herself utterly still, her look conveying what that old and silent one from the terrace had conveyed over the roses and dahlias? An awestruck José Matias understood. And he desperately puffed to keep his cigarettes glowing like a lighthouse, to guide her beloved eyes in the darkness, to show her that he was enraptured there, all hers and faithful!

He never walked along Rua de São Bento in daytime. How would he have dared in his shabby boots and jacket frayed at the elbows? Because that young man, accustomed to the refined dress of sober elegance, had fallen into the misery of tatters. Where did he even come by the bit of money he needed every day for his wine and cod in taverns? I have no idea. But let us sing the praises of the divine Elisa, my friend! With great delicacy, and by clever and shrewd means, she, a wealthy woman, had sought to establish a pension for José Matias, a beggar. An intriguing situation, wouldn't you say? The grateful lady settling monthly allowances on her two men: her physical lover and her spiritual lover. Matias, however, guessed the source of that dreadful charity, and he refused it without a scene or an outburst of pride, even moved as he was, even with the tears in his eyes inflamed by brandy!

So only in the dead of night did he dare to walk down Rua de São Bento and slip into his doorway. And can you imagine how he spent the days? Following, spying on, and sniffing around the supervisor of Public Works! Yes, my friend! He harbored an insatiable, frenzied, inexorable curiosity about that man whom Elisa had chosen. The two previous ones, Miranda and Nogueira, had entered Elisa's bedroom publicly, by way of the Catholic Church, and for human ends besides love—to possess a home, perhaps children, stability, and a peaceful life. But this one was merely the lover whom she had singled out and supported only to be loved physically, and in that union there appeared to be no other rational motive save the coupling of their two bodies. Consequently, Matias never tired of studying the supervisor, his figure, his clothes, his habits, anxious to learn what that man was like, that man whom Elisa had chosen from the host of men in order to feel complete. For the sake of propriety, the supervisor lived at the other end of Rua de São Bento, across from the market. And that part of the street, where Elisa's eyes would not surprise him in his indigence, was José Matias's vantage point early every morning for observing and trailing the supervisor when, still warm from the heat of Elisa's bedroom, he would exit her house. Afterward he did not quit his surveillance; no, cautiously, like a thief, Matias watched him from a distance. And I suspect that he pursued the man in that manner less out of perverse curiosity than to ascertain whether—in the midst of the temptations of Lisbon, overwhelming for a supervisor from Beja—her lover remained bodily faithful to Elisa. As a service to her happiness … he kept an eye on the lover of the woman he loved!

A passionate refinement of spirituality and devotion, my friend! Elisa's soul was his and perennially received his perennial adoration, but now he wanted Elisa's body to be no less adored, nor less faithfully, by the man to whom she had entrusted her body. However, it was easy for the supervisor to be faithful to such a beautiful and wealthy woman who dazzled him with her silk stockings and diamond earrings. And who knows, my friend? Perhaps this faithfulness, this carnal homage to Elisa's divinity, was the last happiness that life granted to José Matias. I believe this to be true because one rainy morning last winter, I spotted the supervisor buying camellias from a florist on Rua do Ouro, and spying him from a corner on the other side of the street stood a gaunt, ragged José Matias, a look of affection, almost of gratitude, on his face! And that night, while shivering and stamping his soaked shoes in the doorway, his gentle, loving eyes riveted on the dark windows of Elisa's house, perhaps he thought, *The poor thing! What a dear! She must have been thrilled with the flowers he bought for her!*

This went on for three years.

Finally, my friend, the day before yesterday a breathless João Seco showed up at my house in the afternoon, saying excitedly, "José Matias has been taken to the hospital on a stretcher with pulmonary congestion!"

It seems that he was found at dawn, lying on the sidewalk in his threadbare jacket, gasping for breath, his moribund face turned up toward Elisa's balconies. I hurried to the hospital. He was already gone. I accompanied the attending physician to the infirmary and lifted the sheet draped over him. At the opening of his dirty, torn shirt he had—tied around his neck with twine—a small silk pouch, as frayed and filthy as his jacket. It no doubt contained a flower, or locks, or a snippet of Elisa's lace back from the days of their first wondrous time and afternoons at Benfica. I asked the doctor, who knew him and pitied him, whether he had suffered. "No! He experienced a comatose moment, opened his eyes wide, exclaimed 'Oh!' in great surprise, and then he breathed his last."

Was that the cry of the soul in fright and also in horror of dying? Or was it the soul exulting for finally recognizing that it was immortal and free? You don't know, my friend, nor did Plato, and neither will the last philosopher on the last afternoon of the world.

*

WE'VE ARRIVED AT THE CEMETERY. I believe that we should keep close to the casket. It's really rather peculiar for this Alves Capão to be following our poor spiritualist so emotionally. But, good heavens … look! Over there, waiting by the church door, that individual of solemn mien in tails and an off-white outer coat. It's the supervisor of Public Works! And he's carrying a big bouquet of violets. Elisa has sent her physical lover to accompany her spiritual lover to his grave and cover him with flowers. But, oh my friend, let us believe that she surely would never have asked José Matias to scatter violets over the supervisor's corpse! And it's because even without understanding Spirit, without realizing happiness from it, Matter will always worship Spirit, and will always treat itself with brutality and disdain, notwithstanding its own joys! How great a consolation, my friend, this supervisor is with his bouquet for a metaphysician who, like me, has critiqued Spinoza and Malebranche, rehabilitated Fichte, and proved sufficiently the illusion of sensation! For this reason alone it was worth escorting to his grave this unexplained José Matias, who was perhaps much more than a man … or perhaps somewhat less than a man. Yes, sir, it's cold. But what a beautiful afternoon!

Glossary to "José Matias"
(in order of appearance)

GEORG WILHELM FRIEDRICH HEGEL (1770–1831): German philosopher and an important figure of German idealism.

RUA DE SÃO BENTO: this main street tells us early on that the story takes place in Lisbon.

COIMBRA: the centrally located city on the Mondego River; site of the oldest university (founded in 1290) in the Portuguese-speaking world.

CRAVEIRO: I found no Craveiro in Eça's time.

THE MISERIES OF POLAND: perhaps a reference to the January [22] Uprising of 1863 in the Russian-occupied sector.

LES CONTEMPLATIONS: a collection of poetry by Victor Hugo published in 1856.

GIUSEPPE GARIBALDI (1807–82): Italian nationalist; wounded during the August 29, 1862, Battle of Aspromonte (southern Italy).

INÊS DE CASTRO (1325–55): Galician noblewoman and lover of King Peter I of Portugal.

PASSEIO PÚBLICO: the vast promenade of nineteenth-century Lisbon that was demolished to make way for the present-day Praça dos Restauradores and Avenida da Liberdade.

ERICEIRA: a seaside resort and fishing village on the western coast of Portugal, some twenty miles northwest of Lisbon.

ALPHONSE DE LAMARTINE (1790–1869): French writer, poet, and politician.

THE ALENTEJO: the region that covers most of the southern half of Portugal.

BENFICA: area, in Eça's time, on the northern outskirts of Lisbon; it also figures in his Lisbon novels *The Maias* and *Cousin Bazilio*.

INTROIBO AD ALTARE DEI: "I will go to the Altar of God." It was the beginning of a Roman Catholic Mass in Latin.

RUY BLAS: the eponymous protagonist of Victor Hugo's *Ruy Blas* (1838), a drama about a commoner in Madrid who dares to love the queen of Spain.

COLARES WINE: from the region west of Lisbon on the Atlantic coast.

SETÚBAL: a city some thirty miles south of Lisbon.

SANTARÉM: a city on the right bank of the Tagus River, some forty miles northeast of Lisbon.

FOZ: São João [Baptista] da Foz, resort near Porto famous for its fortress.

SAINT JOHN CHRYSOSTOM (349–407): early church father known for his preaching and public speaking.

MYSTICAL ROSE (ROSA MYSTICA): a traditional title of Mary in

Catholic Marian devotion because she is deemed the queen of spiritual flowers.

CATCHER OF BULLS (*PEGADOR DE TOUROS, MOÇO DE FORCADO, IN PORTUGUESE*): the Portuguese bullfight differs from the Spanish in that the bulls are not killed; they are caught by a group of eight men (*forcados*) and grappled to the ground.

CARCAVELOS: an area midway between Lisbon and Cascais that was known for its wine.

GRAÇA: the highest point in Lisbon.

THE FURIES: the female deities of vengeance in Greek mythology.

BEJA: a city in the Alentejo region.

[THE LITTLE GIRL'S] STUMP: "a short, pointed roll of leather or paper or wad of rubber for rubbing on a charcoal or pencil drawing to shade or soften it" (*The American Heritage Dictionary of the English Language*, 5th ed. [New York: Houghton Mifflin Harcourt, 2011], 1732).

BARUCH SPINOZA (1632–77): a Jewish-Dutch philosopher of Portuguese Sephardic origin (he was also known by his Portuguese name, Benedito [Bento] de Espinosa).

NICOLAS MALEBRANCHE (1638–1716): a French priest and philosopher who sought to demonstrate the active role of God in every aspect of the world.

JOHANN GOTTLIEB FICHTE (1762–1814): German philosopher who became a founding figure of the philosophical movement known as German idealism.

The Gentle Miracle

AT THAT TIME Jesus had not yet departed from Galilee and the gentle, luminous shores of Lake Tiberias. But the news of his miracles had already reached Engannim, a rich city with strong bulwarks amid olive groves and vineyards in the land of Issachar.

One afternoon a man with fiery, effulgent eyes passed through the cool valley and proclaimed that a young prophet —a handsome Rabbi—was walking the fields and villages of Galilee, preaching the coming of the Kingdom of God and curing all manner of human ills. And while he rested, sitting by the Fountain of Orchards, he still related that on the road to Magdala this Rabbi had cured the leprosy of a Roman decurion's servant merely by extending the shadow of his hands over him; and that on another morning, while crossing by boat to the land of the Gerasenes, where the balsam harvest was beginning, he had brought back to life the daughter of Jairus, an important, learned man who expounded the Sacred Scrolls in the Synagogue. And since astonished field hands everywhere, and shepherds and swarthy women with jugs on their shoulders, asked him whether that Rabbi was, in fact, the Messiah of Judea, and whether the sword of fire shone before him, and whether the shadows of Gog and Magog, walking along like the shadows of two towers, flanked him, the man grasped his staff, shook his hair, and—without even drinking that cold water that Joshua had drunk—pensively set out under the Aqueduct and soon disappeared in a copse of almond trees in full bloom. But a ray of hope, as delightful as dew in the months when cicadas sing, refreshed those simple souls, and then all over the green plain, as far as Ashkelon, plows seemed to dig more readily in the earth; the stones of the olive and wine presses turned more easily; children gathering anemone branches peered along the roads to see if beyond the corner of the wall or under a syc-amore a bright light would appear; and on stone benches by the gates of the city, old men stroking their whiskers no longer raised the old adages with such wise certainty.

Now, living in Engannim at that time was an old man named Obed, who came from a self-important Samaritan fam-ily and had sacrificed on the altars of Mount Ebal. This Obed possessed numerous flocks and numerous vineyards, and he was a man with a heart as filled with pride as his granary was with wheat. But an arid, burning wind, that wind of desola-tion which at the Lord's command blows from the forbidding lands of Assur, had killed the fattest sheep of his flocks; and on the hillsides where his vines twisted around elms and ele-gant trellises, it had only left in its wake—scattered about the stripped elms and stakes—ravaged stumps, shoots, and grape leaves eaten by a rugose fungus. And Obed, crouched at the doorstep of his house with a corner of his cloak drawn over his face, fingered the dust, lamented old age, and pondered com-plaints against a cruel God.

But no sooner had Obed heard about the young Rabbi from Galilee who fed multitudes, drove out demons, and righted all misfortunes than he—a learned man who had traveled in Phoenicia—immediately concluded that Jesus must have been one of those wizards, so common in Palestine, like Apollonius, or Rabbi Ben-Dossa, or Simon the Subtle. Even on dark nights those men converse with the stars, whose secrets for them are always clear and easy to fathom; with a wand they drive away from the grainfields the horseflies generated in the mire of Egypt; and with their fingers they grasp the shadows of trees, which they drape like beneficent awnings over the threshing floors at the hottest time of the day. Jesus of Galilee, a younger man with surely more powerful magic, could, if Obed paid him generously, stop the dying of his livestock and make his vineyards green again. Obed then ordered his servants to set out and search all of Galilee for the new Rabbi and, with the promise of money or jewels, bring him to Engannim, in the land of Issachar.

The servants tightened their leather belts and headed toward the route of the caravans, which skirts the shore of the lake and extends as far as Damascus. One afternoon they caught sight of the fine snows of Mount Hermon against the background of a western sun as red as a ripe pomegranate. Later, in the coolness of a pleasant morning and under a flight of turtledoves, Lake Tiberias shimmered before them—transparent, veiled in silence, bluer than the sky, and bordered in its entirety by flowery meadows, dense orchards, porphyry rocks, and white terraces amid palm groves. A fisherman who was lazily untying his boat from a point of grassy land shaded by oleanders smiled as he listened to the servants. The Rabbi from Nazareth? Oh! Since the month of Iyar the Rabbi, together with his disciples, had gone down to the banks where the River Jordan flows.

The servants, on the run, followed the banks of the river as far as the ford, where the Jordan, still and green, widens into a broad pool to rest and sleep for a moment in the shade of tamarind trees. A man from the tribe of the Essenes, dressed all in white linen, was slowly gathering salutary herbs at water's edge while cradling a lambkin on his lap. The servants greeted him humbly, because the people love those men with hearts as clean and clear and innocent as their garments, which are washed every morning in vats of purified water. Did he know of the travels of the new Rabbi from Galilee who, like the Essenes, preached gentleness and cured people and animals alike? The Essene murmured that the Rabbi had crossed the oasis of Engaddi, and afterward continued farther beyond. But where *farther beyond*? Gesturing with a twig of purple flowers that he had picked, the Essene pointed to the lands of Beyond-Jordan, the plain of Moab. The servants forded the river, and they searched in vain for Jesus, tramping along rugged trails as far as the cliffs where the sinister citadel of Makaur rises. At Jacob's Well there rested a great caravan that was transporting myrrh, spices, and balsam from Gilead to Egypt, and while filling their leather buckets with water, the camel drivers told Obed's servants that in Gadara, right around the new moon, a wonderful Rabbi, greater than David or Isaiah, had cast out seven demons from the breast of a weaver-woman, and that, at the sound of his voice, a man whose throat had been slit by the criminal Barabbas had risen from his grave and gone back to his garden. Hopeful at that news, the servants immediately hurried up the pilgrims' route to Gadara, a city of tall towers, and still farther, to the springs of Al-Maliha. However, that morning Jesus, followed by a crowd singing and waving branches of mimosa, had embarked on a fishing boat and sailed across the lake to Magdala. And so, Obed's now discouraged servants passed again over the Jordan on the Bridge of Jacob's Daughters. One day, having reached the lands of Roman Judea, their sandals torn from trudging the long roads, they crossed paths with a somber Pharisee who was returning to the city of Ephraim on his mule. With devout reverence they stopped the man of the Law. Had he, by chance, encountered that new Prophet from Galilee who, like a God walking Earth, performed miracles? The Pharisee's face, with its aquiline nose, darkened and wrinkled into wrath that boomed fury like a proud drum.

"Oh you pagan slaves! Oh you blasphemers!" he exclaimed. "Where have you heard tell that prophets or miracles exist outside of Jerusalem? Only Jehovah wields that power in his Temple. Ignoramuses and imposters hail from Galilee."

And since the servants flinched before his raised fist, which was completely wrapped with sacred distichs, the furious doctor jumped down from his mule, and, with stones from the road, he pelted Obed's servants, yelling, "*Racca! Racca!*" and adding all the ritual anathemas. The servants fled to Engannim. And great was Obed's grief, because his sheep were dying, his vineyards were withering, and yet, radiantly, like a dawn behind the mountains, the fame of Jesus of Galilee grew, his renown full of consolation and divine promises.

Around that time, a Roman centurion, Publius Septimus, commanded the fort that dominated the valley of Caesarea from the city to the sea. A gruff man and a veteran of Tiberius's campaign against the Parthians, Publius had become rich on plunder and pillage during the revolt of Samaria; he also owned mines in Attica and enjoyed, as a supreme favor from the gods, the friendship of Flaccus, the Imperial Legate of Syria. But a source of sorrow was eating away at his powerful prosperity, like a worm that eats at a succulent piece of fruit. His only daughter, more cherished by him than life and riches, was dying a slow death from an unknown illness, one beyond even the learning of the physicians and magicians that were consulted on his orders. Pale and sad like a cemetery moon, without complaint she would smile wanly at her father, wasting away as she sat beneath an awning drawn over the fort's high esplanade, her sad, black eyes fixed nostalgically on the blueness of the Sea of Tyre, on which she had sailed from Italy in a luxurious galley. Now and then a legionnaire positioned nearby between battlements would leisurely aim an arrow aloft and pierce a great eagle flying on serene wings in the gleaming sky. And for a moment Septimus's daughter would watch the bird floundering until it flopped, dead, on the rocks; afterward, sadder and paler, with a sigh she would once again gaze at the sea.

Then, hearing the merchants of Chorazim sing the praises of this admirable Rabbi, so powerful over the spirits that he healed the tenebrous ills of the soul, Septimus dispatched three decuries of soldiers to search for him throughout Galilee and all the cities of the Decapolis, as far as the coast and as far as Ashkelon. The soldiers stowed their shields in canvas bags, stuck twigs of olive trees in their helmets, and quickly set out, their iron-clad sandals echoing on the basalt pavement stones of the Roman road that divided the whole Herodian tetrarchy, from Caesaria to the lake. At night, their weapons flashed on the tops of hills, in the midst of the flickering flames of raised torches. During the day, they invaded villages, combed leafy orchards, probed haystacks with the tips of their lances; to placate them, frightened women hurried to offer them honey cakes, fresh figs, and bowls of wine, which they downed in one gulp in the shade of sycamores. Thus did the soldiers ransack Lower Galilee, but of the Rabbi, they only discovered the luminous furrows in people's hearts. Tired of the fruitless marches and suspecting that the Jews were hiding their wizard so that the Romans could not avail themselves of his superior magic, they unleashed their fury throughout the pious, submissive land. At the entrance to bridges they stopped pilgrims, shouting the Rabbi's name, and tore veils from virgins; and at the hour when water jugs are filled at wells, they would invade the narrow streets of towns, break into synagogues, and with the hilts of their swords sacrilegiously smash the *Tebahs*, the holy cedar cabinets that housed the Sacred Scrolls. On the outskirts of Hebron they dragged hermits from their caves by their beards to wring from them the name of the desert or palm grove where the Rabbi was in hiding, and two Phoenician merchants coming from Joppa with a load of malabathrum, and who had never heard the name of Jesus, paid to each decurion one hundred drachmas for that crime. Country people, and even the intrepid shepherds of Idumaea who bring white lambs to the Temple, fled in fright to the mountains as soon as the weapons of that violent band sparkled at some bend in the road. And at the edge of terraces, old women shook their disheveled hair and called down imprecations upon them, invoking the vengeance of Elijah. Thus, wreaking havoc, did they roam as far as Ashkelon: they did not find Jesus and retreated along the coast, their sandals sinking into the burning sands.

At daybreak one morning, while marching in a valley near Caesarea, they sighted on a hill a dark green laurel grove, in the midst of which rose the fine, bright portico of a secluded, white temple. An old man with a flowing white beard, crowned with a laurel wreath and attired in a saffron-colored tunic, stood on marble steps holding a short three-stringed lyre, gravely awaiting sunrise. Down below, waving olive branches, the soldiers shouted to the priest. Did he know a new Prophet who had appeared in Galilee, one who was so adept at miracles that he raised the dead to life and changed water into wine?

Serenely extending his arms, the serene old man exclaimed over the dewy greenness of the valley, "Oh Romans! So you believe that prophets working miracles appear in Galilee and Judea? How can a barbarian change the order instituted by Zeus? Magicians and wizards are peddlers who speak hollow words to inveigle money out of gullible fools. Without the permission of the Immortals, nary a withered branch can tumble from a tree, nary a shriveled leaf can be shaken from a tree. There are no prophets, there are no miracles. Only Delphic Apollo knows the secret of things."

Then slowly, their heads bowed as in an afternoon of defeat, the soldiers withdrew to the fortress of Caesarea. And great was the despair of Septimus, because his daughter was dying without complaint as she gazed at the Sea of Tyre. And yet the fame of Jesus, healer of grave ills, grew and grew, always more consoling and fresh, like the afternoon breeze that blows from Mount Hebron that, as it passes through gardens, revives and raises drooping lilies.

Now, between Engannim and Caesarea, in a solitary shack nestled in the hollow of a hill, there lived at that time a widow, the most miserable of all the women in Israel. Her little boy, an only child, was completely crippled, and had passed from the meager breasts at which she had nursed him to the tatters of the rotting straw pallet where he had lain for seven years, moaning and wasting away. Illness had also shrunk her—in the rags that she had never changed—and made her darker and more twisted than an uprooted vine. And misery flourished as abundantly on them as did mold on broken pieces of pottery lost in a desert. Even the oil in the red clay lamp had dried up a long time ago. In the painted chest neither grain nor a crust of bread remained. In the summer, the goat had died for want of forage, and then the fig tree in the garden had withered. Since they were so far from the village, alms of bread and honey never reached their door. And only blades of grass, picked from cracks in rocks and cooked without salt, fed those creatures of God in the Chosen Land, where even birds of ill omen ate their fill!

One day a beggar entered the shack and shared his scant fare with the distressed mother; and sitting for a moment by the fireplace while scratching the wounds on his legs, he told of that hope of the woebegone, that Rabbi who had appeared in Galilee, and who made—in the same basket—seven loaves of bread out of one loaf, and who loved all the little children, and dried all tears, and promised the poor a wondrously resplendent Kingdom of greater abundance than Solomon's court.

The woman listened with hungry eyes. And that gentle Rabbi, hope of the destitute, where was he to be found? Ah, that gentle Rabbi! How many yearned for him and despaired! His fame had spread through all of Judea, like sunlight that reaches and gladdens even an old, faraway wall, yet only those fortunate followers chosen by him could behold the brightness of his face. Obed, who was so wealthy, had sent his servants throughout Galilee to look for Jesus and make promises to lure him to Engannim; Septimus, who was so almighty, had dispatched his soldiers as far as the seacoast to search for Jesus and to bring him, on his orders, to Caesarea. As the man wandered, begging on roads, he had come across Obed's servants, as well as Septimus's legionnaires. And they all returned from their quests defeated and empty-handed, their sandals ruined, without having discovered in which wood or city, in which hovel or palace, Jesus was hiding.

Evening was drawing near. The beggar took his staff and went down the rugged path strewn with heather and stones. The mother returned to her corner, more stooped, more abandoned. And her little boy, in a voice weaker than the whisper of a bird's wing, asked his mother to bring him the Rabbi who loved all little children, even the poorest, and who healed all ills, even the most longstanding ones.

Clutching her head of disheveled hair, the distraught woman exclaimed, "Oh my son! How can I leave you and tramp the roads in search of the Rabbi of Galilee? Obed is rich and has servants, and in vain did they search for Jesus on beaches and hills, from Chorazim to the land of Moab. Septimus is powerful and has soldiers, and in vain did they hunt for Jesus, from Hebron to the sea. How can I leave you? Jesus is a long way off, and our grief, our sorrow, lives here with us, inside these walls, and inside these walls holds us captive. And even if I found him, how would I convince such a desired Rabbi, for whom the rich and the powerful sigh, to journey across cities to this wilderness in order to heal such a poor, paralyzed little boy on such a ragged bed of straw?"

With two tears streaming down his face, the child murmured, "Oh Mother! Jesus loves *all* little children. And I'm still little, and with such an awful sickness, and I'd like so much to be cured!"

And the sobbing mother said, "Oh my son! How can I leave you? The roads to Galilee are long, and men's pity is short. I am so shabby, so feeble, so forlorn that even village dogs would bark at me on sight. No one would pay attention to my request, no one would show me where the gentle Rabbi is staying. Oh my son! Perhaps Jesus has died. Not even the rich and powerful can find him. Heaven brought him, and Heaven took him away. And with him have died forever the hopes of the woebegone."

From among the black rags, the child raised his poor, trembling little hands and pleaded softly, "Mother, I do so wish to see Jesus!"

And then, slowly opening the door and smiling, Jesus said to the child, "Here I am."

Glossary to "The Gentle Miracle"
(in order of appearance)

LAKE TIBERIAS: an alternate name of the Sea of Galilee.

ENGANNIM: a town of the tribe of Issachar.

ISSACHAR: according to the book of Exodus, a son of Jacob and Leah (the fifth son of Leah and ninth son of Jacob) and the founder of the Israelite tribe of Issachar.

MAGDALA: a small town on the western shore of the Sea of Galilee, the home of Mary Magdalene.

GERASENES: peoples from Gerasa, the chief city of the area where Christ drove demons out of two possessed men.

JAIRUS: a synagogue leader whose daughter Jesus raised from the dead.

GOG AND MAGOG: peoples who appear in the book of Revelation. In the accounts of early Christian writers, they were apocalyptic hordes.

ASHKELON: an ancient Canaanite city on the Mediterranean coast, birthplace of Herod the Great.

OBED: son of Ruth and Boaz and grandfather of David.

SAMARIA: an ancient city in Israel, located in the mountains of Samaria; its ruins are near present-day Palestine.

MOUNT EBAL: a mount located north of Shechem (a Canaanite city and first capital of the Kingdom of Israel), opposite Mount Gerizim.

ASSUR: ancient capital of Assyria.

RUGOSE: rough and wrinkled leaves (applied to botany).

APOLLONIUS: Greek philosopher and mathematician (15–100) from the town of Tyana.

BEN-DOSSA: Hanina ben Dosa, first-century Jewish scholar said to have effected miracles by his prayers.

SIMON THE SUBTLE: Simon the Sorcerer or Simon the Magician, who wanted to buy the miraculous powers of the apostles Peter and John (Acts 8:9–24); root of the word *simony*, paying for religious gain.

MOUNT HERMON: mountain range between Syria and Lebanon, probable site of the Transfiguration of Christ.

[MONTH OF] IYAR: eighth month of the civil year and the second month of the ecclesiastical year in the Hebrew calendar.

ESSENES: members of an ancient Jewish ascetic sect during the second Temple of the second century BCE.

ENGADDI [EIN GEDI]: a town situated near the Dead Sea.

MOAB: son of Lot by incest with his daughter.

GILEAD: a mountainous region east of the Jordan River.

GADARA: a city southeast of the Sea of Galilee.

DISTICH: a unit of verse consisting of two lines.

PUBLIUS SEPTIMUS [GETA AUGUSTUS]: Roman emperor, 189–211.

PARTHIAN EMPIRE: an ancient political and cultural power in the area of present-day central Turkey to eastern Iran.

TIBERIUS [CLAUDIUS NERO]: 42 BC to 37 AD, Roman emperor from 14 AD to 37 AD, one of the greatest of Roman generals.

[GAIUS VALERIUS] FLACCUS: first-century Roman poet.

CHORAZIM: an ancient village in Galilee where, in the gospels of Matthew and Luke, Jesus performed "mighty works."

DECURY: a division or body of ten men (Roman History).

DECAPOLIS: a group of ten cities on the eastern frontier of the Roman Empire.

HERODIAN TETRARCHY: a form of governing by four, instituted after the death of Herod the Great (when his kingdom was divided among his three sons and his sister, Salome).

JOPPA: ancient fortified city on the coast of Palestine, some thirty-five miles from Jerusalem.

MALABATHRUM: a tree whose leaves are used for culinary and medicinal purposes.

IDUMAEA: Greek form of Edom, an ancient kingdom in New Testament times.

The Catastrophe

I LIVE ON THE CORNER of Pelourinho Square, directly across from the Arsenal. Even before the war and our disasters, I lived there—second floor, right. I never liked the location. While I was not a bucolic type, my ambition had always been to reside a long way from these sad blocks in the Baixa, in a district with more air and more horizon, with a back yard, a freshness of foliage, and a plot of land, where, amid trees and the rustling of leaves, I could have rosebushes and welcome birds on summer afternoons. But when I inherited from my aunt Petronilha, I bought this building across from the Arsenal. Because of the shops and warehouses, the buildings there are properties of higher income than those of other neighborhoods, so as investment of capital a building in the Baixa is more profitable than a pretty house in the Buenos Aires or Janelas Verdes districts. At least that was the counsel given to me by experienced landlords.

Besides, I had planned to rent the building and go off to live with Maria and my brother near Vale do Pereiro, in a pleasant, agreeable little house that had caught my eye. But when our misfortunes struck and the enemy army occupied Lisbon, the difficult times and the need to economize forced me to abandon that plan to live in the country, and so I am still here—on this forlorn second floor on Pelourinho Square, across from the Arsenal. I came here at a bad time because, I believe, this proximity to the Arsenal made me feel all the bitterness of the invasion with greater intensity. Of course, the people who live in Buenos Aires, Janelas Verdes, or Vale do Pereiro also suffer, and painfully, from the presence of a foreign army in Lisbon. Although the first wave of terror has passed and the city is little by little resuming its normal outward appearance, with coaches and tramways in circulation, a listless mood still weighs over the capital: the air is charged with something subtle and oppressive, like an intolerable atmosphere that spreads through squares, penetrates houses, leaves a sour taste in the water, makes the gaslight seem dark, and introduces into the soul an obsessive, continuous sadness.

Occasionally, when people do get out, occupied with some concern and distracted by it, they forget the great disaster surrounding us; however, the street-corner presence of an enemy uniform suffices immediately for the soul to be crushed by the idea of the defeat and end of our motherland. I don't know what it is, but—by way of example—ever since the foreign flag has been fluttering at the top of some building or other, it seems that this blue is not of our sky and is akin to a London-like haze. Nevertheless, elsewhere, in other districts, it's enough for people to isolate themselves at home in order to avoid this ambient desolation. Since there is no motherland, there is family: people close their doors, everyone gathers around the inviting oil lamps of living rooms, and they talk. The recollection of misfortunes unfolds like a painful relief, and the prospect of hope deludes them like a passing happiness as they remember friends, as well as acquaintances, who died bravely in battle. Sometimes the recollection of a heroic deed seems like the sensation of honor kept intact; afterward, quietly, still around the oil lamps, their whole beings throbbing, a little conspiracy is hatched in an undertone *en famille*.

And the dream of redress makes the reality of the catastrophe bearable. But as for me, I cannot even avail myself of this isolation, because unless I close the windows, bury myself in constant darkness, and live by the gaslight when the July sun sparkles outside, I cannot help seeing before me, like an odious memento, the foreign sentry at the door of the Arsenal, tramping the earth of our motherland.... And it is precisely this sentry who makes me so indignant. Surely others in foreign uniforms—all those officers of the battleships that are in anchorage—spend the livelong day in the bright insolence of their ostentatious dress. Anyway, that doesn't bother me. In the coming-and-going of those officers there is something hurried, uneasy, that gives me the idea of a short-lived occupation, of squadrons that are going to weigh anchor, of humiliations that are going to depart forever. But that sentry, that eternal sentry, who seems to be always the same one, has an air of immutability, of perpetuity that blackens my heart. Every step that he takes in his rugged leather boots affects me like a lugubrious echo in my soul, and his monotonous marching, back and forth from sentry box to sentry box, causes me to feel that there will never stop being a foreign sentry on Portuguese soil. And I cannot tear myself away from the spectacle!

As I shave in the morning, my razor held in midair and my face covered with swirls of lather, I am startled by the small soldier who looks bundled up in his large blue cloak, with his patent leather cap and his weapon on his shoulder—one of those weapons that doubled the size of ours, and that from a distance massacred entire regiments in lines of defense! So now I know almost all of the Arsenal's sentries. For a period of time they were Navy guards; now they're always soldiers of the line. And there is one type who especially makes me indignant: it is the robust, strapping, and well-built youth with his resolute face and bright eyes. I always say: it was his kind who conquered us! Recalling our own soldiers who are inexperienced, dirty, timid, bored, and stunted from the bad air of the barracks and the unhealthiness of their food, I don't know why I see in that superiority of kind and race all of the explanation of the catastrophe.

Formerly, before the invasion, seldom do I remember having watched the Arsenal's sentry; however, I do remember having chanced to see one upon passing by the window. If it was raining, I was bound to glimpse him huddled up in the sentry box, fixing his dull, sad eyes on the torrent of water; if the weather was balmy, it was his pacing and slouched shoulders that impressed me, as well as the measured laziness of his strides—a continual, patent expression of tedium and fatigue. And afterward, at the end of two hours of service, it was a greater lassitude, a brutalization, a vile way of gawking at everything—oxen, mule-drawn carts on rails, fishwives peddling their wares, hucksters, the tent opposite him—that made conspicuous his lack of nerve and vigor as well as of disciplined stability, firmness, persistence. And this vision of soldiers back then seems to expand and encompass the entire city, the entire country! It was this lugubrious somnolence, this tedium, this lack of decisiveness, this cynical indifference, this relaxation of energy and of will power that, I believe, led to our ruin. Even today there occasionally ring in my ears those frequently repeated accusations during the time of our struggle—that we had no army, no squadron, no artillery, no defense, no arms! Nonsense! What we didn't have were souls. That is what was dead, extinguished, dormant, denationalized, inert. And when in a State souls are debased and spent ... what remains is of little value.

I will never forget the impression made on me the day I learned that war had been declared on us and that an army, organized beforehand, was mustered for the invasion in the south and in the north. It was the birthday of my poor friend Nunes, who at that time lived on the Rossio. Since the afternoon that a panic hovered over the city the truth is that, ever since war had broken out in Europe—a war so violently provoked by Germany when it invaded Holland—never in Lisbon, at least among the majority of the population, had there been fear that the *situation would reach us here in our neck of the woods*, as people used to say then.

Not even when the aged Lord Salisbury, almost on his death bed, proclaimed his great manifesto and declared war on Germany, and when we thus saw our only defender so engaged in a fight in the North, did we consider ourselves in danger. And nonetheless there seemed to have arrived the terrible day on which the small nations would disappear from Europe. Therefore, on that fatal afternoon when the entrance of an enemy army at the border was officially announced, the entire city became petrified, caught up in a delirium of terror. And the first thing people did was run to churches! They already imagined enemy regiments spilling into the streets. I don't believe that they had even entertained the idea of a serious resistance. It was said at first that we would venture to engage in battle near Caminha, or in Tancos, solely to show Europe that we still retained some vitality, but it was merely a feint, because the idea would be to withdraw to the lines of Torres Vedras and defend Lisbon. Besides, I wasn't privy to the secrets of the general staff or of the government, and I only know what was being talked about quietly by the scared groups that filled the streets.

That night I went to the Rossio. Nunes was giving a *soirée*. The same somber gloom of the street held sway in the parlor. In faces and voices there was something like a confused expression of fright and terror—a singular way of asking, *Well?*, with wide-open eyes in pallid countenances.

Despite there being two rooms, the parlor for visitors and another for games, everyone was gathered around the sofa, like a flock that feels the presence of the wolf. The lady of the house, who had a soldier son in Tancos, betrayed—despite her décolleté blue dress—a face of stupefaction and swollen red eyes, inasmuch as she had been crying all day. And in the women, and in the men, a kind of insurmountable depression stood out in the silent acceptance of the future defeat, in the inert passivity of feeble souls. Since we had no news, absurd rumors abounded; there were continual moments of silence, lugubrious silence that produced the sensation of the ceremonious retirement on days of funerals. Poor Nunes, looking wan, paced back and forth in the parlor, with the tail of his frock coat flapping as he nervously rubbed his hands intending to distract us from those painful concerns by proposing that we do something. There was a request for a quadrille. A gentleman sat down at the piano, but the first measures of lancers sounded and were quickly lost amid the general buzz of frightened conversations: no one sought a partner, no one danced. Someone remembered a game of forfeits, a charade in pantomime, and startled faces smiled, murmuring with effort, "Let's do that. It's not a bad...."

But everyone remained seated, their hands still, their feet heavy.

I went into the games room to chat with a few individuals. There were journalists and politicians, and from their language you could feel spirits lagging in all of them. Not a one believed in possible resistance, and, faced with danger, egoism rose up, ferocious and brutal. Hate for the enemy was violent, less for the possible loss of the free motherland than for the personal disasters that defeat would bring: one feared for his employment, another for the interest on his government bonds. Until then the State had provided the country with bread, and in the loss of the State was seen the end of the daily bread. But this indignation in words seemed to exhaust the entire amount of patriotism that those souls could offer, because in each proposal that their terrified words suggested—cede the colonies in exchange for an immediate English alliance or grant the cession of two provinces—there lay, at bottom, the immutable idea of surrender, the horror of battle, the anxiety of not losing their employment, and not losing the interest on their government bonds. And besides, with each one feeling the egoistic weakness of his soul, they all instinctively judged the country to be seized by the same depression. The idea of an uprising en masse, the formation of a national guard, of militias, was received with a shrug of shoulders: Why bother? Nothing can be done! We're crushed!

I remember that while they were talking like this near the game table, on which lay the forgotten cards of the peaceful hand of omber, I stepped over to the window. The whole vast dome of the sky was clouded over with a whitish mist, but under the Arco do Bandeira there opened a great blue expanse, like the circular entrance of an immense portico, and in the center shone a large moon, sad, mute, and pale. The hill, off to one side with its castle, was faintly silhouetted over the blue pallor of the background. An immense sadness seemed to descend from that setting, and a vague compassion for the country's misfortunes invaded my soul. Without knowing why, I felt myself gripped by an anguished longing—the longing for something that had disappeared, that had ended forever, and I did not know what that something was. Down below, the darkened Rossio stood out, mute, in the illuminated rows of shop displays. The square itself, around the column bathed in moonlight with a pale streak, looked dense with people. But not a single shout rose, nor a single voice: it was a dark mass that seemed caught up in lethargy, carried away by the instinctive terror that causes animals to huddle together, awaiting the storm with resignation. And from the tall, desolate, white houses there issued the same sensation of terrified forbearance and selfish fixation on an obscure fear. All of a sudden noise came from the direction of Rua do Almada: it was like a rhythmic euphony or chant that you felt approaching in the air. Lights from torches, giving the appearance of a tail of sparks, appeared at a corner of the Rossio, and a group materialized marching in lively fashion to the beat of a patriotic hymn whose rhythm moved it along at a quick pace:

> *War, war, war is holy,*
> *For holy independence ...*

There were maybe twenty marchers, and—from above, from the window, because of their high hats—they looked like boys from schools or one of the societies that abounded then in the city. They continued all along the Rossio, waving their arms and raising their voices in an appeal to the dark crowd. But no response greeted them; the entire mass of people only crowded together to watch those solitary, enthusiastic youths pass by. Shops soon doused their lights and closed their doors, fearful of a riot, and in that cold silence, which came from the indifference of the people and the stillness of their faces, it seemed that the singing died out on its own, that enthusiasm waned, like a flag falling along the flagpole for lack of a breeze. When the marchers approached the Dona Maria Theater, the hymn had nearly ended, and the torches were dying out. It vanished, all of it, and got lost in the obscure mass of people like a short-lived effort of heroism in the midst of vast public indifference. I went back inside, thinking, with a lump in my throat, that we were lost forever.

Finally, since night was drawing near, it was necessary to do something to dispel that all-encompassing atmosphere of dread. Nunes, Correia, and I sat down to play omber in the game room. In the parlor certainly they had also felt the necessity to shake off the ladies' frightened torpor. We heard a piano scale, muffled chords, and shortly thereafter, a voice—which I recognized as that of a cavalry officer—rose up, tender and plaintive, singing a recitative from Fromental Halévy's opera *La Juive*:

Sleep, for I am keeping watch, seductive image …

That melody, that morbid voice of longing, struck me then as singularly strange at such a moment. It was like an outmoded, ancient sound, the voice of an extinct world, drifting through in dreams. Around the table the monotonous voices droned on: I passed, I dealt cards. From down below, from the Rossio, came the same dull noise of the crowd that filled the square, and in the parlor, in the amorous languor of the accompaniment imbued with refinement, the lieutenant's voice again rose:

Sleep, for I am keeping watch, seductive image …

Already at that hour the enemy army was treading on the ground of the motherland! Poor lieutenant! We ran into each other later. At the time I had joined up with my national militia companions. And what a militia! All we had for uniforms were make-do overcoats! And for arms? Hunting rifles! But nonetheless, on that cold April morning we kept going in a torrential rain. It seems that a great battle was being fought, although we didn't know anything about it. We were near an abandoned, run-down shack halfway up the slope of a hill that blocked our view of the front, and we hunkered down there for two hours—drenched, our knees in mud, after having marched all night, beside ourselves with fatigue and hunger, and bunched together so as not to doze off. All around us a deluge fell from a low, lugubrious sky; and the old shack and its four posts seemed completely enveloped in rain, as shrunken and sleepy as we were. In the distance, artillery boomed; other times it was sharp volleys like the sudden tearing of a big piece of faille silk. But we didn't even see the smoke in that foggy, rainy air, nor do I know where we were, or what we were defending.

Commanding the company was the same lieutenant who had sung a line from *La Juive.* Sallow, steadfast, and muffled in his cloak, he paced back and forth, no longer looking like the lieutenant who twisted his mustache next to the piano and rolled tender eyes at the most poignant passages. All of a sudden, a dull gallop was heard on the wet earth: it was an officer, his uniform in disarray, his sword in hand, his face inflamed in the heat of battle, a handsome fellow with a thread of blood trickling from an ear. He halted his horse, bellowing with rage.

"Who's commanding this detachment?"

"I am, Captain," replied the lieutenant, coming to attention.

"Damnation! Circle around the left, behind that old shack, and establish position on the road, next to the trench!"

And he left at a gallop. And then we followed in double time, in the mud, where our feet sank, making a brutal effort to climb over terrain that made for sluggish going, panting in the downpour and the roar of the artillery that now seemed to be drawing near. We passed in front of the run-down shack; there were ambulance wagons at the door, and inside, the screams of the wounded. It was the first time that we heard those heart-rending cries of abandoned pain, and in the detachment we felt something like a jolt, a hesitation—it was our flesh, that of our compatriots and our countrymen, who resisted in the face of that harsh reality of death and pain!

"March!" bellowed the lieutenant.

We reached the road but didn't see a thing. Across from us was a dim row of poplars; farther down, there were other trees, a hermitage on a mountaintop, and, throughout the entire valley, the rough, inhospitable fog from the incessant rain. We came to a halt: the distance darkened another detachment. So we stayed there, in the same standstill, stuck in the rain, shivering in mortal fatigue. Not even a sip of brandy. My swollen feet were killing me in soaked boots. And as I thought about the days of peace when it was from the armchair in my office that I would watch the rain falling, I found that I was furiously angry at the foreigner, in a frenzy to march onward, with a brutal desire for carnage. And desperate on account of that standstill, I accused—in the hallucination of my despair—the generals, the government, all who held the upper hand and were not ordering me to march. That indecision was abhorrent. Our clothes stuck to our bodies, and we felt water running down our legs, our hands freezing on the barrels of our rifles; and the sharp, biting wind trapped in the valley blew all around us.

Suddenly a deafening noise erupted. It was an artillery battery, galloping to take up position. It passed by like a whirlwind in the fog, rain, and mud, and to yells, to bucks of the horses, to jolts of the gun carriages; and, in a furious burst of whiplashes, it shook and got lost in the mist with a dull, muted sound on the drenched ground. Unexpectedly, a fusillade breaks out on our right, and now we feel the whistling of bullets. We instinctively duck, in that cowardly recoil of green militia.

"Steady!" shouts the lieutenant.

A soldier in front of me collapses onto the mud like an empty sack. Motionless, dead. Now we see little clouds of gray smoke, which the rain scatters and the wind disperses. All of a sudden the lieutenant falters and falls to his knees: he's wounded in the arm, but he shoots up like a spring, brandishing his sword like a wild man, yelling, "Fire!"

Afterward I don't remember much. The tremendous sound of the artillery disoriented me. It's like a dream, like in sleepwalking, that I fire at random into the gray fog that covers everything in front of me. Suddenly, at my side, the lieutenant falls again, and rolling over on the ground, he shouts in a fury of death throes, "Finish me off, boys! Finish me off, boys!"

But it was in that moment that we felt ourselves enveloped, absorbed by a black mass that was descending like a waterspout in the violence of the elements. We quit the position on the run, chucking our arms in the midst of a deafening outcry. Afterward, I have a vague recollection of that enormous swarm of combatants breaking up, dispersing into groups. There are around a hundred of us in the middle of it all, running, tripping, floundering in the mud, trampled underfoot. I have a hazy awareness that it's the defeat, the flight, the panic of the militias, and I flee—I flee with a fierce bitterness, shouting without knowing why, longing to find a corner, a house, a hole. And I recall seeing, during that mad rush in front of me, a bareheaded officer, a resolute, disheveled figure yelling at the top of his voice, brandishing his sword, trying valiantly to check the flight. The tide of people overpowers him, though, batters him, and I feel, vaguely, my boots slipping over his inert, crushed body.

Oh! Damned war!

*

HOW I RETURNED TO LISBON and found myself in my house, I really do not remember. However, I do recall stopping in the Rossio and seeing it jammed with a horrible crowd, which was the entire populace of the environs seeking refuge in their flight before the enemy. It was a chaos of wagons, livestock, belongings, and shouting women; a brutal, scared mass, swirling about itself, clamoring for bread under the implacable rain. It was in Lisbon that I learned, in bits and pieces, all the details: the enemy squadron on the Tagus River; the city without water because the Alviela River canal was closed off; the insurrection in the streets; and a crazed populace going from degradation to fury, now dashing against churches, now demanding arms and joining to the confusion of the invasion the horrors of demagoguery. Bitter days. All my hair turned gray.

And to think that for years we could have prepared ourselves. And to think that, like England, we could have created corps of volunteers, making a soldier of every citizen, and preparing in that manner, beforehand, a great national army of defense, armed, equipped, energetic, and having gained, in the practice of discipline, the pride of uniform.

But what good does it do now to think about what could have been done? Our great misfortune, I repeat, was the abasement, the inertia into which our souls had fallen. There was still a time in which all adversity was attributed to governments. A grotesque accusation that no one would dare to repeat today. Governments could perhaps have created more artillery, or more and more ambulances, but what they could not have created was an energetic soul for the country. We had fallen into indifference, into imbecilic skepticism, into disdain for every idea, into repugnance for every effort, into nullification of will. We were cachectic! The government, the Constitution—the very charter that was so scorned—had given us everything that it could give: freedom. It was under the protection of this freedom that the country, the motherland, the mass of citizens, had the duty to render their nation prosperous, alive, strong, worthy of independence. However, the country had not lost the habit of living at the doors of convents, and since there were no convents the country turned to the government, expecting from the government all that it should have exacted from itself, demanding that the government do everything that it behooved the people themselves to do. They wanted the government to clear its lands, wanted the government to create its industries, wanted the government to write its books, wanted the government to feed its children, wanted the government to erect its buildings, wanted the government to give it the idea of its God. Always the government! The government was supposed to be the farmer, the industrialist, the merchant, the philosopher, the priest, the painter, the architect—everything! When a country thus abdicates all its initiative in the hands of the government and folds its arms, expecting civilization to provide it with ready-made bureaus, like the light that comes from the sun, that country is in trouble. Souls lose their vigor, arms lose their custom of work, consciences lose precepts, brains lose action. It's as if the government were there to do everything: the country stretches out in the sun and makes itself comfortable in order to sleep well. It awakes, as we awoke, with a foreign sentry at the Arsenal gate. Ah! If we had known!

But we know now! This city seems like another. It's no longer that funereal, beaten multitude jammed together at the Rossio on the eve of the catastrophe. Today you see a resolve in attitudes, looks, and faces; each look springs from a contained yet brave fire, and chests rise as if now they really do contain a heart! No longer do you see throughout the city that base idleness, for everyone has the calling of a lofty duty to fulfill. Women seem to have felt their responsibility and are mothers, because they have the duty of raising citizens. We read our history now; we work now; and the very façades of our houses no longer have that stupid appearance of faces without ideas, like on that moonlit night; now, behind each windowpane, you sense a united family, organizing itself with resolve.

As for me, every day I take my children to the window, put them on my knees, and show them the sentry. I show him to them, pacing slowly, from sentry box to sentry box, in the shade that the building provides against the hot July sun, and I imbue them with horror, with hatred of that foreign soldier. I then relate to them the story of the invasion, the calamities, the fearful episodes, the bloodstained chapters of the sinister history. Afterward I point out to them the future: and I make them ardently wish for the day when they will see—from this house that they inhabit, from this window—a Portuguese sentry once again pacing on Portuguese soil. And, for that, I show them the sure path, the one that we should have followed: to work, to believe, and, being small by virtue of territory, to be great by action, by work, by freedom, by knowledge, by strength of spirit. And I accustom them to loving their motherland instead of scorning it, as many had formerly done. How I remember! We used to go to cafés, to the Guild, cross our legs, and between puffs say lazily, "This is a mess! This is a waste! This is an igno-ble country.... It's going to the dogs...."

And instead of striving to salvage the "this," we would ask for more cognac and head over to a brothel. Ah, cowardly gen-eration! Well were you punished!

But now this new generation belongs to others. This one no longer says that the "this" is lost. It keeps quiet and waits: if it's not animated, it's focused. And then not everything is sadness. We also have our holidays. And for a holiday everything will do: December first, the granting of the charter; July twenty-fourth, anything, provided that it celebrate a national date. Not in public—we still can't do that—but everyone in his own home, at her own table. On those days more flowers are put in vases, the chandelier is decorated with greenery, the pretty old flag is brought out, as is the coat of arms that used to make us laugh and that today moves us. And afterward we all sing *en famille*—softly, so as not to attract the attention of spies—the old hymn, the Hymn of the Charter, any hymn.... And a great toast is made, to a better future. And there is one consolation, an intimate joy, to think that at the same time, in almost all the buildings of the city, the generation in the making is celebrat-ing inside their parlors, in a quasi-religious way, the old-time holidays of the motherland.... And later, at night, gathered around the oil lamp, like a class in national history, I tell my boys this story ... of a patriot.

Glossary to "The Catastrophe"
(in order of appearance)

PELOURINHO SQUARE: In present-day Lisbon it is Praça do Município.

BAIXA: Lisbon's reconstructed downtown (or "Lower" town) after the November 1, 1755, earthquake.

VALE DO PEREIRO: on the outskirts of Lisbon in Eça's time; a street by this name still exists in the area to the northeast of Avenida da Liberdade.

ROSSIO: the broad square in the Baixa that was, and is, the heart of Lisbon. The column of King Dom Pedro IV rises in the middle, and the Dona Maria II National Theater, named after his daughter, stands on the north side.

SALISBURY: Lord Salisbury, Robert Cecil (1830–1903): British statesman who served as prime minister three times over a period of thirteen years.

CAMINHA: a town in the northwest of Portugal, north of Viana do Castelo.

TANCOS: a town in the center of Portugal, in the district of Santarém.

LINES OF TORRES VEDRAS: lines of forts and other military defenses built in secrecy to defend Lisbon during the Peninsular War. They were ordered by Arthur Wellesley, Duke of Wellington, and constructed between November 1809 and December 1810.

LANCERS: a set of quadrilles danced in sequence.

FROMENTAL HALÉVY (1799–1862): French composer known principally for his opera *La Juive*, 1835.

ALVIELA RIVER: a source, via the Alviela Aqueduct, of Lisbon's potable water supply. Its headwaters are in Serra de Aire e Candeeiros in the district of Santarém, some forty miles northeast of Lisbon.

COAT OF ARMS: the Portuguese word is *quinas,* which in the singular could simply be defined as "shield" or "[Portuguese] flag." However, the plural (the prefix *quin*) expressly states five, and one Portuguese dictionary describes a *quina* as follows: "Each one of the five shields that constitute part of the Portuguese coat of arms" [*Cada um dos cinco escudos que fazem parte das armas de Portugal*]; *Dicionário Prático Ilustrado* (Porto: Lello and Irmão, 1976), 987.

The Falling Snow and Other Stories was designed in
Garamond with Mrs Eaves display type and composed by
Kachergis Book Design of Pittsboro, North Carolina.